EPIC CURES

ALSO BY TOM SHEEHAN

NOVELS:
An Accountable Death
Vigilantes East
Death for the Phantom Receiver

POETRY:
Ah, Devon Unbowed
The Saugus Book
Reflections from Vinegar Hill
This Rare Earth & Other Flights
The Westering

MEMOIR:
A Collection of Friends

NONFICTION:
A Gathering of Memories, Saugus 1900-2000
(with John Burns)

Of Time and the River
(with John Burns and Robert Wentworth)

EPIC CURES

To Ruthie,
Just from your computer
Course, and from where I
spend most of my hours,
at the computer, whence this.
Please enjoy
Tom Sheehan

A COLLECTION OF STORIES BY

TOM SHEEHAN

Press 53
Winston-Salem, North Carolina

Press 53
PO Box 30314
Winston-Salem, NC 27130

First Edition

Cover design by Kevin Watson
Cover art by Jeff Fioravanti
Tom Sheehan photo by Rich Garabedian

The author wishes to thank the editors of the following publications in which these stories first appeared, in the presented version or an earlier version:

Aethlon, "Sacrifice Fly"
Duct Tape Press, "The Boy Who Dug Worms at Mussel Flats"
eastoftheweb (London), "Banjo"
Electric Acorn (Dublin), "The Lobster That Wouldn't Sleep"
Fiction Warehouse, "In the Company of Angels, the Company of Men" and "Last Call for a Loner"
42 Opus, "Humboldt Haven"
Literary Potpourri, "The Rescues of Brittan Courvalais"
Muse Apprentice Guild, "Tylen Brackus"
Prose Toad, "The Old Man of the River"
Slow Trains, "The Undies Pennant"
Small Spiral Notebook, "Aces & Eights" and "The Canoeist"
Snow Monkey, "Flesh of an Unwanted Fish"
StorySouth, "The Idylls of Staff Bickerston"
The Paumanok Review, "Knickers" and "Rural Free Delivery"
3amMagazine.com (Paris), "One Oh for Tillie"
Triplopia, "The River Thief"
Tryst, "Charnley and Leonard the Blind Man"

Printed in the United States of America

ISBN 0-9772283-2-0

DEDICATION

*For all who labored in Raytheon's vineyard with me,
including those memorable cohorts and story tellers
in their own right:
Larry Bucaria
Nick Capecci
Ron Doucette
Sal Giambaressi
John Henigan
Joe Latvis
Ed LeBlanc
Don Savio
Peter Steckowych
John Taflas
Jim Tuson
and Charlie Poulin, who gave this book its name.*

*And with a special tug at my heart for Billie, Mikey,
Jasper "Jeep," Alexa, Bobby and Travis, and those
who follow in name or trend.*

CONTENTS

This writing of tales has never been a game,
no matter how many times I've lost.

~ Tom Sheehan

KNICKERS

I was fighting it all the way, wearing knickers, me, twelve going on thirty it felt some days, dreams about Ginnie Wilmot practically every night now, the *morning dew* being the vague remnants my father spoke about with a smile on his face, new hairs in my crotch, my mother wanting her boy *to look neat*, my father looking at the horizon almost saying *this too will pass*. It was his one-shoulder shrug that carried verb and noun in its arsenal. I had early discovered that he did not need a lot of words.

My mother was looking at her choice of two hats, checking them out in the mirror on her bureau. A dried flower was creased in cellophane in one corner of the mirror; I'd heard some reference about it but had declined interest. My father's picture, him in a Marine uniform, was framed in a second corner, my sisters and me in another, in our Sunday best a year earlier. A palm frond from Palm Sunday twisted itself across the top of the mirror. I think the hats were as old as I was. I knew she would pick the purple one.

Her eyes announced the decision prematurely; again, an article of speech. Much of the time we were a family of silence, where looks or shrugs or hand gestures or finger pointing said all that was needed. My cousin Phyllenda had given the hat to her. "You'll look great in this one." I could never tell my mother Phyllenda's boyfriend had swiped it from a booth in Dougherty's Pub in Malden Square where he'd go of an evening or two. I'd seen them talking an evening on the porch, Dermott's hand up under Phyllenda's dress and it not yet dark.

A May Sunday was a bit snappy this early with the sunrise. "There will be hundreds of people at Nahant Beach today." Both the radio in the bedroom and the kitchen were on; her music almost mute in the background. She looked out the window across Cliftondale Square, across the green of the traffic circle and the new green of elms already leaping at full growth against the sky. On the third floor we lived, yet not as high as some of the elms. Gently a nod was spoken, an affirmation. "They are waiting for summer at the beach," she added. "They go walking on the beach looking for it. It's over the horizon a few weeks yet. We will go right from church. You will wear your new green suit." At length it had become her trip-hammer approach, the hard music. In that voice I felt the agencies of iron and slag at a mix. "You don't know how proud I am of you in your new suit. And two pair of pants, at that." For sure, iron and slag in her words, the new and the dross. At her lighting up about the new suit, I cringed. *Two pair of pants* seemed eternal, would carry me into high school, into football, the mold of the locker room, pal-talk growing the way my older brother would nod, owning up to all I had heard. Hell, there'd be knickers, for God's sake, for girls, lots of them prettier than Ginnie Wilmot who once sat across a log flashing her white underpants at me so that something happened in my throat, something so dark and dry and dreadful that I can taste it yet.

Simon Goldman it was who sprung the suit on my mother, little shrunken Simon with the poppy eyes and the red face, on Saturday morning collecting his due of pennies she yet owed on a parlor set. "It's green herringbone tweed, my Helen," he said, in that possessive delivery he must have developed early in his game. "It has two pair of pants. For you yet cheaper than anyone. Resplendent he will be in it. Resplendent. No boy in this whole town has a suit like it. And the famous golfers wear knickers, I've seen them in newsreels at the theater. Hogan and O'Brien and Downey, McDevitt and Fitzpatrick, McHenry and that Shaun whoever from Swampscott." He was inventive, you had to admit. I'd have said a liar as well as a schemer. "Two pair of pants. Green. Herringbone. Think of the message."

His eyes almost fell out of his head, dropping Ireland almost at his feet, dropping it at her feet. I almost pushed him down the stairs, he was at it again, selling her, saying it was a bargain, saying you people are climbing the social ladder on my advice and merchandise. Truth is, she cautioned me once, only once, on how I should remember Simon. "I found him," she had said, "he didn't find me."

The worst part of it all, putting on the suit, the knickers with knee length socks, was having to take off my sneakers. I thought they were welded to me. I thought I'd wear them forever. I belonged in sneakers, foul or fair, "But not in your new suit." It was as if her whole foot had come down on the subject. My father lifted his chin, flicked his head aside, gave off a mere suggestion of a nod, shrugged his shoulders. *This too shall pass.* With a knife he could not have carved it deeper.

In my new greenery we headed for Nahant Beach, me in my green knickers, four sisters all dolled up in the back seat of the old Graham, the titters and snickers behind their hands, my unsworn vow becoming animate at the back of my mind, a prowler on the outskirts of a campground.

Up front, in her purple hat, a purple dress with a big collar, a black pocketbook with an over-scored but lustrous patina, my mother looked straight ahead, playing now and then with the knob on the radio, trying to catch La Scala or New York out for a morning stroll.

She stared at nothing she might wish to have. Beside her, between her and my father in a car borrowed from my uncle, was the second pair of green herringbone knickers. Not knowing why they were there, I nevertheless felt my father's hand in it. I wondered if there had been an argument's movement along with the package, or behind it. Arguments I had heard, about dozens of things, then quiet discussions. Once it had been about the radio one could hardly hear. "Music has shaped me," my mother once said, "from the very first touch to the very first clench of fist." That's when I knew she loved the brass of a band or an orchestra, not just the oompa of it, but the cold clear energy of horns clearing their throats with melodies one could only dream of.

"Toot the horn," my mother said. "Now there's Dolly Donovan." Her wave was thorough and friendly. No message hung on its signal. "She'll be at the beach. Maurice will bring her." I did not deflect a message in that pronouncement: it came anyway. Maurice bid and Maurice done. Some laws, it seemed to say, were carved in stone. It could have said *Life is more than being made to wear green knickers*, but I wouldn't let it.

In the rearview mirror I caught my father's eye. "We might as well see what Forty Steps looks like today, and then come back to the beach." The gears downshifted as he swung the corner down Boston Street in Lynn. We had come over the bridge spanning the Saugus River. In my nose the salt was alive, and pictures came with it. The gulls, by the hundreds, whipped a frenzy. Waves dashed on the rocks of Nahant, especially where Forty Steps climbed upward from the froth of water. The lobster boats, working yet, bobbed out on the Atlantic. Under sunlight majestic white sails of sloops and schooners and sailboats from Elysium, Islands of the Blessed and Marblehead darted like skaters before the wind. On that same wind brigantines and caravels and corsairs leaped from my reading, taking me away from green knickers and Nahant all the way back to Elysium and Ginnie Wilmot, the salt spray clean and sprightly, and the dry vulture of taste yet in my throat from one glimpse of white underpants. Would that mystery, that sight, never go away?

The Graham, brush-painted green, lumpy for the tour of Nahant where Cabots and Rockerfellers and Lowells and Longfellow himself once sat their thrones, cruised along the Nahant Causeway. In the slight breeze you could feel the sun bleaching stones, sand, the inner harbor's glistening rocks throwing off plates of light like the backs of hippopotami caught in a satin lacquer. People dressed for church and late dinners and nights on the town walked along the beach, their best clothes akin to badges of some sort. "My, look at that white hat with the huge brim," my mother said, pointing out a woman holding a man's arm, three children at their heels. The girls were still giggling behind their hands, restrained while my father was driving, on their best behavior. Once on the beach they would become themselves. And I would set about de-suiting myself.

When we strolled over to the Forty Steps, the waves talking to us, the crowd of people on all approaches, I saw other boys in knickers, but no herringbone green tweed. No iron mother holding her whip and her pride in one hand. A few giggles and *harrumphs* I heard, the way my grandfather could talk, making a point or two on his own. No question in my mind they were directed at my pants more than the whole suit. These people could also nod, shrug, gesture, make sense without words. I wondered what made me want to read in the first place, seeking all the adventure of new words, in this wide world of the body's semaphore, so expressive, so legitimate.

I knew it wouldn't take long, not at Nahant, not at the edge of the great ocean itself, not here where the Norsemen and Vikings and Irish sailors were flung to, across the seas, with Europe behind shoving them relentlessly. My parents, arm in arm, walked on pavement, the girls broke free with yells, I fled down to the rocks at the ocean's edge. With an odd gesture, my mother lifted a hand to her face, as if surprise dwelt there to be touched, to be awakened, to be lifted for use. That's when I knew she was the smartest person in the whole world. She had seen it all coming, had practically choreographed the whole thing, and my father thinking he was in control all that time. At last she had measured me against all other boys in knickers. And found something wanting.

Green is as green does, I could almost hear myself say as I slipped on the rocks heavy with seaweed still with salt, still with water, still with an unbecoming dye residing pimple-like, blister-like, pod-like, in its hairy masses. It was more like sitting down in puddled ink, that intentional trip, trying to be a loving son, finding it so difficult in green knickers, obeying more primal urges.

"What a mess you've made of yourself," she said when she saw me, that hand still in surprise at her face. "Go up to the car and change your pants. I brought the other pair along," *so you could get rid of them also,* she seemed to say. My father had found the horizon to his liking, the thin line of boyhood and manhood merging out there on the edge of the world; no shrug of the shoulder, no sleight of hand, but a look outward that was as well a look backward. I saw it all.

I'm so shit lucky, I said to myself, loving them forever, and then some.

ONE *OH* FOR TILLIE

I t didn't announce itself, the difference in the room, but it was there, of that he was positive. It wasn't the soft caress of the new blanket, or the deep-sensed mattress he'd never slept on before, or the grass-laden field-laden air entirely new to him pushing through the open window and tumbling like puppies on his face. If he opened his eyes he'd know, but he had kept them shut—enjoying the self-created anxiety, the deliciousness of minute fright that he'd conjured up. There was apprehension and a plethora of mental groping going on that had taken hold of him. Being alone was also new to him, but being aware of a presence *did* make a difference, if he could only believe what he was telling himself. At thirteen he knew you sometimes had difficulty believing yourself.

But the fact of *presence* suddenly hit him its full force, though it had an argument attached to it. He didn't want to leap wildly out of bed (there *was* a chance he could be embarrassed), so he pretended again, this time *emergence,* slow and oh so deliberate *emergence*—from his woolen cocoon, from a dark and mysterious Caribbean cave close upon the jungle, from under the lashed canvas aboard the ship of an evil one-eyed captain of pirates, from behind the dark curtains of a magician or castle wall. What he could not do was look out of the back of his head, though he tried, trying to move the slits of his eyes, now finding morning by its faintness, so that he could see behind him.

Cautiously he moved, as if by his innate stealth he could fool anyone into thinking he was motionless or asleep or unconscious. His right ear found the pillow, telling him he had moved far enough. He opened his eyes and the girl Tillie was sitting there at the small desk, or the woman Tillie, or whatever you'd call her Tillie. She had not said a word the night before when he met her rocking away on the porch, staring straight ahead, not acknowledging him, not once looking up at him, just rocking her slow rock. Twenty or thirty she could have been, but he wasn't sure of how to make that measurement, what elements to compute with. Where she had been in a blue dress and yellow sweater on the porch, she was now in the most simple of night dresses or nightgowns through which in a widening swath morning's faint light moved and made soft mounds, pleasant roundness of her flesh. Her breasts lifted themselves right there under the slight cover and his eyes had found them immediately, the nipples dark the way they had been the night before. Still she did not look at him, still she said no word, made no sound, and kept one hand secreted on herself. At once he knew she was not a danger, not a fearsome threat to him, though he could not tell how he knew. High on her forehead was a scar showing its whiteness, a very human and vulnerable scar that said that she herself had been hurt, had suffered pain at some time. On her left shoulder, faint but red, rose a birthmark. It looked to be wings open to the wind, it said she was susceptible and not ghostly. The speechless mouth was formed with pretty lips puckered on themselves, full. Hair was a soft blond, though it tumbled about her head but in a not ugly fashion.

Even in the pale kiss of dawn her cheeks had much color in them, at least heightened from that of her face. Her eyes as yet showed no color, but were not malevolent or fearful though they carried the same sense of distance in them others had shown, a long reach into something he could not begin to understand. A coarse achiness crossed through his chest and he wanted to swallow. His mouth was dry.

For the very first time she turned slowly to look at him and dawn caught itself in the eyes looking at him. Something unknown had softened her mouth, made it elegant and wet and shiny; a word had not done it, or a smile or any movement on his part, but it was rolled like a smooth petal and had a lovely pout to it. He fought to remember everything that had brought him here, to the Cape, to this room, in front of this girl who had not yet uttered a sound.

As she stood dreamily, slowly in the light of the false dawn throwing itself upon her, particles of morning faintness falling with some kind of fever all over her ample body, and as she looked naked in that soft reach with the darkness at her midsection and at her breasts, yesterday all came back in its crowding way. He was surprised at what he remembered so quickly even as she began to move from her place. A phenomenal silence hung about them in this house that had promised so much of sound.

It had been a slow, easy, green morning at that, yesterday, and had been since the very earliest part of daylight when his father had gentled him up with a push at the shoulder. "Don't run," he had said, "but walk to the nearest exit." The constant smile came with the voice, and over that broad shoulder, it seemed, he could hear the birds of Saxon in their small riot of gaiety, a sure sign of the day, its goodness, its promise, the sun having already laid bare most of the secrets his room had but a few hours earlier when he pitched awake in the darkness. His newsprint ball players on the walls, as if they had sprinted into position, long-legged and gangly and floppy-panted, were now the icons they were meant to be, Williams and DiMaggio and Slats Marion full-figured in a splash of sunlight, suddenly each one three-dimensional across the chest, shadows behind them, life-emerging; for a moment he thought Billy Cox would loose the ball in his hand all the way across the room to first base. He heard the birds again, as if scattered in flight from their roosts, raucous and noisy as fans at a game, the way he pictured the Sooners breaking away from the line to become propertied. Sleepily he locked on to the second sun of his father's smile, tried to remember what they had been saying in the other room as he had dozed off and on the night before.

It had been Mel's voice, deep and rugged, carrying the whole diaphragm with it, the words coming square and piecemeal as if each one was an entity, which had first penetrated his move into sleep.

"Mike'll love it down there, Bill." He paused, let the weight of each word have its way. "He'll have the whole farm to run around on. Charlie and Mav will keep him busy with the cows and the chickens and the gardens. Nothing heavy, for sure, no barn building or rock walls to set up, but enough for him to break out. Hell, he's starting to grow like a weed and Mav's cooking will put admirable meat on his bones. And there's always new life coming around the corner." From the last he got the implication that Mel thought he was much younger than he really was. Most older folks had that way about them, he agreed to himself.

Quietly and sort of pleased, he knew they were talking about his summer and him, him thirteen, lanky, a stick of bones just finding a hair or two in his crotch, the wonder of a host of things either pressing down on him with almighty force or trying to come through his very skin, other messages scratching for light. Mel he could see as clear as ever; blond, muscled, the blue Corps uniform rippling across his chest and upper arms like a sail under attack of the wind. Once, according to his father, Mel had been a desperate youngster, fully at rebellion, always rambunctious, in the darkness of home beaten by his father for much of his young life, until the man had had a heart attack with a strap still in his hand. "Mel was looking for a payback for the longest time," he'd said, as if to cover a lot of ground with a few words, as if Mel was due as much room for whatever transgressions had been yet accounted for.

"He can stay the whole month of August if he wants... and if he likes it," Mel had continued. "All summer for that matter. It'd be one less mouth to feed and he'll come back bigger and stronger, maybe so you wouldn't recognize him come the end of August." That square and stubborn chin of his usually moved slowly when he talked, and he would have bet few cries ever leaped from his mouth, even when his old and mean father was beating on him. No, sir, not one to cry, that Mel, all blond and good looking and packed full of muscle, who walked like a bomb might go off if he got triggered wrong. It sounded great to be going down to his farm with him, even if Liv was going along, and her a teacher at that. "There's something about the earth or the elements or whatever you want to call it, that gets deep into you down there in Middleboro. It's high green all summer, wild growing making up for winter coming down the road, vegetables leaping up out of the ground like they've been shot, cream as thick as molasses and Mav's ice cream every night of your life makes it all so perfect you can't believe it even when it's happening. It's a dream much as anything that I know of, an aura, a feeling. I don't know if it's the food or the air or if it's in the damn water, but it's something that'll pop his backside as good as a ramrod. Hell, I bet he sprouts an inch or two just this summer. You got a ball player coming on your hands, Bill, and you've got to give him room."

He'd known that Mel had been left a large piece of property down the Cape way from his butcher of a father because Mel was all that was left of the Grasbys (a brother drowned in a small pond when he was only six, a sister killed in a car crash at only sixteen when she had been drinking and another sister not seen around these parts for more than fifteen years), that an old couple, Charlie and Mavis Trellbottom, worked it for him while he was still working on his enlistment, that Mel was on his long leave of the year, that Liv Pillard, his girlfriend, was going down to the farm with him for just about all of his leave. The aura and taste of a farm suddenly flooded him, his head being jammed with smells of hay and new cut grass and barns wet with whatever steamed up barns and made them dank and memorable other than horse or mule sweat or a cow's splatting wildly across a dense plank floor. All the sounds came back, the clacking and strapping sounds and the noisy wetness you get conditioned to, and the aging by which wood speaks so eloquently and so disparately as if the popping stretch of boards and the checking of beams is each one unique unto itself, each one a message of age and sorrow, a cry.

"Barns bend but never break," he'd heard his father say once after such a visit, and such came fully at him. He'd been but once, to Billerica that time with a cousin for a long and adventurous weekend, and parts of the quick visit had stayed with him; rafts of bees or hornets at their endless commotion and business, spiders dancing on silver rails so high in the peaks it made him think of circus trapeze swingers, hay dust so thick in his nose at times he thought he might not be able to breathe, another near secret odor that had to be leather almost making its way back to life, the moan of a solitary cow, a stool being kicked over and milk sloshing its whiteness on heavy planks, in one corner of the barn the close-to-silent scurry of a mouse with a cat arched in mid-flight as if its bones were broken.

Suddenly, not knowing why, the way things had been happening lately, Liv Pillard eased herself into his mind; tall, bosomy, hipped, standing in the door of a classroom watching her students return from recess, skirt full against her thigh, pushed by her rear, her mouth the reddest mouth he'd ever imagined, the long auburn curls in a slow dance about her neck whenever she moved a fraction of an inch. The graceful lines of her calves, at her hips, had more meaning in them than he could fathom. A hundred times she had smiled at him, he figured, because his father and Mel were long-time friends, because their roads high and low and often had drifted through Parris Island and Quantico and Nicaragua and Philadelphia and the Boston Navy Yard, because they played cards from cribbage through every realm of poker with the same dead-earnest intensity no hand or prize could shake and could drink beer for whole weekends at a time without seeming to move; had the same set of the chin, they did, jutting and chippy, asking for it one might have said, proud, bearing absolute silence at times, whole unadulterated reams of it that could threaten a body as much as could a fist. Their competition was in place of a war, it being a time between wars.

Shopping, picking up supplies in special stores, getting the oil checked a couple of times because of gauge trouble, the ride to the farm was a long and convoluted trip. Liv and Mel sat up front in the long roomy roadster, him in the back, the sun and the wind pouring down over them, Liv's hair caught up in them like a pennant, every which way flying and catching gold and throwing it away as if she were philanthropic. Now and then he closed his eyes with his head on the seat, her perfume not less than gentle in his nose but new and mysterious, new grass smell edging it out, the perfume coming back, more new grass and occasionally lilacs loose about the road, once in a while her head out of sight, and he wondered if she slept fitfully as he did. A trucker honked at them as they passed, then honked again and pointed at the car to his striker craning his neck to see the car as it pulled away, Mel throwing his hand in the air as a nonchalant goodbye. He himself had no idea of what was so special about the long-hooded Packard, except that it was long and black and speeding to a grand farm in Middleboro with animals and strange crops and all the ice cream he'd ever want, and him leggy and sprawled across the back seat, and Liv's perfume coming relentlessly at him.

Mel slowed the car at the crest of a small hill, and then stopped. "There it is, kid," he said, his jaw pointing, his sharply hewn nose pointing, a readable smile on his face.

Land spread itself everywhere, whole patches of it cut up and divided by more greens and yellows and rock walls and punctuating tree lines than he could imagine. It spread from horizon to horizon and coming from his own private library of National Geographics were unrolling pictures of the pampas and the savanna and a sense of space at once so vast and so intimate it walloped him, like *a hand aside the head.* He heard his grandfather's voice, some letters of words, some syllables, bent in half by the tongue and others stretched for all they were worth, lifting themselves out of a forgotten cave, a grotto or cairn he had put aside for too long, a place where stone took on new dimensions and new spirits, the slight figure of the small man in a forgotten doorway, the booming voice so often attributed to the *upstart young poet Yeats now knocking heads asunder.* Cluttering on top of Liv's resurgent perfume came the sweet odor of more new cut grass, somewhere a whole crop of it, and then a vaguely refined field smell came rolling in, dutifully at recall, coming from the green sea of a field on a crest of combers; clover from that other visit he realized, where the barn had been memorialized, ripe as the Atlantic itself, rich as brine. In the middle of all laid out before his view was a long sparkling white house, the main part of two floors and sundry additions plunked like excess punctuation, also white, easy and casual afterthoughts at a glance, which had been appended at random, he surmised, or had been required by different men and different needs.

From the chimney of one of these, squat and like a hen coop, the one farthest from the main house, smoke rose slowly, its column meandering ever so slightly, uninterrupted for all intents, lazy as the beginning of this very day had been. A wide porch spread out on the two sides of the house he could see, and promised more at each of its further ends. A horse and wagon, piled high with perhaps hay, a shade of yellow not yet seen in the fields, crawled across the front yard; its facing side was gray and neutral and had no contour top or bottom, but belonged, picture-perfect.

A shed off to the side had the same color, weathered, beaten and angled, wearing a thousand storms for sure. It leaned into its own existence. Time was trying to mark this place and this event for him, time and what else was working along with it; the indelibles indeed were afoot but he could not bring them all the way home, could not decipher them the way they should be: a painting inching itself into reality, another clutch in his gut as if something were being pulled out of him, a tendon, a muscle, a useless organ through the eye of a pore. An emptiness carved its hollow way through his stomach. He felt cheated somehow, but could not lay identity on it.

A woman on the porch shook a mat or a small rug over the railing. Her motion was quick and lively, and seemed to be the only thing moving. Liv's perfume came again, more than lilac, more than any petals known, more than recall could demand. And with it the realization that taste had been introduced. In such a short time, taste had been introduced; it caught itself at the tip of his tongue, lingered, left. It was not a sweetness, he knew. He tried to recall it. It came to him that a variety of borders had been built around him in his short life and were being broken down, but he could not determine the extent of them or the extent of the breakdowns. At the edges of his senses, likewise at the point of division, identity of a number of things for a new moment was unknown.

Then, the way ideas are crystallized, from a small world controlled by an inner energy, the great merger came, the meshing of sights and scents and somehow reachable mysteries. It pushed together the picture-perfect wagon and the woman at dusting and the sudden ebullient clover and the inviting spread of the house and the wide issue of fields going off to where stars waiting night were hanging out and the mix of planets. Liv's perfume crawled down the back of his neck and Liv looked up at him from the front seat and he looked down at her and saw one absolutely splendid nipple of her twisting standing alone in the cup of her gaping bra like the knob on the gate lock in the back yard at home. The rush was upon him.

Her teeth were as white as the house. His stomach hurt. Wind whirled in his ears.

Holding her hand visored over her eyes, the two o'clock sun slashing down on the side of the house and across her stance, the woman on the porch had seen them coming down the slight ramp of road. Brown hair was piled on top of her head and pulled into a bun. Near sixty at least, she had a wide forehead, comfortable eyes which traveled easily over the three occupants of the car, a mouth that was as soft as prayer, and arms bare right to the shoulders. An elaborate pinkness flowed on her skin, a rosy pinkness, gifted more than earned it appeared, and it softened everything else about her—eyes, mouth, the angles of her joints. Almost as a salute, one shoulder dipped subtilely as if a sign of recognition, or acceptance. Pale blue, front-buttoned, her dress wore remnant perspiration in dark patches, at both arm pits, at the belt line, at one breast, perhaps something wet had been held close to her body, perhaps something wet and dear. The boy could see that she moved very deliberately, bringing her arm casually and gracefully down from her face. That same hand waved at them but he could tell mostly at Mel, for a smile came with it. He thought of the ice cream promised, for this must be Mavis Trellbottom. Into a dark recess the wagon had most likely gone, for it was out of sight and there were doors of all sizes in the barns, and the yard was quiet and serenely peaceful.

She yelled, "Mel!" full of surprise and endearment, and then in a cry two octaves higher, "Charlie! Charlie!" and not *they're here* but "Mel's here." The voice was as sincere as her face. The boy felt she would have yelled "Mel" even if the president were with them.

Even before Charlie came into view, Mel was out of the car and had picked the rug-shaking woman named Mav right off the deck of the porch. Slippered feet showed, much of her legs, a flash of underclothing, and her hair sort of brown in another minute might have come loose from the top of her head. A featherweight, the boy thought, as Mel swirled her about, more than warmth written all over the pair of them. A small stick of jealousy stabbed at him, a jab a lightweight might have tossed, but jealousy none the less. She enjoyed the roughhouse greeting, it was evident.

"Hi ya, Duchess!" Mel had yelled, then hugged her tightly to his frame. On his face, as innocent and as real as morning sunlight on a green leaf, was expressed the most honest emotion the boy had ever witnessed. Even at thirteen, short of experience in the world, he realized that look would not be seen by him very often in this or any lifetime. Another message in the air, another barrier broken, another lesson to be learned plain as dealt cards.

Suddenly he was aware that much of the classroom was at hand. This very summer, this very farm, these people now caught up in his very breathing, would grant him a whole new range of knowledge. He would in no way be able to hold off what was surely coming at him. He looked at the people around him. Liv was still locked to her seat in the car, her face catching the sun at such a generous angle it played games with his eyes. Mav was still caught up in the arms of the young Marine dressed in chinos and a blue polo shirt that seemed to measure his biceps. An older man, unhurried, deliberate in walk, gray haired but moving with an obvious strength, denim straps wide over his shoulders, wearing army boots with the issue buckles still in place, probably rock-solid and not arguable and, more than likely at one time or another, the undisputed King of the Hill among his acquaintances, was striding across the yard. Charlie Trellbottom was a strider, all the way a strider. Energy lifted off him as easy as steam off the swamp back home, and would have been solid-looking to the most casual observer; white hair as thick as goodly pelt, face weathered, wood-burned marked like one of the barns standing behind him in the sunlight, shoulders almost as wide as Mel's. No way was this strider really like my grandfather, who was probably the same age, but he did evince the same kind of energy. A band saw smile cut itself across his face as he said, his voice a flawless timbre that made the young visitor think of old tools they didn't make any longer, "The Marines have landed, Tripoli is saved."

The two hugged and slapped each other like old teammates after a long separation, and the boy could measure the immediate sense of warmth rushing through him. They shook hands all around. He *was* welcome! The air could have hailed him: *Welcome, Michael,* and said, *This is another home for you.* He pretended he heard that from some corner of the yard, the guinea hens roosting in the trees and now squawking like ladies in a knitting circle, a rooster strutting his 5th Avenue stuff, a lift of steam almost audible off a hundred surfaces.

The slight creak he heard in a pause of the welcomes and a moment of other truce brought his eyes to a pair of toes moving up and down, back and forth, at the far left corner of the porch. Patent leather shiny as gills, yellow socks dandelions could have painted. That's all he could see of a third person, one which incidentally had not been mentioned either at home by Mel or in the car on the drive down. The creaking sound said *rocker* to him, and Mavis, noting the tilt of his head, the eyed interest, said, "That'll be our daughter Tillie, but she doesn't say a whole lot." He thought it most apologetic and that it didn't sound like her; already his mind made up that she didn't make excuses, didn't beat around the bush, said what was on her mind no matter the audience or how the cut of it went.

Mel introduced him to Mavis and Charlie and without the slightest hesitation she hustled him off to his room, pushing the tote bag into his arms. On the way off Charlie said he'd take him for an initiation ride on the wagon after supper. There was an actual chuckle in his voice. Liv had slipped her arm around Mel's waist and the sun glanced a halo off them. As he turned to go with Mavis ahead of him, as Charlie turned away for some obvious chore, he saw Liv slip a hand into Mel's pocket. The feeling he had had in the back seat of the car came back to him. It's none of my business, he tried to say to himself, but he couldn't manage it. He also wanted to say that there were so many things he didn't know about, but wouldn't shoot himself down so quickly, not that he even wanted to. He wasn't all the way stupid! Time would see to that.

Mavis Trellbottom, in her blue dress splotched darker in spots by perspiration, took the stairs easily. The oak steps and risers talked incorrigibly under her feet, not a whimpering under weight but a composite of a little anger and a lot of tiredness, the tiredness of holding on, nails and pegs clutching at centuries, a statement against over-use or abuse, a statement of time. The noises were distinct, individual, as if they were on slow-played piano keys or singular strum of a string, and he cold easily pick out the separate notes. On a bet he could identify the source of each one of them, even with his eyes closed. A hazy picture leaped up in his mind of black-haired, wild-eyed, tart and acidic Jamie Stevenson in the back of the Cliftondale School classroom at home shooting his mouth off, crying abuse too, although only when it suited his purposes. Sometimes Jamie, when tromped on, would not utter a sound, and this house might sometime also do the same. But proof had been initially offered that this rambling house would be one of sounds, that it would never be truly quiet, even at sleep. If it were suddenly, without wind or cause, to shift sideways, he thought, there'd be beams creaking, lintels stretching their whole selves with accompaniment, joists threatening his ears, all with their unique notes.

A delicious odor of richness, like piccalilli let loose of jars, followed them up the stairs. With it, or because of it, he knew beans and brown bread from Abie's red brick oven and hot dogs and the same piccalilli. His senses kept stretching themselves all over the place just waiting to be tested. The walls were papered with a small flower pattern with a pink background. Two pictures of revolutionary soldiers hung on the stair walls. A mirror in a gold frame filled the wall at the head of the stairs, and five doors gave promise to the next life, choices set out for his undertaking.

"I've put you down the end so you can hear the farm as it wakes up in the morning. It's new for you, as Mel tells me, being up there just outside Boston. Must be tough for a boy to grow up there when there's so much of this. You'll like it here because it was Mel's room when he was a boy and he always loved it. Now don't be bashful...anything you want just give me a yell...food, more blankets, anything. The bathroom is over there. Charlie and I are at the other end on the first floor and Tillie has the room above us. You'll be all by yourself. If you like sounds, night sounds or morning sounds, cows, roosters, chickens, guinea hens, this is the place for them. Mel used to make up stories all the time when he visited. Made his own joys he did when he was down here." She was right on the money, he thought, as if she had read his mind. There'd be other special things from her. Her last statement brought him all the way around to Mel's father and what he had heard of him. To be away from Saxon and his father must have been a real treat for the young Mel, and this kind woman showing him the ropes must have known all of what went on back there. She'd never spill that knowledge though, of that he was sure as dawn. If his father had beaten *him* what would his life be like right now, what would he have become? That vision left him hurriedly, but the awful taste lingered as he measured up the room.

His room had a nice enough bed with a pile of blankets, a chest of drawers beside one window, a small desk and chair, a small table with a big white bowl on it and a white pitcher, which he swore he had seen pictures of. A rack at the side held two towels and a face cloth. A big stuffed chair loomed out of another wall as if it had just appeared out of nowhere, it was so big and so out of place in the room. The walls had a green-tinted paper that was very comfortable on his eyes, though he could discern no apparent design. There were three doors to the room. Mavis drifted out of one of them saying, "Find your way back when you're ready and we'll have something to eat. Mel's always hungry."

He had settled himself into the room, put his things away, explored doors, gone down a hallway quietly, came back, went another way. He saw the room where the girl must sleep, pale green walls, white curtains, no pictures. He heard Mel and Liv behind the door of another room at their honest noise, which must have carried on from the car as quick as you could think, crept back quietly so as not to disturb them (or be heard being more like it), went down the stairs, saw the girl Tillie close up for the first time really.

In a short while he heard all about her, as if all of them were apologizing to him for springing the surprise of her on him. They took turns in telling him about her at the table where Mavis had presented her broiled chicken dinner. Tillie, in a yellow dress, her hair tied up atop her head, her skin as white as Mavis's was pink, but in that same gentle fashion, moved, ate, reached, but said nothing. Her eyes did indeed have much of distance in them, or depth, like a bottomless well came one image through his mind, and never once came across his eyes paired up, or acknowledging him. That's when he first noticed her breasts, center-darkened against the dress's pale yellow material, the way a nipple would announce itself, broad and darker as a picture might show, at times at play behind that so thin retreat. Her hands were delicately shaped, the nails neat as a made bed.

Mel had said, "Tillie had a very bad accident a few years ago, when she was just twenty-one. She was engaged to a great kid, whom I'd known a long while. He was in the Corps and he called and said he was on his way home on a quick leave and was driving up to see her. She rushed off in her car to meet him and hit him head on at Bailey's Crossing just south of town. He never came out of the car alive. They had to cut him out and she didn't know until almost two months later when she came out of a coma."

"Hasn't spoken a word since," said Mavis. "She hears us, knows us, loves us, but just can't talk— won't talk. It may be that what we're saying right now doesn't even register with her, at least not fully. We don't know. Even the doctors don't know, haven't helped a whole lot except hold out for the promise of something good to happen." The slackness in Mavis's jaw at that moment was an infrequent lapse, he thought.

Charlie nodded at him. "We don't know what will bring her out of this, but we're positive something will happen before we pass on. She's a wonderful girl. She's filled our lives for us, even now when we have to do so much for her."

He liked Mavis and Charlie immensely. Charlie's eyes were like some exorbitantly costly gem, and with the light of the sun still playing in the room they took on more warmth and life.

They absolutely shone when he looked at his daughter, when he spoke of her. Tillie still made no move that acknowledged any presence in the room. She continued to eat, robotic, he thought, just the way she rocked for hours on the porch—rocking, nodding, touching her toes, pressing on them, lifting back her head bare fractions of an inch, as if practice was the art of perfection. Her listlessness seemed overpowering to him. He wondered how he'd ever become as accustomed to it as were the others, even Liv, more beautiful than ever, her face shining with a hidden light of some kind, whose perfume crawled down the back of his mind in a slowly tantalizing swallow. "Hope is as beautiful as she is, Mike. It's one of the loveliest of contemplations in life, I'm sure you'll find that out, if you don't know it at this moment. I think Mav and Charlie would say right now that it's the best thing in their lives, that it's just as beautiful as Tillie is."

Nothing it seemed could be more beautiful than Liv, and he had heard her behind the door in that long secretive hallway, the music of her wordless voice, the mystery of what posture she had been in, what stance, what exposure. Pictures spilled all over his insides and he wondered if he had given anything away. Every sound he had heard he could remember. Did his face show it? He looked at Tillie, his mouth open, hoping for refuge, for escape. She did not move, though the darkness at her breasts was deeper than it had been minutes ago.

Mavis put more chicken on his plate. He looked into her eyes and saw the faraway there too, the long, long tunnel out into space or down into earth. A smile flickered across her mouth, as if she had shared a secret with him right in front of the others. He could not find it. If it was there in front of him, he could not find it, but the slightest curve of that hidden smile was given him again. God, she was as warm as his mother was! And like his mother, could leave messages right out in front of other people's noses. It wasn't always that he could read them, at least not right off the bat, but something would come of every communication. His father was direct in his messages. There'd be nothing here at this table from his father. It would be unsaid. A girl had been hurt. A boy had died. Things had changed. It was like war. After a while the sounds of battle pass.

Now this girl, this speechless girl, this silent Tillie of the accident, came slowly toward him. In the narrowness of dawn, in the narrowness of the small bedroom, she came towards him. Liv, that other girl, that other magical figure, had drifted in and out of his mind, with her whatever stance or position trying to break free from behind that door of yesterday, with her music of sounds shifting its notes in his mind in absolute total recall, every living breath of it. Liv, that other girl, had come at him and gone away. This girl Tillie moved so effortlessly, as if she needed no energy, oiled, lubricated at every joint, almost a spirit of movement, everything that the barest of dreams had dared came sliding towards him. Again, in the false dawn, she looked at him, as she had not looked at him on the night before. He saw distance closing itself down in her eyes, saw the telescope of time working its long way in, collapsing hours, years, the screech of tires, the impact of metals and rubber and blood, how sound must have suddenly stopped for her that night. He saw space there moving irretrievably away; none of it would ever come back, none of it could ever come back.

He understood, for the first time in his life, silence of the unborn, the unknown, the calamity of graceless death. He knew at length what wailing and keening were that he had heard so much about, heard the longing one should never hear, heard it all coming from silence as she slid in beside him. With the whitest of arms, the very fairest of arms, oh so deliberately lovely, she lifted the thin blanket of his cover and lay down beside him. Warmth, as good as coals, flooded him, all the length of his body. Patches of flesh were suddenly hot, burning their way onto him. He didn't know where they were, but someplace against him. An entirely brand new odor he'd never known and would never forget for as long as he lived came rolling over him. With the same ease of her advancing motions, hardly movement at all, grace be it for a name, she placed one of her darkly auburn blazing-reddened nipples against his mouth, adjusted it oh so casually, caress of longing someplace behind it. She spoke. Tillie spoke. She said the sound *"Gently"* as if it had come out of some mysterious and solemn rite, old as all the centuries themselves, as if it had been said the same way before, and at the same time as if it might be a most serious order or command. His mouth opened. His lips were dry. Her hand reached to hold him softly by the head, cupped him to nursing at that wetting place.

He did not know how long he lay still, the horrific heat against him, or if he slept, if she moved, if he moved. There was newness now and hands everywhere and a mouth not his and a gentleness and a fire he'd never known and sounds beyond them. Sounds were in the air and the wash of the morning whispering at them, and hands again, instructive hands, hands at his hands, movement of hands, knowledge, moisture, life exploding a whole arsenal of secrets. The back of his head filled with aromas bent on attacking him but were so startling and so smooth they might not have even been there in the first place, only dared to be. And finally a small and barely audible *"oh,"* a lovely *"oh,"* a remarkably beautiful *"oh,"* an *"oh"* worthy of all speech and all language, leveled across the room as though it might barely reach over the thin shroud on the bed or might go on into all of time itself, the first *"oh"* that Tillie Trellbottom had given up in seven long years.

He didn't remember her leaving or his falling asleep again or waking up more than two hours later and the house silent again down into its dampest roots, down into its deepest part of being a house. Then a rooster called out bright as a bugle, a surly cow answered, a horse, in the high trees the guinea hens began a noisy clamor. Other sounds came that he could not identify. His father's face loomed in a shadow and he suddenly knew what his father had meant about waking up in the morning under a tepee. A languid tiredness rolled through his body, but he was sharply awake and extraordinarily hungry. It made him move quickly to the wash basin.

Only Mavis was in the kitchen and, as if she had timed his schedule, placed a plate of ham and eggs and home fries at the table for him. "You'll not be this late again because Charlie won't let you. He's been gone for over an hour with the wagon, Mel and Liv have gone for a walk. Tillie will probably stay in her room for much of the morning."

Mavis continued to move even as he explained that he had been tired and had fallen back to sleep. She wore flat shoes, white ankle socks and had on a neat gray dress not yet adorned with dark stains. But that promise was there even if the fluid motion she did things with was no surprise to him, as if that grace of hers was part of her own private language. There was so much to language that was not said, that was left unsaid but known. Ideas came cramming into his head, it seemed volumes of them; where they came from, what they sprang out of, he had no idea, at least not a direct idea. It might be too that he'd explode, so much moved on him and in him. He breathed on his plate to ease the canister of his chest and the threat that was building itself there. He wanted Tillie to come into the room, wanted that desperately and could feel the want riding on his face. He wanted to see her eyes again, wanted to see how she was dressed, wanted to see what he could remember. He kept his face to the meal, low over the table whenever Mavis might turn towards him. Redness must surely sit on it for there was heat still resident on his skin.

The morning sun, still angled, still in a wake-up attitude, spilled all over the table and the countertop and lit up much of the room. A vase of purple flowers had taken over what the sun hadn't grabbed, lilacs he said to himself, knowing he would not have noticed them on another day, but the perfume of them carried

42

its vital message. All this *whatever* he deep-voiced to himself had opened all his pores, all his nerves. Things so shortly occurred, so shortly known, came slowly out of some private place he had put them. Perhaps they could no longer be managed. Tillie had said only, *"Gently"* and *"Oh,"* and nothing else, of that he was positive. It said a mountain had been moved, a roadblock torn down and done away with. It said *miracle* in a very small and private way as far back in his mind as he could put it. Another aroma, he realized, was in the room; it did not say *purple flowers* but said *her.* To leave the room at that moment was important to him, but he could not manage it. It would be escaping from Mavis. It wasn't right. If only Tillie would walk into the room or call down and say she was going to stay in her room forever, then he could move. How would her voice sound in the morning air? How would Mavis turn around and look at him if Tillie spoke? What would Mavis say? Would she scream at him? Would he run? Would Charlie or Mel come after him? Would Liv wag her finger at him, even after he had seen *her* nipple stand like the gate knob? He remembered sweet skin against his mouth; *that* was talking in another way. He remembered air being in short supply. Suffocation had been a possibility. He began to shake and finally realized he was frightened. Down here there would be no way to turn, nobody to turn to. There was no assumption of help. A violation had taken place and punishment was in order. His father would be furious. His mother would cry.

Mavis gave him seconds. She must have eyes in the back of her head, he thought.

"Charlie will be back in a short while. He'll take you to the high field on the wagon. You'll have your license by noon." A deep chuckle came with the promise, and then she moved about the room, sunlight falling on her, sunlight following her. She was warm, she was a magnet, she was another aura in his young life. He couldn't begin to mark all that had come at him in such a short time. Was there no end to it? Was this a confidante in motion, this woman in front of him? Her gray dress had the neatest edges, her skin was still of a blessed pinkness, and they cut across each other the way designs cut, the way advertisements move within themselves. "A horse is a horse is a horse, as they say." She spoke with her hands full and didn't use them to make added expression, to accentuate. "Be good to Blackie and he'll be good to you. He wears the wagon. The wagon doesn't wear him. Don't tell Charlie I told you, but he still has trouble cutting left, so mind your fence posts and the corner of the barn if you head off to the low fields. Keep the reins honest in your hands. The answer is in your hands. That's all I'm telling you. Now here he comes."

She wasn't even mad at him. That was amazing. She must know every breath taken on the farm, the source of every sound. His mother would. She'd know everything there was to know; who sneezed or coughed in the night, who cursed in the back yard or took the Name in vain, who suddenly got too big for his hat or his britches. Nor was Charlie angry, still wearing a smile bright as a new saw. Charlie made off with him as if he were abducting him. Before he knew it, he was away from the house, away from Mavis and the kitchen, and Tillie had not called out to him, had not said another word. Perhaps he could breathe now, now that nobody was angry at him. Swinging around he saw the high field spread out before them, not really high but it was on a risen slope of land and kept a firm contour, a place to itself, and Tillie barely hung on at the back of his head.

The clover was rich, the sun was warm, his high and commanding seat gave him a great survey. In his hands the reins had meaning, he soon found out. Blackie was a gallant giant of a horse, black as despair, black as hopelessness, he thought, with ears that flicked like broad knives at the flies, like a pair of hands waving. Electricity from him came in surges down the leather of the straps, a great amount of electricity, and a great amount of power. The wagon seat made him think he was on top of the world. Life was somehow ennobling, for all he had come through, spreading it and himself in great patches of experience. Blackie now and then pranced and danced as if to speak unsaid words. He seemed to say, *"You have the reins but I have the power."* It was not like that with Tillie. She had coaxed and coached and guided him, but also had the power of every move. Pieces came back at him, then chunks of her and chunks of heat and great masses of moisture and an ache and an emptiness in his chest as if he had cut all ties with the human race. It was all so unfair to feel this way. After all, she had spoken, the miracle of miracles; she had used language, she had told him how it was supposed to be, how she wanted it to be. Suddenly he wanted to lash out at Blackie, to drive very hard, to leap past all of the fields, to be *home, to be away from all of this. Is she thinking of me back there in her room,* came a live and ringing thought in his head, like he was talking to himself. It was so confusing, so much of all of it so unnecessary. But a restless edge kept cutting into him, making unknown demands. Finally, relenting, he took himself back to his room even as Charlie loomed beside him bigger than much of life. He brought back what he had seen of her, and how he had closed his eyes at first, and then filled them endlessly even in the faintest light. He remembered how it fell across her whiteness, how shadows get rounded and curved, how light falls into darkness and answers fall away with the light. There'd been mounds of whiteness and expanses and crevices and openings, and her hands had argued at first, and then pleased. His had argued and argued, until, light making more of her whiteness, they had begun a new life of their own, had traveled and touched and been instructed. How empty now his head felt, how dry his mouth, and Charlie was pointing to a pile of logs across the field.

They loaded the logs on the wagon as Blackie kicked at dust and knocked at flies and swung his tail in the air. Sweat ran down his chest; he could feel the little balls of it flowing on his skin. He smelled different. Charlie would know it in a second, how it leaped from under his arms and made itself known, telling tales, telling everything sweet and unsweetened, everything calm and hysterical, ratting on him. His perspiration felt like little balls of steel cruising on his chest. Oh, Christ, would this ever end? he said.

As they unloaded the logs in the yard, Mavis and Tillie sitting on the porch, bees working the air, buzzing, the sun working, sizzling on hard surfaces, heat beginning to touch everything, the guinea hens raucous in the trees, his muscles found other meanings. He dared to throw some of the logs a bit farther than he ought. Mavis watched, Tillie didn't, rocking her chair back and forth as part metronome, sporting yellow socks he thought were disgusting to look at; she had such lovely lines to her legs. He threw another log beyond the pile as he recalled how the lines of her legs met, how they rolled into and out of darkness. Mavis smiled at him, waved them on to lunch, turned on the porch like a judge who had made a quick decision. He thought of his mother preparing a small speech on transgressions.

Lunch, though, was quick and quiet, and Tillie said nothing and he said nothing and Charlie said they'd get another load of wood. They worked at the next load for over three hours, took a swim in a small pool in a stream on the way back, unloaded the wood just before the supper call was made. After supper he sat on the porch steps near Tillie with a huge bowl of ice cream. Once in a while he looked up at her as she rocked and slowly ate her ice cream. The whole yard seemed to fall into a temporary silence, as if it had somehow been earned.

It was announcement when he said, "That was a lot of work today, Charlie. I know I'll be in bed early tonight." Charlie laughed a small laugh and nodded at him. Mavis said, "You'll be surprised how much you grow in one summer down here." Tillie rocked her chair. He was going across that void again, he knew, across the darkness to that other light. There was no other way.

For hours he lay way over on one side of the bed, waiting, making camp, the tepee up and the tepee down. The center pole seemed bigger. He'd never have a laugh with his father about this, but he'd try to share it with him somehow. Maybe years down the road. Maybe masked like a story. He'd not brag, though. You don't brag about miracles. You have nothing to do with miracles except letting them happen and knowing what they are when they do happen. He thought of dress blues and manly chevrons and quick and immediate leaves, and Mel and Liv in their room and how they had all but disappeared from the earth in such a short time. This was like a hotel for them and Liv's hands were live hands, which he had seen. Was everybody like that? If Mavis and Charlie went to bed together at the same time, who would start things off, who would reach if they were to reach? Charlie was tired too. The gray of Mavis' dress had gathered dark blue of perspiration into it. Did it run on her like little steel balls? It made sense to have odors because they were so distinctive, said so much, gave so much away. Liv's nipple was not like Tillie's, he was sure. Tillie's stuck out like a bullet. It had been so real and now it wasn't. Was it possible that she had never been there in the first place? The air told him different. She was in the bedclothes, the smell of her. That was real. Who made up his bed? Was it Mavis? The tent came down.

Moments later, just after midnight, he pitched camp again. He caught her on the smallest bit of breeze coming down the corridor. Silence was still her marker. There was not the slightest creak of the floorboards, and the door he'd left wide open. She moved as she had before, and soon said, *"Gently"* again, and later *"Oh"* again, and he obeyed every gesture and made some of his own with the breath caught up in his chest like a ball of fire. He did not think of Mavis or Charlie or Mel or Liv or his mother or his father, but he did think of the young marine rushing home to this lovely whiteness. It made tears, too, like little balls of steel on his skin, and in the faint streak of dawn, as she took her mouth away with her, she said, "Today we'll have a picnic."

She was not in the kitchen for breakfast, and he ate hungrily along with Charlie. He was ravenous. Food odors leaped at him in quick announcements and there was nothing he did not like or could not identify in an instant, so sharp were his senses, so deep his sudden concern for aromas and the things that walked on the air, which pulled at him. Other revelations had mounted their stands (only two days old and it promised to be one hell of a summer); his shoulders felt wider, his upper arms thicker, his wrists stronger. Time no longer had any urgency to it. You could say handling the logs had done it, but he wouldn't hold just for that. He had paid his way, it was true, had made his contribution. It was like the artifice of mental reservation, you could talk about two things at the same time, and both of them would fall into place. His father would be pleased at the general nature of things, though the crux of it unknown; nothing would be said directly for the first time, but eventually notice would be in the air. It'd be like shaving or jock itch or sudden stains on his shorts that would demand no explanation. Of this he was certain; it would be unsaid, as so many important things were, unsaid but accepted.

Charlie said they would spend one more morning on firewood, and would be back for lunch. At lunch, the sun living amongst them, splashing on every surface, she sat stiffly at the table and he was certain only he was aware that the great distance in her eyes had closed down on itself. It was *that* different. Suddenly he knew how difficult it was to speak sometimes. Profoundly he knew he was moving into one of the great events of his life. As long as he lived some parts of these moments now building about him, now filled with stark and rich aromas, now filled with color, now waiting on sound like a dream trying to be recalled, would have a special place with him. He knew that the two nights here on this farm, and their implausible emergence, would somehow fade away, and that others, if they were to come, would fade away also, but these moments would stand.

And it was gray-blue Mavis who began the moment when she looked at him and asked, "What are you *men* up to this afternoon?"

The word *men* was firm as an oath as she said it. It was not a negligible word. It was not an easy word. It was not thrown out to be cute or to question. It carried more than mere conviction; it carried absolute knowledge, it carried every sound of the night, every shadow, every bit of memorable whiteness, it carried all the resurrection she had waited on for such a long time. It was almost a salute, yet her mouth gaped in awed wonder and her eyes shone with an ancient thanksgiving and her heart leaped in her chest, as Tillie said, "Mike and I are having a picnic."

Charlie nodded, the long wait done.

CHARNLEY AND LEONARD THE BLIND MAN

*S ilence is the color
in a blind man's eyes*

Leonard wondered if it was some kind of contest, if it smacked of more than what it seemed. He had heard the poem a hundred times, Charnley always walking around with the book in his shirt pocket or back pocket suddenly reading it to him, again and again, and Leonard, the Blind Man of North Saugus, let the words sink in and become part of him, part of his sightless brain. Just like Charnley had become part of him. Charnley's face he could not picture, nor eyes, nor beard, nor jut of chin, but settled on the imagination of Charnley's hands and could only do so when he felt his own slim unworked hands, the thin fingers, the soft palms, the frail knuckles, how the fingers wanted to touch a piano but couldn't, or a woman, but who wants a blind man.

Charnley, he noted early, walked with a heavy step, a plod on the earth or trod surface, so that the framework of the old building vibrated and made echoes of itself. Charnley's hands must be robust and huge, Leonard thought, because he had been a farmer at one time, a tenant farmer, a milker of cows, a digger of land, a puller of weeds who just happened to read poems. Just think about that, he said to himself, think about the farmer, think about the distance between two men, how wide it can be, what narrows that distance, sound or silence? What kind of providence can a poem bring?

Silence is the color
in a blind man's eyes, sounded again.

Though Leonard initially could not begin to visualize the poem on the page (not with the sensitivity or capture of Braille or the impressions of an old copper etching he'd known), perhaps not ever, he thought, the way the verses were built, the white space supporting the sounds. This, even as Charnley repeatedly explained the structure, often testing Leonard's patience to the darkest limits, the words building on a pad in his mind, a pad conjured up in an instant. At first they collected in a bunch that he had time to separate and sound off on. What the hell, if he had anything he had time, a whole ton of time.

Then the words, each one in turn, eventually assumed a hazy kind of identity and a place alongside another word or two. Sense came of some of them finally, and then one night, alone, a clarity, as if a shell of awed proportions had gone off in his head, exploded its sound and meaning in a dazzling display of whiteness. His brother Milward had once tried to explain the properties of a white phosphorous shell to him, the heat and the dazzling light and the rush of energy traversing a forward slope of a mountain in Korea. The nearest thing to them Leonard had ever known, to both Milward's description of white phosphorous and this final poem, was pain. He used to tell Charnley his gall bladder attack was a poem because that had struck him awake on several nights at full alarm, fright leaping through his body, a stabbing in his guts, a poem of pain fully understood down to its root and rhythm.

> *his red octaves screaming*
> *two shades of peace*
> *in sanguine vibrato*

Charnley had said, "I'll stop at the end of each verse, each line, so you can see, can visualize, how the whole damn poem is made." As if a piece of punctuation or explanation, he added, "Don't let my rambunctious choice of words upset you. I am not very selective, not schooled. I only mean by them what I'm trying to say." At that moment Charnley's voice was heavy and anvil-like, canyon stuff, back-of-the-barn deep, not a classroom voice, not a poet's voice, no obtuse edge to it, no carriage of partial mystery, no forecast of shadows. It was the no-nonsense voice of a farmer who knows the land is an enemy of wild proportions or the friend of a lifetime in one swift reaping. Patience, it could have said, all the rough stuff not withstanding.

"But your voice changes when you read the poem," Leonard said, "the sound changes, you get cryptic, short-tempered, and don't tell me I'm getting short or I'll kick you the hell out of here! You think I can't see you, don't you? Well, I know when you're standing in the doorway or in front of one of the windows. One room, one door, seven windows, I could find you in a damn minute."

And for his own punctuation said, "And don't shrug your shoulders like that. I know what you're doing when you do it. And your voice changes then, too. I could call you an Octavarian." He tittered, less than a guffaw it was, half full of respect, measuring, playful, reaching. "Hell, man, sometimes I can see better than you." His fingers tapped slowly on the tabletop, a radioman sending out his own code.

Charnley only smiled, yet standing in the doorway on this visit so Leonard could find him in that shadow of shadows, that deep shade of an eclipse of the whole man. He'd been in the shadows his whole life; his dimensions raw and few but known.

a purple strike lamenting rivers
and roads lashed in his mind

One day a year earlier and there's no one there, and then a voice says, coming off the front walk of the one-room house that used to be the old North Saugus School, "I'm a new neighbor now. I'm Charnley. I come to live with my daughter Marla in the old Corbett house. I have a poem here about a blind man I'd like to share with you. I like to read some poems. Not all poems, just some of them. I've watched you walk all the way to Lynn to see your brother Charlie and all the way up the Pike to see your brother Milward, some days your cane flashing like a saber, the sun giving respect to its duty. This poem reminds me of you and I wonder what you might have to say about it."

Leonard's quick words leaped out of the darkness. "You followed me?"

Charnley spoke as if he were plowing the land, trying to make the furrow straight, the endeavor simple. "No, you were going my way, so I went along with you, some ways in the rear, but then I went past both times, to see Ma Corbett in the nursing home in Lynn and off to an old friend's new home in Lynnfield, but not far from Milward's place."

Charnley read him the poem for the first time.

like a crow's endless cawing
of blackness anticipates nothing

"That's a goddamn love poem," Leonard shouted, "and I don't even have a girlfriend. What the hell are you trying to do to me. What are you saying?" There was no way he could fathom Charnley's face, what lurked in a half smile or the set of eyes, how his mouth was framed, the lips readable. If he dipped one shoulder in a half shrug, was it a signal he could interpret?

"Everything is love, Leonard, or no love. Everything. You don't need a girlfriend to have love. I don't have a girlfriend. My wife's been dead two-three years now. I love this poem. You made me see what it's like, this poem. I just want to know what it does for you. If it does anything. I am never sure of things like this, such argument or reasoning. You sow a seed, take care of its bed with tender care, it grows. If it doesn't, better find out why."

"You're like a damn busybody hen, popping in here, following me like I was a damn cripple or something, sticking this poem in my ear. I never had a poem in my ear."

And now, for all my listening,
it is your hand on my heart

"I'm trying to be a friend, Leonard. I wanted to share something with you. I'm just an old farmer who loves this poem."

"Not outright pity, I take it."

"None at all. I don't give a damn if you never see another shadow in your whole life, if that's what you want to hear from me." Leonard knew he was blocking one of the windows, the idea of sunlight failing around him, a personage of shadow.

the mute fingers letting out
the slack where your mouth
reached

They had, with that declaration, become friends for one long year. Charnley would come and read the poem, always reading it from the book, never having it memorized, saying he couldn't do it. Leonard never told him he had it memorized, had said it a thousand times a day it seemed for months on end, at first the words cluttered on the pad and then standing like singular statues. There would be a pot of tea on the old kitchen range, converted to gas by his brother Milward, and the tea would hit the one room as if it had been sprayed with pekoe or oolong or something else Asian, a cutting swath of clear acid in the air, hitting the sinuses, clearing them, drawing Leonard and his friend to the stove on cold days or to the small porch on warm days, the late sun spilling on their feet, the poem following the way a shadow comes along or moves ahead of a body proper.

Leonard said one day, the wind bitter and cold outside, the windows rattling, "Why don't you ever read one of the other poems?"

"It would only dilute this one, Leonard, cut right through it. If I know one poem in my life, it's worth it, and I know this poem because you know it. It's real for me. It's like my wife, my one woman forever. I'll not dilute her. Not for one damn minute. Not forever. The same as having a best friend. There's only one of those. Everyone else has to get in line.

your moving away,
a pale green evening down
the memory of a pasture

Came the day eventually, in the sock of winter, they said the poem like a duet at work, the words falling in place with unerring accuracy, rhythmic, shared, together, almost one voice, the room expanding around them, a spring pasture coming to them, silence coming at them, one word and then another word hanging in space like they were parsing each one in the midst of the air, a letter at a time, a slight whoosh if need be, the rush of a consonant or its soft command on the lips, sibilant, syllabic. The blind man and the sighted man said *silence* as if they stood in the middle of a mausoleum, and the word hung there for them and then died away and became itself. All around them they felt the word become itself. When they said *color*, some long minutes later, Charnley had his eyes closed and Leonard had his wide open, and they knew they were twinned in this sound, this nothingness. Leonard was ferociously at ease.

The next day the knock at the door was timid, feminine, like feathers, Leonard thought, pigeon feathers in the eaves. It was Charnley's daughter Marla. "I have news about my father." The tone of her voice abounded with that news, harbinger, omen. "I found him this morning in his bed the way he wanted to go, peacefully, in the darkness. That's just what he said to me one night recently, 'Peacefully, in the darkness.' He also said that when it comes on him he wanted you to have this book." She placed the book of poems in Leonard's hand. "He said you'd know what to do with it."

She was a smaller shadow than her father standing in the open door, the wind rustling behind her, death hanging back there in the darkness of the day as if it were words ready to be spoken, dread highlights hunting the darkness. The old schoolhouse had no echoes, no vibrations, the sills socked home tightly on the granite bases. Half the size of her father, Leonard thought, yes, perhaps half the size.

Leonard motioned for her to close the door. "Shut the death out," he said, and his fingers found the page of the poem where that route was worn like a path. Listening for her steps, seeking minor vibrations if there were any, he offered the open page to Charnley's daughter, their hands touching. An electrical movement passed through them and he remembered a static charge coming at him once from a metal file cabinet at Milward's house.

Her voice was soft, hesitant. It would take her time. He had plenty of time. Now Charnley had all of it. Against one window she posed a smaller shadow, but a whiteness lurked in aura. Leonard thought of the white phosphorous Milward had spoken about as Charnley's daughter Marla sifted through the poem. He tried to picture her small hands holding the book open. There was something delicate he could almost reach, fragile, silken, but it was lost in the poem as she spoke it, her breath instead nearly touching him, cinnamon with it, and perhaps maple syrup, yet day and night all coming together in the one essence:

Arrangement by Tones

Silence is the color
in a blind man's eye,
his red octaves screaming
two shades of peace
in sanguine vibrato
a purple strike lamenting rivers
and roads lashed in his mind,
like a crow's endless cawing
of blackness anticipates nothing.
And now, for all my listening,
it is your hand on my heart,
the mute fingers letting out
the slack where your mouth
reached, your moving away,
a pale green evening down
the memory of a pasture.

It was faint but indelible, he decided; discoverable, he assented; mild but ascendant, he owned up to; and Leonard the Blind Man knew how soft and delicious it was on her tongue, at her lips, coming from her mouth, the poem, the poem her father had found for him.

THE LOBSTER THAT WOULDN'T SLEEP

It had happened again and bright-eyed, thick-chested Judd Farro, half-clad in the yellow foul weather gear of his trade, couldn't remember how many times it had happened over the years. The sea, obviously, has its own rules and regulations, he thought, its own machinations, and you don't really count on them. But here, in its own great mystery, the lobster with the bold X on its backside was caught anew in one of his traps, big as life, healthy, and as if daring to say Here I am again. The X was indelible, unmistakable, and struck him with an awed intensity.

Judd Farro, lobsterman, knew the sea in his knees and in his heart: the endless rock that caressed him in the shift of tides and the swells at play, either out on the broad expanse or lodged in port softly bumping in that slow-time dance against the dockside. And there was, too, the endless ache in his heart when he was not out on it. That he didn't know the sea as well as he should in his mind was completely acceptable, for with the sea came the immutable laws governing it and all those who toiled on it, like he and his kind, and the absolute idiosyncrasies that played with those same laws. But even so, Judd was comfortable with his lot in life, skipper, owner, husband, father, a man who celebrated the vast sea itself; who was iron-fisted, muscled, beaten brown by sun and wind and salt. Much of his lot in life he had gotten from his father, a lobsterman before him, who had plied his way in and out of the small estuary that was the Saugus River, just north of Boston, to gather his crop from the great Atlantic, to do his great battle of survival out there on the *Father of All Oceans*.

It was his father, Ivan Farro, an oak slab of a man, legendary on the river and in the trade, whose words were very early carved into young Judd's mind, along with the great guffawing laughter that came with his introductions: *We're the Farros, lately of Egypt, now of Saugus.* People warmed to the genial and hardworking giant, and the father's ethics and strains passed clearly to the son.

It was Ivan Farro, at a party one evening at his home when Judd was just a boy, who first lined up a dozen lobsters and declared, "I am going to put all these lobsters to sleep in the middle of the kitchen floor." The heart and soul and meat of his trade, and most undoubtedly of all there with him, inched about on the old birch flooring with the clumsy gait of elephants, dark little out-of-this-world creatures with their claws tied back by broad-banded elastics. Some were bigger than others, but all were keepers to this hardy band of men who fought the sea for these ungainly treasures.

Some of the lobsters appeared as if they could just drill their way down through the floor, so rambunctious they were in their actions. Others appeared not so boisterous, perhaps a bit weaker, having less desire for survival.

"Hey, Ivan," came one strong but gargled voice. "Those 'uns on the end ain't *weaks,* is they? You could told if you gave 'un a hotfoot!" His own laughter preceded all other responses. Judd couldn't see who said it, but he guessed at Herb Comeau. Because of his line of site, he couldn't see Herb in the kitchen, but a hazy flavor of him crept into his mind, small, cigar-y, white-toothed all the time in that part of his mouth where the cigar wasn't clutched, all of the sea on him the way it was on his father, the signature of the river and the sea and the salt and the lifetime under the sun, and the smell of the boats, the unmistakable mix of diesel and salt that brands some men for life.

Ivan shot back, "Should I take their boots off before I light them up, or do you just want me to put the whole dozen of them to sleep like I promised?" He held a lobster out as if it were a token of his promise.

Judd, watching from the second floor landing of the old colonial keeping room of the house they lived in, almost leaped to attention again at his father's words. He craned his young neck to see into the kitchen from his place between the balusters. The broad back of his father bent over as he knelt on the floor. Judd shifted his position a few balusters and saw his father pick up one of the lobsters, still struggling for the open sea, for the sea bottom and its myriad food, its claws trying to menace the grip that was on it. Slowly he began to rub the back of the lobster, riding the knuckles of one hand up and down the dark green but splotched back of the deep crustacean, the ugly grasper of sorts, the clawed menace the likes of which had once gotten desperate hold of Judd's little finger and almost kept it. Perhaps a full minute his father rubbed, all the time keeping up a constant run of chatter that Judd could make no sense of: *The sea is full, but the pan is clean. The waves are rough, but the butter's keen. You've been done in by baits and chums, now sleep, me Bucko, until eternity comes.* All the while he rubbed, he repeated the words, sometimes changing his delivery, sometimes bringing them almost to a tune, now and then a lilt, now and then like a deathbed vow in a voice as serious as Judd had ever heard, chambered, dark, resonant, the echo of the sea somewhere in it, bottom talk that Judd could only sense but knew was real. Much later in life he'd think of the words *mystical* and *mythical* and all they conveyed and how either seemed for that time to be the most fitting, for he was watching his very own father in this strange rite, his very own father taming the terror of the deep. The once-vicious grip on his little finger came back in clear recall and he could feel it all the way up his arm as he knelt on his elbows. He loved that giant of a man as he loved nothing else in life, except, of course, his mother.

"Now sleep, Bucko," said his father, "until the pots aboil," and he placed the lobster on its head and the two points of its claws, like the Tricorn, an even and balanced position which Judd had never before seen a lobster in, upside down in this crazy world. He remembered riding the swing in the Ballard School playground that way and how the blood had rushed into his head and made him so dizzy he had fallen off the swing and had taken a good whack on the back of his head. Now here this lobster remained perfectly still and there was no sound from the kitchen except the claws of the other eleven lobsters trying to find their way home. Judd's mouth hung open and he was afraid that he'd have to hold his breath as long as the lobster stood on its head. It was almost as if an enjoyable panic was toying with him. He was certain that he could breathe if he wanted to. Well, almost certain. He took a quick breath to prove himself right.

The lobster stayed in that clumsy position, not one claw moving, the thick tail motionless, and his father reached for a second creature at his knees, and began the words again: *The sea is full, but the pan is clean...* and before Judd could believe it there were eleven lobsters standing on their heads on the kitchen floor, and not a word from Herb Comeau or Lance Kujawski or Dave Penney or any of that intrepid band, or from their women, suddenly drilled to silence by the still parade. Judd could smell rising up to him the salt and the diesel and the acrid edge of whiskey and tired beer in the mix. And the mass of clams in the buckets and the oatmeal his mother had fed the creatures the night before to clean them out. And the exciting newness and freshness of sugar and butter corn he knew would be his on the next afternoon, corn all the way down from Middleton or Danvers or from a little stand his mother had found way out in Georgetown, a nice ride's worth on a Sunday morning.

To Judd the array of motionless lobsters looked like sentinels on guard duty, for his father had arranged them in a perfect row, using the edge line of one piece of birch flooring as the crown point, a place where lobster heads bent at neatness and sleep. And mystery.

But the last lobster was a rebel, a far more desperate creature than its companions, something of a different order or a different breed, resistant, stoical, culled for this very one and special moment, for even as Ivan Farro carried on for the fortieth or so time the ritual of his words, singing them, praying them, uttering them almost as oaths, cajoling, entrancing, the last lobster did not do his bidding. Even when his father's voice came as an old sea ditty, rollicking in its words, full of creaking beams and sounds that were never port sounds, that last-stand lobster waved its claws in the air, snapped its tail at Ivan's hand, called the sea onto itself, failed to buckle under.

At length the other lobsters had fallen over, Herb said he was hungry, Ethel Bridgeman had turned the heat up under the big pots on the stove, and Lance and Dave began to gather the other lobsters from the floor.

"Not this one," said Ivan. "Not this Bucko! This Bucko's going back in tomorrow." His voice was strictly serious. He held the lobster over his head. "No quitter, this one. No, siree! I'm going to mark him and if any of you guys bring him up in your traps, do him and me the honor of chucking him back. This guy's a tiger!"

He took a knife from one of the drawers and scratched a large X on its backside. Then he took an indelible marker off the shelf and drew the X right over the etched mark. "See here, guys." He held the lobster out toward them. "See my mark. If you bring him up, toss him back in. He's earned his time. Do me that favor." He found each of their eyes with his own eyes, and the promises were silent, and absolute.

And the party had continued and the pot had boiled and young Judd Farro had fallen asleep at the head of the stairs.

All of it he remembered again as he looked at the marked lobster, the X as plain and as bold as the night of the party so long ago. Whether it was the same one was doubtful, but you never knew when it came to the sea, rules or no rules. Perhaps a new breed had been uncovered, or set in motion by his father, perhaps a new *Genus Exus Homarus* was abroad on the deep. He remembered so clearly the night of the party and the alignment of sleeping lobsters. And the strange one who wouldn't sleep like the others, and the storm that beat at the coast very suddenly a few cold months later and his father going down into the depths forever, and the smiling little Herb Comeau from Moncton or Memramcook or wherever he was from with his now eternal cigar, and Josh Billings and his son Peter, and Eddie LeBlanc and the Fewers and the Donovans and the Capeccis and the Savios and the Gallivans and others from the Saugus fleet. If he said all of their names any more it would hurt him, so he cut some of them off, but an ache as big as the sea itself had settled on him once more.

Judd Farro held the lobster over his head and yelled to Yancey Dewey off his port bow. "Hey, Yance. I got that big old sucker again!" The old mythic lobster, a dark green and splotched character swept up from the drama of the sea, serious as a clutch of dark bones, was waved in the air, a semaphore of impractical sorts. When Judd, at length, heaved him over the side, the splash was gone quickly.

Suddenly Judd was in the middle of a grand reverie. This hard-working man, who fought against the hard sea, all things around him buffeted by the fishing laws and the Maritime Laws and the low catches of the times and the often bare scratching for survival that colored every moment of his days, was caught in a reverie. But the reverie he enjoyed. It said it had captured him up as if scooped by a great fist. It said that someone was standing right beside him. It said someone was sharing the deck with him, sharing the slight cut of the breeze on his skin and the roll of the deck marking its meter at his knees and his hips, and sharing the wide expanse flattening out beyond everything just the way Kansas grass or Iowa grass surely must go on forever, or the void out past all the stars. And the soft and hollow ache coming anew in his chest.

Yancey Dewey, pulling and yanking at his own traps, yelled, his voice carrying cleanly over the water. "The sleepless monster takes the bait again! You can bet one thing on it, Judd." He stood straight up from his task on the deck of his boat, a mark of punctuation for his words. "Your old man's got a hand in this. Said he'd never let go and he sure hasn't."

The endless roll of the sea was yet broadcasting itself at Judd Farro's knees, at his hips, swinging its mythical and timeless magic, and far over the small white caps running under the most patient of winds, from a distance without measure, from either that far not-so-illuminated point of reference on the horizon or from the confines of his own mind, he heard the chant his father had sung: *The sea is full, but the pan is clean. The waves may be rough, but the butter's keen. You've been done in by baits and chums, now sleep, me Bucko, until eternity comes.*

Judd Farro, deep within himself, as far down as he could go, knew that the sleepless lobster would come again into his trap, that the indelible marking would endure, until the time came when he would be stretching out for it himself, the sea all around him. The sea had its laws and regulations.

THE BOY WHO DUG
WORMS AT MUSSEL FLATS

First, a small sail bobbed out on the water. And then it disappeared, as if it had been erased. Bartholomew Bagnalupus did not blink at the contradiction his eyes gave him. Things like mist and eyespots and vacuums of sight existed. *Been there, had that,* he thought, as he swung his short-handled curled pitchfork into the earth of Mussel Flats. He'd have another bucket of worms before the tide drove him off the flats.

Out on the bay the light sail boats tossed easily and ran ahead of the small breeze, and in the slash of waters promising to cover the stretch of Mussel Flats before the day turned over on itself. Young Bartholomew Bagnalupus, sixteen by a few weeks, thought the sails looked like napkins off his mother's table, the way they folded in triangles, ran the breeze as if the front door had been opened and whipped them from the table. Contrast lurked not far from his mind as he dug in the muck for worms, at four cents a piece from the bait shop... the white sails out there and him on his knees here in the muck.

The sun, insisting it lit fires, cussed its way across Bart's shoulders and upper back. Because the bucket was only half-full of worms, gray water, sand and minute debris, it made him drive his short angled fork into the muck of Mussel Flats in the way only he could attack it. His grandfather, the Great Bartholomew, had shown him how to worm when Bart barely came free of diapers. "On your knees, boy, 'cause that's the way the good Lord wants you serving. On your knees and your eyes wide open. Never forget that."

Now his eyes shook open and salt touched at every crevice of his body. He thought it to be iodine, a penetrating thinness with stiletto point. His body ached as it did every afternoon, his knees sore, sneakers sopped and loaded with mud, the sun barely past ignition, his mind filled with the being of salt, with his grandfather, with the waters of the ocean that had taken his father.

If railroad tracks plied this end of town, people would have said Bartholomew Bagnalupus lived on the other side, just a worm digger, clam digger, hauler of kelp.

At the back of his mind, some awareness pulled him into another consciousness. At a different level, more pronounced, it was a severe yank, and one he knew would be folly to ignore. *Be alert to your own voice,* old Bartholomew had said. *Be alert.* He stood up to get a better view of the small bay now growing under the tide, the tide's reach coming in over the flat land. As he put his hand up, a visor over his eyes, stories of old Bartholomew flooded him and he fastened onto the first legend of the old man now sitting in a chair in the sunroom of his daughter's house.

As a youngster of eighteen, in the little village of Pratolino outside Florence, his grandfather's Saturday task demanded he take horse and wagon and crops about fifteen miles to the market for sale. Repetitious and boring, it offered little escape from the centuries-old drudgery of the rock-strewn farm. The Cohorts had disappeared long ago. The Legions too. Adventure went with them. Pieces of mountains came up profusely through farmlands. Italy rendered little but continual labor. So one Saturday morning Bartholomew Bagnalupus, yearning for more, hearing the voice inside his body, sold the crop, sold the wagon, sold the horse and bought a ticket on a ship headed for America. Seventy years later, three wives later, fifteen children later, thirty-five grandchildren later, he still demanded attention from his youngest and last grandchild, and the fourth one to bear his name.

There had been a sail out there and now it was gone. Bart dropped his pitchfork and raced toward the water. His sneakers, filled with salt water and muck, caused him to struggle in some parts of the flats. Out on the water he saw the half-silhouette of a capsized sailboat, but could see no movement. Shortly, he knew, he'd be in the water so he took off his sneakers and dungarees at the banking. Then he thought about his wallet. Pulling it from his pocket he placed it under a large flat stone that would be there when the tide went out again. Bartholomew Bagnalupus, fourth of the name, worm digger, from the other side of the tracks, dove into the water off Mussel Flats and cut his strong arms through the water like a propeller.

As if a buoy had found release from a tangled underwater line, a girl popped to the surface a few yards from the overturned sailboat. Air and noise and blubbering came from her mouth, and one arm swung like a hen's broken wing against the water. A few strokes brought him to her side. He grasped her in his arms and pulled her close to the boat.

Bart held her against the hull and felt her body pressing back at him, the curves and softness he had only dreamed about. Blond tresses swung like leather traces, thick, knotted and rope-like, over her eyes. The one arm that had swung idly now wrapped about his neck. Her lips gave off promise. Against him her breasts bore softly. A knee, lightly, accidentally, not quite harmlessly, touched at his groin. He felt the new action in his body. Even above the salt in his nose, at his eyes, a new essence came to him, filling his head. *Listen to your body*, old Bartholomew had said.

He listened now and it was the girl who spoke. "God, you smell good," she said as her second arm swung limply about his neck. Her whole frame pushed against him. "Thank you for jumping in. I'd have been all right except for the line that caught at my foot. But I think I've hurt my arm. Do you always dig out here?"

Bart did not answer. Had she smelled salt-residue, shaving lotion, pasta, sauce from the back of the stove, the harsh cut of liberally dosed garlic, the riches of his mother's kitchen? He knew what she smelled like. An aroma leaped anew, with a smooth edge, and then a cutting edge. It filled his head. If he had socks on they'd have been knocked off his feet. And her body, despite being in the water, rode warm and fresh and totally new in experience against his body, floating against him the whole length, all the curves and the new softness bending to his bends, following his contours.

Wearing only his skivvies, he suddenly became aware of an erection starting on its route. What an embarrassment! Yet her eyes told him something, even as a voice came to them over the water: *Marcy, are you okay?* Her eyes closed once, she leaned against him the whole way, and said, "You're precious."

The voice came from another boat. It was Marcy Talbert's father, the banker, the man who owned most all of Pressburn Hill off the old pond, who owned Vinegar Hill and Applepine Hill and Cutter's Pond itself and practically half of Rapid Tucker's Pond. The broad, heavy-chested man jumped into the water and lifted his daughter into the other boat and climbed back aboard. His hand came down to Bart Bagnalupus. "Come aboard, son. I'm damn glad you were around."

Bart did not accept the hand, his erection still somewhat in place. "Thank you, but I left my wallet back there under a rock." *I'd be embarrassed to hell,* he thought. Over his shoulder he looked, back at the expanse of Mussel Flats. Time and tide had closed down on him and the rock, now under water.

"Not going to find it now, son. Come aboard." His hand came back down to Bart. His eyes gleamed big and pleasant and the face seemed kindly though he had not shaved this day. "I know you're in your skivvies, son. She told me. It's okay. She don't mind; I won't mind. She's mine and she's precious, even if a little headstrong."

A father's eyes looked down at him, not a harsh banker's eyes, and no banker's hand extended fully to him, but a father's hand. "I'll have to dive for it," Bart said. "It's all I have and my mother needs it. My father drowned in his boat a few years ago."

"You the one always digging for worms out here?" The hand came again, still fully extended. Bart took it and the big man hauled him out of the water in one swift movement. His erection failed, and disappeared. He felt shrunken and weak and his breath suddenly came in loud gasps. The banker threw a blanket over Bart's shoulders. "Your father the one who tried to get that other crew out of the storm when their boat went under?"

"Yes, sir, that was him." The girl Marcy stared at him, first at his face and then at his crotch. Redness ran all across his face. She smiled again. A haunting and passing beauty glowed on her face. Bart felt he'd never see this same loveliness again in his life.

"Knock it off, Marcy," her father said. "Why don't you kiss him and let it go for now."

Bartholomew Bagnalupus said to himself, *I better listen to this man the same way I listen to my grandfather. He says things you have to find for yourself.*

"That arm looks bad, Marcy. We better get you down to see Doc Smithers."

The girl with the soft lips, the warm frame, the deliciously new body, spoke up. "I won't go see that drunk. He's always peeking down my blouse or up my skirt. Take me to Doc Higgins. He tends to business."

Bart listened. Learning came at him from every direction. This girl showed herself beautiful, willful, and independent. Gray-green-hazel eyes had really knocked his socks off. Her father threw Bart a pair of swimming trunks. Bart put them on. Marcy still smiled at him.

They ran ahead of the breeze, all the way into the marina. Banker Talbert drove them to Doc Higgins's office. Marcy wore a few bruises. Bart only had a chill. Then the banker drove Bart home. He spoke to his mother. "He saved my daughter's life, Mrs. Bagnalupus. He's not hurt, but if I were you I would not let him out of the house before tomorrow. Doc says he might have a reaction. Keep him inside and rested. He'll be okay tomorrow. Tomorrow's a great new day. You and your son please come to dinner at my house tomorrow evening. My daughter demands it and I concur. I'll come and get you at five-thirty."

He looked at the two teenagers sitting on the steps. "I think they already have some kind of mental correspondence." His eyes were light and friendly. At the end of the porch, an old man rocked away in an old rocking chair, alert, nodding.

Early the next morning, when Bartholomew Bagnalupus clomped out onto the muck of Mussel Flats and the tide had gone out to sea, the rock he had hidden his wallet under sat on the mud like a pancake. Someone had stuffed the wallet with hundred dollar bills. At first he thought just about handing the wallet to his mother, seeing the glow on her face. Then, seeing Marcy's face and the face of her father, he began to wonder how he would handle it all.

All along his body, though, he felt the newness of the girl in the water, knew the smell of her in his nostrils, heard her saying, "God, you smell good." If he told the old man in the sunroom, he'd nod and smile, nod and smile.

THE IDYLLS OF STAFF BICKERSTON

This is such an old story with me, about Staff and his rules in life, how they were never formed, but came of themselves, like up out of the ground along the lake, perhaps like frost heaves, not belonging but suddenly there. I am compelled to tell you about him. Once there was a man, his name was Staff, and I came upon him once, fully live, marveling at the lot given him in this life.

It was a tall, sunny day in Spofford, New Hampshire, a breeze off the Northeast, the few clouds in the sky moving like boats out on a vast ocean. Porched, comfortable, knowing the breeze as fresh as a sassy child as it punched through the screen, Staff Bickerston watched his seven-year-old son Marco fire pellets of some sort from a crude slingshot at the last few panes of glass in an old hen house. Like an afterthought the hen house sat out alongside the house, and back from the road, eyesore of eyesores to many but tolerable to Staff. It had been, when he was Marco's age, his clubhouse, rendezvous, lair, and "trysting place with the angels," as he had once told his own father. That clutch of wood, he currently assessed, leaning now, awry, its right angles at elsewhere, would soon be a pile of dust and debris heading back into the earth again, going as it always had at its own speed, first gear, down low, birth to oblivion. He could nearly measure the pace of that journey.

There were readable parallels, or contrasts. Now, too, the grip on his own home was threatened, with a near unbreakable string tied to the local bank and its chief administrator and old acquaintance, Lowell Stratton. Lowell was long-faced and Yankee, cut out of an old black-and-white picture of early America, Colonial early; Staff was somewhat of a redhead, blue-eyed, medium height, medium weight, but broad-smiled. Somewhere along the line he was an import. One shake of his head and the quiet but consistent threat that was Lowell puffed away, and Lowell's long Yankee face disappeared. Oh, he could always drink like that. Oh, that he could!

Earlier in the week he had examined a pellet of Marco's ammunition, then also attracted by its sheen in flight. Bringing the sun over his left shoulder, he spoke aloud, nobody around him, his voice steady but quizzical: "Here I am. I'm peering at it, shining it up on my pants, holding it up at the perfect angle to catch the sunlight glint of its polish, but boring through that rich exterior for the core, the stone's essence, the beauty of its exterior aside. Where is it from? What has it to tell us? What has Marco taken from it? What has it given to him?" Pausing, the small stone still aloft, blessing all that had come unto him, he added, "Have another drink, son."

Staff marveled at his son's skill, for the shiny pellets hit with unerring accuracy some of the remaining panes. Marco was both an impish and inventive child having, Staff much earlier had determined, much of his father's graces for entertainment. As the pellets flew in their near-flat trajectory, they gave off a shine or quick luster. Staff wondered what the material was. Enriched mica, he said to himself, fully satisfied with that assumption, and felt again the near-potable breath of breeze on his face. I could get soon inebriated on that stuff, he thought. Not a whiff of preservative or toxic crap in it. Just a drink off the top layer of the lake.

To all but a few people in Spofford, plunked precariously around a small New England lake, Minot "Staff" Bickerston was a loser in more ways than one. The first thing, they would say, was the little grasp he had on the art of maintenance, the art that most Europeans brought with them when they came here across the span of near four centuries. Give a structure a good footing, take care of it by some rules of order, and it might last unto eternity. Much of Europe still stood tall, though its roots had traversed more than twice as many centuries, but Staff Bickerston had neither the sense of planning, nor the energy or aptitude, others would say, to preserve what had become his, the big house on the lake, with a goodly spread of ground about it. That he was an idler or a loafer from his earliest days had earned him the nickname of Staff, always at hand to lean on. Acquaintances said he was lazy, an out-and-out idler, a leaner in life. His best friend, Nathan Hawkinns only nodded, and said, "Staff's a dreamer. We all dream, but he goes places the rest of us can't get to. Or don't dare." Nate's insider's smile used to drive people crazy, when he'd say things like, "Staff pays more attention to a sawbuck in his wallet than a hundred bucks in the bank, because the sawbuck has presence."

Countless times, though not at harangue, neighbors had heard Staff's wife Mathis say, "The grass needs cutting, Staff. It's getting to be too seedy. And the porch needs painting."

"You're apt to be right on both accounts, Mathy," he'd say, a chuckle evident in his voice, "and one of these days I might accord some attention to your observations, though I possess serious reconsideration on the matter."

The neighbors would smile, as they knew Mathis smiled, for Staff Bickerston was, as Nate had said, more dreamer than doer. It was his cut in life, and he paid it a due course of honor. It was pointed out that Staff didn't paint much or well, nor handle wood's qualities or potentials any better.

"Grass," he might have said, "as well as bush and brush, have as much right to grow as the trees in the forest. We keep trimming and cutting back and what we really achieve is the reduction of oxygen production in this world floating through the stars." Long before the Rain Forest perils had come upon us with the huge slashing of South American forests, Staff had blown the whistle on loggers. "Our last gasp at air might be from the last leaf left, the final pittance of osmosis. God forbid you have to live on the air your lawn gives off. Talk about troubles at your own due."

Most people didn't listen to a Staff Bickerston. It would admit too much for both sides of the equation.

From the eighth grade on he had worked in Leon Culbertson's grocery store, never going any place else in the intervening years, never hoping to go, missing one day in all the time. The pace of groceries was his speed, braced to fit merely three meals in a day, and never a continuous onslaught. People seemed to tolerate him at times, as if it were a sly brand of pity; a few loved him, none disliked him with any fervor or vengeance.

But the bank had come at him. The bank had ceased to listen to him, as he fell behind in partial or total payments, rushing at the last minute to save his equity, to buy a purchase of time. "Oh, Mathy," he'd say, "one day it'll be over. It will be ours again, to give to the boy, to give him a start."

"You know what he will do with it, Staff," Mathis countered, the smile at her mouth even as she spoke. "That's the only thing stops me from going out of my mind... he'll own up to it just as you do."

"You love us both?"

For a moment she mused, a piece of sunlight falling across her face, giving her eyes a touch of shadow, and a sense of the old beauty he had always seen in her: cheekbones shiny as new coins, one small scar over her left eye granting perpetual youth of accident. Staff saw the moonlight, like a blade of light, falling across her face out on the lake years ago, the night he knew he was in love with her. He could feel the sense of water drifting through her fingers the way it did that night, the wind with jasmine in it coming to him through her hair as dark as the night sky, the way her skirt rode lightly and daringly on her thighs.

"Where did you go just then," she said, "back to the lake? Oh, Staff, you're such a beautiful dreamer and I love you for it, but sometimes..." and she closed her eyes and saw the look on his face that same night when her heart beat faster than it ever had and she knew he was in love with her. They had celebrated that moment all their married life. The moment, for a moment, was real. It warmed her.

LOWELL STRATTON SAW Mathis across the diminutive Spofford rotary traffic circle and hailed her. His long legs took him quickly to her side. His hair, she noticed, was thinning, a small breath of air parting it in more than one place, and long hours of work sat in his eyes. Lowell, it was known, never went home early to Lila Theis, his wife. She suspected no one would.

Those thoughts were on her mind as she said, looking up into his face, "I know what you're going to say, Lowell, that we're late again, but Staff will get something done again. He always does." Never cute, hardly ever precious, Lowell seemed a bit softer, the breeze at his hair making him vulnerable, susceptible, and, even for a banker, somewhat tolerable.

Once they had dated, seemed a century ago, but Staff Bickerston had ended that promptly. Long ago Lowell had admitted that Staff for once knew what he wanted and took care of the situation.

Lowell noticed her smile was still the loveliest smile around the whole lake, realizing once more she could charm him at a moment's notice. For twenty years she had had that power. All her cares, all Staff's shortcomings, had not creased that lovely skin; and her eyes were yet the softest blue he had ever known. There had been times when he thought he could see the back of her mind. "I know what the old skinflint pays him, Mathis. I do his taxes, and I don't know how Staff will get by this time. Things are really serious. It's rolling all around us, cutting corners, tightening the belt. Even old Culbertson's getting to feel it. He's been the Rock of Gibraltar forever it seems. I just don't know how Staff'll do it this time. It might be the last leg."

"Lowell," she said, her hand touching lightly the sleeve of his suit coat, "you are a very honorable man. Staff has always said you were a most honorable man. Your father was hard but fair, and you are a cut of the same cloth. We know you are patient. Whatever comes to pass will come to pass. Staff's family has had that house for almost a century now. I don't think he will let it go without some rather amazing effort at retention. He knows he will owe forever, or almost ever. But the dreams keep him going. It's what he does best, and there's something to be said for that. He will never die from stress or a heart attack. It's simply not in his make-up."

"Oh, Lord, Mathy, how well I know that. There are moments, I'll frankly admit, when the tonnage comes down on top of me and I wonder what Staff would do in the same circumstance. I swear there are times, right smack in the middle of my day, when I can hear him talking me out of a blue funk or a frazzle. Sometimes I hear him say, sort of an aside, 'Go fishing, Lowell. The trout are biting at flies,' or 'the bass are looking for silver lures,' or 'go put your skates on, Lowell, and make a little breeze of your own.'"

"Come see us, Lowell. You're always welcome. The porch is made for conversation. Staff says that all the time. Come by for coffee some night, when the breeze talks itself across the lake. Those nights are magic for the soul, he says. I might tell you about his putting some old glass panes in the old chicken coop, just so Marco can break them with his slingshot. They are cuts of the same cloth, those two."

"God, Mathy, only Staff would do something like that. Only he would think of it in the first place. Yes, I'll try to make it pure social, but I can never promise in this business. Some hard things get hammered home every day. Last week we had to foreclose on Jed Akins at last. Near broke both our hearts, but had to be done."

"What's he going to do now, Lowell?"

"It's probably going to beat him into the ground, but I think he's going to live in a spare room at son Ethan's, over in Coldwell, by the river." There was no pain in Lowell's eyes that Mathis could see, but she knew it was there. "At least he'll have a view of the river. Staff would say that is important, wouldn't he?"

"You pick things up quickly, Lowell. Come see us, an evening or a night when the breeze is right." She walked off on her errands.

MARCO NEVER MENTIONED the sudden appearance of glass panes in the old chicken coop. He just assumed that his father had replaced the glass for his entertainment. Vaguely he could remember his father saying he saved the glass from the old greenhouse that had long ago ceased to be. Staff had stacked the glass in a corner of the cellar. "We'll have need of it someday." There was no way of accounting for it, but that someday was here.

The lure of the hill out back pulled at him again. Where the chicken coop had been his father's "place," Marco had a spot of his own, and he slipped into the brush and climbed the small rise behind the house. His own place was a cave so small and so slight that only he could get into it, perhaps seven or eight feet deep and four feet high. The cave actually had been formed by three huge stones, which had been brought against each other long ago. Time had set a mound of vegetation growing over the stones, and hiding the cave. In his mind he called it "His Columbus Place," being the first one, he believed, to find it. One wall was always damp, but the air had a magic touch to it, and the same silence he found in church he found in the cave, an awed and overpowering silence, as if a huge hand had transferred it.

It was here that he found his ammunition, finding some of it in small round stones on the floor of the cave or chipping it off the top of the wall where its deep-seated shine attracted him on his first visit. An old cobbler's hammer he'd found in the cellar sat in a small box with some other tools, and with it Marco chipped away enough ammunition to fill his leather pouch. A few stones, too large for ammo pellets, he left in the box in the cave, thinking about making hatchets out of them later on. The old Indian exhibit of arrowheads and spearheads and hatchets at the library had intrigued him from the first moment he had seen them.

A WEEK LATER Lowell Stratton showed up at the porch, Staff and Mathis enjoying the breeze, the hum of the crickets and frogs coming uphill from the edges of the lake. Out over the lake the evening star was a night light in a spacious room, and slightly downhill clusters of fireflies danced their crazy dance at the edge of Staff's field.

"It's one of those nights, isn't it, Lowell?" Mathis said, as he came up the steps. "I trust it's social and not business."

"I won't mention any predicaments if you don't," countered Lowell. "Felt like a late coffee and Lila Theis wanted to get a good night's sleep for her big day tomorrow over at the Benton Festival. Course, I can't go. So I thought I'd pay my respects." He sat his long frame down easily into an old red Adirondack chair. The chair made a few noises, as if a few nails had loosened up.

"You have a decent day, Lowell?" Staff said. "Maybe an iced coffee might be the trick for you, if you didn't. Be right back." His footsteps sounded down the hallway.

Mathis said, "We still in trouble, Lowell?"

"Hasn't got any better, but I really wasn't going to mention it tonight. Just wanted to cool it a bit. Guess this place is about the best place in town for that. It's probably even better than the lake. I would come by tomorrow, though, and say, if things got real bad, and they are about there now, I swear, I can get a good man to give you a solid price for the place. He's from Alberton, done well for himself, and has asked a few times about this place."

Mathis's breath on the intake was clearly audible.

Lowell felt her anxiety. "There is no shame in selling, Mathis. You can pay off what you owe and get a smaller place. You don't need all these fields, either. They just sit fallow all the time anyway, as if they'll never grow another crop ever, or be used for anything else appropriate."

"That last part bothers me, Lowell. I know it'd bother Staff no end to see this place used appropriately, as you term it. We all know what that means, don't we?" Then her head cocked to attention.

Staff's footsteps came back down the hallway, the breeze humped its small back, the fireflies leaped into a small cloud in the middle of a warm field. At one end of the porch, a trellis covered with roses, near the end of their short stay, made the slightest emanation on the breeze.

Mathis put her hand on Lowell's sleeve. "Not tonight, Lowell. It's just too beautiful. It has to be another time."

"Scout's honor," Lowell said, putting his hand up, the breeze touching his fingers, the essence of rose trying to carry something of Lila Theis in it. He could not find it.

Staff brought Lowell a tall glass of iced coffee. "Hell of a night, Lowell. Hell of a night. You two have a pitch at business while I was out of earshot?" He put the glass into Lowell's outstretched hand. "Tell you this, Lowell, I'd bet you'd be willing to swap places tonight, wouldn't you? It'd be a great trade-off, what I have for what you have, only I'd never make that trade in a thousand years, come I'd have to live in the gutter."

"I came because Mathy invited me again, and because you know I know you have something special and I don't. I know I couldn't even buy it, so no business tonight like I promised Mathy when she said come by for coffee."

Staff pointed off across the field. "See those fireflies out there, Lowell? Know what my father told me about them? Way back, I was younger than Marco, I think, we were sitting here and he said they were the Milky Way in another smaller and infinite universe in constant motion. He said they were stars in their own right, just the motion and speed different from our place and time. Had me full convinced about it. Still think it's possible. Gets me wondering sometimes."

Lowell said, "I was thinking about the roses, Staff. How sweet they smell, and what a short time they're here with us. Beautiful and sweet as all hell and gone as quick as you turn around. Oh, Jeezus, it's hard to say, but Lila's like that, sometimes like it's not worth the damn bother." He raised his glass. "To the roses," he said, "while they last."

Later that night, after Lowell had walked down past the small field, past the clusters of fireflies, and off to town, Mathy and Staff agreed it had been one of the saddest nights they had ever known.

From each side of the coin, they would agree.

TWO WEEKS LATER, just before Mathy was to set the table for the evening meal, Marco outside with his slingshot, Staff sitting on the porch knowing Marco had left two panes of glass untouched, Lowell Stratton came up the road in his car. A tall and heavy-set man in a yellow golf shirt climbed out of Lowell's little sports car with Lowell, as if he had been shoehorned out of the tight seat. The man nodded to

Staff on the porch and looked at Marco adjusting his slingshot in the driveway. When the two men came closer, Marco turned around, adjusted his aim and fired a pellet that smashed one of the remaining panes of glass.

Helluva shot, kid!" the man said. "Helluva shot! I used to be able to do that. You use pebbles or what?"

Marco smiled, slipped the slingshot into his back pocket after looking at the last pane of glass sitting in the middle of the old chicken coop like the last target on Earth. "I get my ammunition out back." He motioned back up the small rise and mound behind the house and the quick burst of brush growing there. "It's kinda secret." He walked back to check out the chicken coop.

Lowell, just coming onto the porch, said to Staff and Mathis, "This here's Abbot Gruden, folks. He's from Alberton and one of those new millionaires we hear talk about. He's pushed me pretty hard on this and since he's such a good customer now at the bank, I am compelled to bring him here. Has a sincere interest in this property and would like to make you an outstanding offer." Lowell's face, long and angular, seemed longer than usual, and redder.

Abbot Gruden jumped right in, even as he stood at the foot of the porch steps. "I gather this is or could be a might uncomfortable, folks. I don't want it to be that way. This is a very attractive spot, I think, not for development but for good living. A lot of things that I once couldn't afford I can now afford. I've been passing by this place for years and always had a dream about it." His glance went back down the driveway and then across the fields that dropped down toward the lake, the arms of the evening sun clasping the whole laketop. He smiled easily at Marco coming back from the chicken coop. His voice was partly an aside when he said, "Like Tom and Huck, I swear."

Staff said, "Come up on the porch, you two, and have some iced coffee. The scene won't change for about another forty minutes, then you'll get another picture." Opening the screen door, he put his hand out and said, "'Case Lowell forgot, this is my wife Mathy and I am Staff Bickerston who is, apparently, deeper in trouble with Lowell and the bank than I would have imagined. I always figured I'd pass back into the land right around here."

A slight but warm smile cut the corners of Abbot Gruden's mouth. "I'll make it quick, Staff. No folderol and clumsy stuff and no feints and quick moves. I'll buy this place from you, let you stay here a couple of years, on me, on the house." His second option at a smile was a bit clumsy. "Did that sound funny?"

"Think nothing of it, Abbot," Staff said. "The point you're making, other than being extremely generous, is you want to become owner of record sooner than later. Is that right? Is that to secure a better buying price?"

"Well, Staff, I didn't make my money by throwing it away." His shoulders were squared as if he were a military man. His jaw was square too, and his haircut, clean above the ears, was brand new. Staff noticed that Abbot Gruden did not talk with his hands, like so many men did. Abbot Gruden's deep voice carried all his messages, and he continued. "This site represents a good investment for me. The value is never going to go down. Land is just not in production any more. Hasn't been since the Big Bang, far as I can see." His gaze went back across the field where both sun and breeze played in the tops of the high grass, at times looking like combers coming at a shoreline. When a small cloud passed over, the grass changed color and Staff and Abbot Gruden both saw and sensed the iridescence change.

Mathis meanwhile was looking at something in Lowell's eyes. She took it to be pain. Her hand touched the sleeve of his suit coat.

Lowell said, "That'd be two years of free rent, folks. That's a generosity I never heard about. That's something I could never handle at the bank. Getting tough enough to do things the way they have to be done now." Mathis knew he could still feel the gentle touch at his sleeve. His eyes showed it. The face of Lila Theis came at the back of her head. She shivered with a momentary chill.

Staff walked down to the end of the porch and motioned Abbot Gruden to follow him. The two men saw Marco standing in the driveway and looking back at the coop. There was a single pane of glass in the coop and the sun was a slash against that pane. It almost came straight back at the two men. Staff said, "He loves it here. He's just like me coming back again even before I go under the grass. I'd love to keep the place for him, but I know I don't have a shot at it much longer. Not now, not tonight, but we might have to talk again about this. You and I, on the side someplace. Fair enough? You've made a decent and generous proposal. I just might have to do what would drive my soul outward."

He leaned to look back at the coop and the slash of sunlight falling off the last pane of glass, shifting positions and brightness. "That's the last one, Marco. Make it a good shot."

Marco, suddenly older, as if he had become his father, said, "Let him try. Said he used to do it when he was a kid."

He held out the slingshot to Abbot Gruden.

The initial touch of warm air Abbot Gruden had known coming on the property, came back over him. He was obviously pleased when he said, "Why not? It's been a long time." Then the exuberance rang in his voice. "It's been too damn long!"

Staff and Abbot Gruden stepped down from the porch as Mathis and Lowell Stratton stood aside at the screen door. Marco handed Abbot Gruden the slingshot. Gruden hefted it in his hand, closed his fist tightly about the crude handle, closed one eye and looked through the Y of the tines at the pane of glass. "Ammunition, please, Ammo Bearer," he said, the voice resonant, in charge, deeper than before, an infantry officer at command. Marco dug into his leather ammo pouch and handed Abbot Gruden a small round pellet, about half an inch in rough diameter. The new shooter placed it into the leather seat of the slingshot and looked down as he gripped it firmly.

In later weeks Staff would tell the story over and over again. "This kind man, this man who had made such a generous offer, looked down at the pellet, then took it out of the leather saddle and held it aloft. He did it just like I had done before, stupid me. There he was, this stranger Lowell brought over, peering at one of Marco's pellets, shining it up on his pants, holding it up at the perfect angle to catch the sunlight glint of its polish. Wondering, I bet, just like I did, where was it from? What did it have to tell us? 'My god,' he says, 'where did you get this?' Marco near jumped out of his skin. 'Out back,' he says, 'in my cave, My Columbus Place.' 'You have any more?' the big fellow says.' 'I got a whole bunch, some of them bigger than that but they're too big for the slingshot.' The big fellow looks me right in the eyes and says, 'Staff Bickerston, you might not have to sell this place after all. You got placer gold here, my man, right in your own back yard.'"

"And we rush off to Marco's hideaway and Marco crawls inside his cave and comes out with his storage box and there's a couple of dozen pieces there, some of them big as golf balls. A couple even bigger. And then all hell breaks loose, and Abbot Gruden, millionaire in general, geologist by avocation, pronounces us probably quite comfortably rich and the mortgage a thing of the past. He's almighty excited and almost out of breath and we have to listen to him. He tells us all that here, as the ice retreated, the Connecticut Valley was filled with a marvelous great glacial lake, Glacial Lake Hitchcock, which extended from where Middletown, Connecticut is now, to just north of where St. Johnsbury, Vermont is. There was a smaller glacial lake in the Ashuelot Valley, too, that eventually drained into Hitchcock. The Ice Sheet rumbled through here, he told us, grinding strong deep grooves, long linear striations, and cone-shaped rat tails into the rock pointing the way, and now he was using his hands to talk, believe it or not, waving them all over heck."

"'Eventually,' he said, 'those ice sleds went on a more southwestward flow. They had Keene and Spofford in mind, I'll bet, as the big ice melted and thinned and began to be controlled by the local topography of the mountains over past Keene on the west and the newer mountains on the east.' He said they were pushing stuff out in front all the time, all kinds of stuff. Even while the huge glacial lake in the Ashuelot River Valley pulled and drew down the buoyant glacier front to a new position, ever sliding forward and calving itself into the lake. Ain't that some beautiful, calving itself into the lake. My, oh my, I can see it now."

On more than one summation Staff ended up by saying, "Beauty of it all is Lowell was about as tickled as we were. It was the only time I ever saw him kiss Mathy, that's for sure."

THE UNDIES PENNANT

Y oung Johnny Templemore, in the summer of his
sixteenth year, at the beach on a Saturday
afternoon with his crowd, was at a crossroads in his
life. Already he had experienced three erections on
the crowded beach, any and all girls driving him into
the mindless frenzy. He could have buried himself
in the sand, or gone into the cool ocean water and
stayed there until midnight. The girl in the two-piece
purple swimsuit was particularly dangerous, and
daring, the way she absolutely was posing for him
with her back against the beach wall, posing for him
alone out of all the guys around. Almost snapping it
at him, he could hear his brother saying, him three
years in the Navy and knowing practically everything
there was to know about girls. He was sure of it.
Three erections told him so.

Now game time was at hand and pal and
teammate Spit Kelly had their attention. Spit had a
way about him you noticed sooner than later.

"So we go off to practice on Monday. We dead sure
have to cap off a great summer, 'cause if we don't,

we're going to forget it in a hurry." Spit looked at the dozen of them, most of them entering their senior year, Johnny Templemore and Greg Wozny and Joey Turner being the only juniors-to-be in the group, babies, just out of their sophomore years, wet and sopping behind the ears. Virgin territory, though not so readily admissible.

"It's got to be different. It's got to be memorable. And it's got to be exciting."

Spit, getting demonstrative, was the fullback on the team and would take on fire. The whole North Shore League knew it and gave Spit a whole handful of respect. He was a ladies' man to boot, a great dancer, a smooth talker, as if every girl he ever met had been waiting for him. The single scar, across his lower lip, almost firehouse red when he was angry or pushing at extremities, marked him apart from the others, marked him dangerous, or at least as a survivor of an unknown and unannounced encounter along the way. But nobody had ever asked him who did it. With his helmet on, the scar burned with a Brandenburg flair and occasionally earned him an extra yard or two with the ball. We had seen that time and again, and in the tough games.

"Now who's got any ideas? Make them good 'cause we don't want to waste our time. We haven't got much more of this weekend. Then it's three and a half months of locking on to football." One fist smacked down into the other hand and people on the beach turned to look at him. Spit, also knowing where the stage was, turned his good side to the crowd.

Johnny Templemore never had any ideas that would excite any of them, except the single one he had of Miss Purple Suit, sitting now with her legs v'd into the sunshine not ten yards from him. That image was his to keep, forever. Spit looked at him and looked away.

It was long and lean Ray Carbury who spoke first. "How about a contest, like who's the first one that gets some nookie tonight?" A smile was beginning. "And can prove it." His eyes went wide with comic expression.

Spit said, "There's nothing special in that. Maybe nothing different at all." Some guys nodded. Some smiled in coy agreement. Some hung their heads. Johnny Templemore was still looking at Miss Purple Suit, his mind filling with unknown images, the other and most foreign territories.

Carbury came back. "What if we set a time limit and a special way to announce it? And we need proof of the whole thing."

"What kind of proof?" Spit said. "Her name on a placard and one of you guys walking around Saugus Center with it over your shoulder? I don't want any part of that."

"Yuh," Dutch Broovert said, "'cause MaryJane would kick your ass all over town if you gave her name."

"And kick it twice as far if it wasn't her," Spit added. But he was thinking, and measuring, and Johnny Templemore figured that Spit was already planning to move on from MaryJane anyway.

Ray said, "What if the winner had to hang up a pair of her panties as a signal."

"Hang 'em where?" Spit put in.

Ray wasn't quitting. "In the Center someplace. Out in the open. Like maybe the statue right on the green. Hang the panties up on the statue's outstretched arm, like a flag or a pennant, like *Welcome aboard, Captain.*" His tittering fell on the sand.

Spit leaped to his feet again. "That's great," he said, "but we have to have some rules. Start making suggestions." He pointed at them, one at a time, locking eyeballs just the way he'd do it in the huddle.

"It can't be a steady," Mark Campio said. "That's got to be off limits."

"It can't be a regular," Bill Brockman added, everybody having a damn good idea of who and what he was talking about, names not being spoken.

"Do we have to know who she is? We'll have to swear to keep her name secret," Eddie Searles put in, already worried about his sister Kate and how she had made the driveway memorable with her boyfriend at least three times already that he personally knew about.

Spit was onstage again. "Of course we have to know who she is. It's nothing otherwise if we don't. The fun will be gone. Hell, we all get plenty anyway. We're all going to put in five bucks for the winner. And we have to swear to keep her name secret, just among us. That has to be part of it."

Dunna Coggs, usually quiet, a great follower but never a leader, feeling a minute opening, said, "The clock has to be set for start and finish."

Johnny Templemore, not yet with a girl, started to sweat. Miss Purple Suit was packing up her things. Opportunity was leaving him on the next bus headed away from the beach.

Spit was smiling and nodding. "That's great. We leave the Center at seven, go our separate ways, and shut the clock off at midnight. The trophy has to be hung before midnight, on the arm of the statue. You climb it or get a ladder, but you have to get it up there. And it has to be there until Sunday morning. How does that sound?"

There was a murmur of approval, and Spit added, "And there can be no previous arrangements. We kick ass on anybody who does. 'Member how we got Tattletale Dick last year on punt returns? We'll do the same thing to whoever screws this up. No cheating. We're a team, aren't we? Are we game?" An adventure and an excitement made merry in his voice.

Johnny Templemore, never with a girl other than minor petting, a clumsy fondling of a breast or two, but full of dreams, walked away from the Center at seven p.m. in a quandary. He was a dead duck, he figured. Sixteen years and nothing to show for it. Now he had five hours and the whole world was coming down on him. Little there was he could do. Couldn't call a girl and say, plain outright, "Want to make love with me tonight so I can win a contest?" And Miss Purple Suit, long gone away from him, came back only in short quick bursts of successful dreams.

At ten o'clock he sat on the front porch of his house a mile out of the Center. He'd be banished forever in the group. Probably most of them knew he had never been with any girl anyway. Now he'd be the *Sweet Virgin running the halfback counter play or the Sweet Virgin sweeping wide with Student Body right* in the first game. He could hear quarterback Chuck Waymore calling the play in the huddle, his eyes right smack on Johnny Templemore and the whole team knowing the score.

With his skin crawling with apprehension and all the boding promise, he snuck into his sister Elsie's room and stole a pair of her underpants. He took sleek black ones, thin, sheer, all the adjectives flying at him. Into a back pocket he slipped them and started out for the Center. Less than a hundred yards down Main Street, a car slowed and stopped beside him. It was MaryElizabeth Harmon, bar none absolutely the best looking girl in the school, sitting behind the wheel of her father's sleek Packard Clipper. An image formed itself in Jackie's mind: she and the Packard formed a fair pair, elusive, beautiful, brand new. Her blond hair was a halo in the dark interior, and he could remember her hips just a few days past walking in front of him down the high school corridor. Miss Purple Suit most likely couldn't hold her hat.

"I thought that was you, Jack," she said. "Where you going at this hour, and what's *that* hanging out of your back pocket?"

Thinking it was his handkerchief, he pulled the pair of panties out of his pocket and held them at the window. Only then did he see what he flagged at MaryElizabeth.

MaryElizabeth said, "I think you better get in here, Jack. You really have some kind of explaining to do, and I don't mind listening." Mystery rode in her voice. She reached over, lifted the lock button very slowly and opened the door for him. He could feel the same sensation he had at the beach. Now he could at least hide in the darkness of the Packard's interior.

He told her everything that happened during the day. And how he had slipped into Elsie's room and taken a token trophy.

The heartiness of her laughter, warm and headily delightful to him, filled the car, and she pulled off the road and went in behind the American Legion building, the parking lot completely deserted. "They'll never let you get away with it, Jackie. If they ever find you out, you're done with those guys. I know it. I could draw you a picture of it all." Her hand was such a soft comfort on his shoulder, he could feel it in his toes.

She placed that hand on his bare arm. It was hot, Purple Suit hot. "I'll give you mine. No strings attached." Her voice was husky, smoky, carrying the unknown, all of it, and bit down into his body with a claw hammer clutch. Easily, without distortion, she slipped her skirt up and wrestled her underpants off. A pair of the loveliest legs ever seen filled the front seat of the Packard.

Her skirt still riding where she had pulled it around her hips, she looked at him. "My God, Jackie, you're white as a ghost. Haven't you ever seen a girl before?" She stared at him. "Never been with a girl, Jackie? I suppose you'd want to touch me, wouldn't you. I don't mind." She took his hand, "Like how I'll show you, and then a little faster if you want." And then, only moments later, her voice still smoky, the unknowns breaking all apart for him, she said, "I suppose you'll want everything, won't you, and on the first night, too. Oh, my, what a lover you are." And later she said he could hang her panties on the statue but couldn't tell anybody her name.

Johnny Templemore climbed the statue and hung MaryElizabeth's underpants on the statue raised for Civil War veterans. As he was leaving the Center, four of the guys rushed at him and demanded the girl's name. Johnny Templemore, understanding more than ever the predicament he was in, relented and let them poke fun at him when he said he had snuck a pair of underpants from his sister's room. They all joked about it and had a big laugh out of his desperation, knowing there'd be more laughs coming, a whole season of them: in the locker room, in the huddle, on the bus going to and coming back from games. Jackie the lover!

The story went around town in a hurry, and Elsie Templemore, passing the statue just before noon, figured her kid brother had come pretty far along in the world, as she acknowledged to herself that the underpants were not hers.

And Johnny Templemore, all these years later, father to six, grandfather to twenty-two, a storyteller from the word go, who for years regaled all with classic stories on his summer porch or in his winter kitchen by the fire, never once told anybody about hanging grandma's underpants on the statue in Saugus Center.

ACES & EIGHTS

Compulsive excitement filled Sergeant Charlie Twohig, down to his toes. Ledo, at this end of the Burma Road, was not a scavenger's post with a limited amount of personnel: it was an army metropolis burgeoning even in the darkness with a kind of stateside activity. The muffled sound of a laboring engine crawled out of a nearby valley, sounding as if it were under wraps, promising more engines up the line with the sometimes slow hum of war. From the edge of night he heard the tom-tom of a hammer beating on sheet metal. Night guards, bent on their watches and patrols, loomed as hulking giants working thick shadows. The heat, floating down out of another valley, at first did not seem to bother Charlie Twohig. Noise and activity meant people and people meant money and money meant gambling. The long haul from North Africa had been worth the trouble; the pigeons, his resolute mind said, were ready for the taking.

Into his bunk he crawled and felt a slight but not new discomfort. His throat was dry and he needed a drink and an itching sensation began to crawl on his hands with the purchase of a seven-day itch. His heart, he swore, was pumping faster than ever and he convinced himself it was more of the excitement. A strange heat was subtilely making way in his body.

Private Jake Breda twisted in the bunk above him. Twohig wanted to talk. "Hey, Jake, you awake?"

"Yuh, Sarge."

"You ever been really excited, Jake? I mean so bad you got sick from it."

"Sure, when I got married."

"Right at the altar?"

"Hell, no, Sarge. When I closed the door behind me at the motel. What have you got to be so excited about?"

"I'm in a streak, Jake. I never felt this way in my life. It ain't I won so much, but I haven't lost since that blackjack game in Ceylon."

"What's it feel like? I never felt really different when I was winning. Never parleyed much to begin with, so can't tell by me."

"Jake, I swear my hands are sweating for a deck of cards right now. Hell, I wished it was morning. I wish it was tomorrow already. I swear I'm going to win big, so big it's burning a hole right through me."

Breda dropped a hand down the side of the bunk. "Give me a smoke, will you, Sarge." Twohig was for the moment a suddenly accessible sergeant.

"Sure, Jake, keep the deck. God, I'm burning with excitement. I wish I didn't have to sleep at all. Tomorrow I'm going to line me up some real good ones. Blackjack, that's what it's going to be. Blackjack. I can't lose. I can't lose. Tomorrow, all day, it'll be twenty-one, twenty-one, twenty-one. I'm in the groove."

He fell asleep dreaming of getting hit and hit and hit with aces and deuces and treys and coming up twenty-one every time out of the gate. He did not see a king or queen all night. Twenty-one, twenty-one, twenty-one.

Parts of the journey that brought him here to Ledo, at the end of the world in upheaval, clamor everywhere, came across his memory with unusual clarity, with unusual color. He didn't think much about Ohio, and only knew the new uneasiness in him as irregular. Odds be damned!

WEEKS EARLIER THEY had been at sea. Sergeant Charlie Twohig, long, lean and dark, with a mysterious ailment, as yet unknown to him, threatening to work its way into his consciousness, leaned against a metal bulkhead of a lead LST and felt the heat sinking into his back, blacksmith's iron if anything. The perspiration falling off his brow he had long been aware of and continually tried to dismiss its presence by constantly shuffling a deck of cards, a veritable extension of his hands... fingers, hands, cards, money, they were partners forever.

Behind him where he gazed, the uncoupled train of LSTs moved with a cumbersome plodding out of the Suez Canal and into the searing brightness of the Red Sea. The indignant, hot and worried cargo was a company of Graves Registration men that, already in the first flush of dawn, felt the slamming of solar heat, the huge and imponderable hammer of it. To a man, they had heard and believed the waters before them boiled under an hour of sun. There was much evidence about them: with explosive quickness of a flare the sun had popped up over Asia and dark welts were maps on their fatigues. It was impossible to sit still and let sweat crawl a horde of ants over the skin, yet it was just as difficult to move about on the boats or find a piece of shade. And the worst was yet to come. It was like a sore throbbing elsewhere.

Behind them the flat oblique shadows of the LSTs lay on the waters of the Red Sea; ahead of them was half the company's final target, India and Burma and the dead. The other two platoons, under Captain Redmond, were to continue on to China. At both ends of the Burma Road the dead needed to be buried.

Corporal Tally Biggs sat beside Charlie Twohig and eyed the deck of cards. He said, his head at a condescending angle, "You know, Twig, if I never saw you with a deck of cards I'd of thought you were naked." Biggs pronounced *naked* as if it were *nekid*, and he had the ungracious habit of speaking with little lip movement, watching guard perhaps on any commitment. An inconsistent green in his eyes likewise operated under a controlled guise. Biggs was not easy to like, and found few fast friends, if any at all, in the ranks of comrades.

"Hell," Twohig said with his Midwestern drawl, "if I didn't have a deck of cards to fondle, you know I'd be bare ass. You wanna cut low card for a buck?" If it was not the sun lighting up his eyes, it was the thought of a gamble, of odds being folded up in someone's camp and might as well be his.

Biggs read him clearly. "No, siree!" he said. "Not for three cuts to your one. I owe you up to my ass now and I ain't getting in any deeper." Always he'd worried about making some outward sign of the cowardice lodged within his thin frame. It made his voice soft and entreating as he said, "Twig, couldn't we get torpedoed out here? Christ, but we're moving slow, ain't we? Couldn't they up and stick a fish right in us?"

"Torpedoes is for boats, not for these little lake-crossing barges. What you really got to worry about is getting strafed by some Heinkel or Junkers or a Stuka, or maybe getting dive-bombed when you ain't got your life belt on." Twohig loved to pull the string that tied Biggs's guts together. "Cut!" He held the deck out. The blue bicycles of the top card caught the sun.

Biggs, aware of Twohig's constant taunts, had spent much of the night dwelling on the idea of swimming in the cauldron of the Red Sea. He hated fish and he hated blood and he didn't know how to swim in the first place. "I ain't cutting, Twig! Not three to one I ain't cutting." The deep green of his eyes had retreated to a thin, watery green and he moved his wrist to mop away sweat lingering at the edges of his eyes. "I don't care how hot it gets, I ain't getting nowhere out of this belt. All's I can do is keep my head from going under if we was to get thrown in the drink."

Twohig moved one shoulder away from the bulkhead and a wisp of air was sucked in behind his back. "Life belts are no good against sharks, Tally. They're the real butchers of the sea. They tell me sharks can amputate a leg quicker'n a doctor can with an electric saw. Cut!" The blue bicycles again.

"Ain't no sharks in these waters! Nothing lives in these waters, nothing at all!"

"Don't be stupid, Biggs. I suppose you never heard of the balance of power. You must be pretty dumb not to know about that."

"What the hell's that got to do with sharks? That's only about countries lining up against each other in bunches to keep out of war. And I ain't cutting!" Slowly he shook his head at Twohig and smiled a treacherously deceptive smile.

"Yuh, and it's all about little ones getting eaten by big ones. It keeps order in things like they don't need traffic cops or anything. They just go on and anything small in the way of big ones gets eaten up. Maybe they do have traffic cops here. I'd guess that's what you'd call sharks. They eat up their share of smaller fish and anything foreign that gets in the water, and you know what, Biggs?"

"What?"

"If you was to fall in the water when we got dive bombed, you'd be foreign. Cut!" The bicycles were rolling.

The deck of cards was there in front of him, the rolling stock. "Trey of spades!" Sweat ran over Biggs's face but he smiled that thin despicable smile of a caricatured rat.

"Deuce. You owe!" Upward in Twohig's sweaty hand the two of hearts lay and a thin blotch of pink was evident on the white of the card.

Angrily, Biggs said, "You're a lousy gambler, Sergeant. I'm the only guy in the whole outfit you can beat." Great desire to punch the sergeant rushed on him, but he knew he'd probably get thrown over the side if he hit him. "Someday I'll beat your ass, but good," and he could see his fists smashing away at Twohig's face the way Henry Armstrong could, or the way Harry Greb used to throw them in the barrooms in New Orleans when he was training for fights. His father always said Harry Greb was a real,

real tiger, standing in the middle of a bar and yelling out, "I'm Harry Greb and I can kick the crap out of any man in here," and going ahead and doing it, his training routine.

Twohig tired of Biggs and wanted to move on to new entertainment. In front of him Captain Redmond's big ears were fire red and sweat was a shadow that covered his whole shirt. Beneath the captain's arms it seemed darker still, dark like patches on tire tubes. Twohig was willing to bet the captain was wearing a tie. With the deck clutched in his hand he moved his left shoulder and saw steam come up from behind his back. With his left foot he nudged the fruit crate Redmond was sitting on.

Redmond turned around and looked at him. The knot on his tie was still tied under the oversized larynx, his eyes were bulging as though the sockets had loosened their properties and the oversized lower lip was more a piece of extra flesh than an integral part of his mouth. Twohig did not like the captain, not from the outset; he was ugly and a phony to boot. Why didn't the man wear his glasses outside the orderly room? If he only knew how much they improved his appearance.

"Sorry, Captain. Guess I need to stretch a bit." Twohig loved to play games with him as much as with Tally Biggs. Biggs's money he liked, but the captain was more fun and he relished the idea of toying with an officer. The idea of the India/Burma assignment caused him some minor dread, and it was lucky, he thought, that the captain was going on to China with the first two platoons.

Twohig the gambler knew what the captain would say, knew him like a book he did. Would he never get tired of mouthing the same pet phrases?

"That's quite all right, Sergeant. We all of us need some stretching, but the road ahead is a long one and we must make the best of it."

It was Redmond clear as a phony bell. Just another echo. Christ, if that ain't just like him, thought Twohig. He can't talk without any of them damn sickening words... *we all of us*, as if he really belonged; *the road ahead... make the best of it.* Just another broken record from officer country.

A licorice sensation ran through Charlie Twohig, and a fluttering joy swam in his head. It was game time. "What is the road ahead, sir? We all of us heard some scuttlebutt back there," he said, pointing over his shoulder back to the African horizon, now a low cloud on the rim of the sea, "but I'm sure we could do with some reviewing." It was not a successful attempt, though he had chosen his words carefully. The homely bastard had hardly blinked his eyes.

When the sergeant had kicked his box, Captain Redmond had been deep in thought about his gambling non-com. Inside his shirt pocket, probably now soaked from the sweat, was a letter from Twohig's wife. There would be no need of reading it again for he had memorized its contents. It was evident she was a more intelligent person than Twohig, though hardly as devious, and he had read between the lines the love she had for the mad gambler. As for himself, he had never had, owned or partaken of a woman for any extended period of time, though he knew how deep the hooks of a good, true love went. The thought that he might help this woman had built a new spirit in him, but he was destined to go to China after the split-up in Ceylon. A deep desire prompted him to do what he could. It would make him feel good inside, this call beyond duty.

112

"We break at Ceylon, Sergeant. First and second platoons go with me to China. Third and fourth go with Lieutenants Tozzi and Milano to Diamond Harbor at Calcutta."

The Guinea Brigade, thought Twohig. If we could ever get to Rome or Naples, they might get something done for us. What the hell use are two damn Guineas out in India? They might as well be on the moon.

"What's our course after Calcutta, sir?" Twohig was irritated. What the hell made Redmond think he was so damn smart? Anybody who ever read anything knows about Diamond Harbor. Damn the sweat! It was making him blink as it ran into his eyes and he'd be damned if he ever wanted an officer to think he was forced to blink when stared down.

Redmond, though he sweated profusely, did not mind the heat. For a long time he had conditioned himself to do without comfort and had forced himself into extreme exposures, both of the body and of the mind. For eighteen months he had been without a woman and he was still able to think of them with great sensitivity and imagination. Even among the married men of his command, no other could say the same. When his time came (he felt the slight rocking of the craft as a warning of a growing need), he would really enjoy his fling. Searching for a woman would be an adventure. Of course, his looks would hold off some women, but they would be arrogant and unworthy. A man had more to offer than looks. When he looked at Twohig he wondered what his wife looked like. Somehow he had formed a picture of her, big of bust and hip, blond hair, blue eyes, skin like buttermilk, and tremendously good in bed. That she was intelligent was unquestioned. That had been divined from her letter. Her use of negatives was clue enough, and the way she slid into comfortable alliterations made him think of her reading poetry on a morning porch by the sea or a wide lake, by herself.

The dark, brooding eyes of Twohig were focused on him. Realizing the contempt behind them, Redmond exerted his station. It would never do to let Twohig know he was either aware of his intentions or that he was reacting to an enlisted man's barbs. "From Calcutta, the Black Hole, you'll go to Dacca, Tripura, Silchar, bypass the Khasi Hills, to Sylhet and on to the far corner of Assam, ending up at Ledo." His eyes were locked onto Twohig's eyes.

Smart-ass! I read Kipling, too. Does he think no one but him ever read? "Do we go near Cooch-Behar, sir?" *That* ought to stir his almighty ass.

"I don't believe so, Sergeant. From my recollection of the map, I think Cooch-Behar is in the western part of Assam." Maybe the interrogating sergeant would take the hint and not push it any more. He'd be able to spell correctly more Indian names than Twohig could think of: Dibrugarh, Sadiya, Tinsukia, Sibsagar, Mahiganj, and he'd even throw in Saikoa-ghat for a plum. The map of Assam and Burma burned in his mind just as clearly as the letter from Twohig's wife. At the moment he had the incredible feeling of being unable to separate them.

"Begging your pardon, sir." Twohig said, as he felt an irking sensation swim through his body, "but I'm willing to bet that Cooch-Behar is—"

Redmond cut him off. "I'm not a betting man, Sergeant, as we all must know by this time." His hand waved in the air as if brushing the whole episode away. "It really isn't too all important." The letter was important and he wanted to get his mind back to it. Introducing Tozzi and Milano to its contents was a thought that had not previously entered his mind. As the craft rocked the little wings of memory started to flutter in his groin, and he was aware of a slight sense of hopelessness for the whole situation. Neither Tozzi nor Milano, both seemingly good young officers though as yet untried, could hardly begin to understand the woman who had written the letter. She loved with a deep and abiding love. Well, maybe they could see that, but the rest would be a mystery to them and the fact that she could be good in bed would never enter their indecent young minds. It would only be time and chance that would force him to reveal the letter, to enlist their aid, but that bore on the unthinkable. Besides, it would deprive him of aiding her all by himself. She had written to him, the company commander. It was strictly his responsibility.

The train of squat craft was now riding easily over a sea of slow, even swells and the sexual impact of its motion made Redmond think about finding a girl among the Ceylonese before he headed off to China. Ceylon seemed much more romantic than China. He pictured a mysterious, dark-eyed beauty standing above him. Her subtle undulations would match the motion of the sea.

Except for the oppressive heat and an occasional alarm when an aircraft came into sight over the flat, hot sea, the trip to Ceylon was routine. Neither submarine nor surface craft threatened them and Twohig managed to bite into Tally Biggs's bankroll for thirty-two dollars. Captain Redmond fidgeted and sweat the whole way, as did his command, but he was frustrated in devising a plan to aid Sara Twohig. The woman was well worth assisting and he couldn't help but think that her bed, in the privacy of darkness, was lonely and pathetic, and certainly bore amends.

The big excitement at the harbor on the northern tip of Ceylon was neither a big blackjack game for Twohig, nor Redmond's seduction of a beautiful and young Ceylonese secretary on the second night. The excitement was Captain John Tracker, who met them when they landed. He, and not Redmond, was to go on to China because headquarters found out that he had lived there for five years when a boy. Redmond could not have been more pleased. Even while he was making love to the olive secretary with hair as black as midnight and a scent about her that moved soft wings in his nostrils, he was thinking about Sara Twohig in that lonely bed in Ohio.

On the last day of June, with the monsoons in season, the –nth Graves Registration Company split into two sections of two platoons each, and the section headed for Ledo in Assam, with Redmond in command, left Ceylon at twilight and moved out into the Bay of Bengal. This side of Africa they had buried their first dead, one of their own, Corporal Eddie Akins, who had followed a girl away from the compound on the fourth day. The next day his body was discovered by a patrol, stripped, slashed, and impaled on a crude bamboo rack tied to a tree. Thousands of burials, and many of them much dirtier than Akins's, lay ahead of them, they knew to a man. Redmond struck Akins' name from the company roster.

At dark the bright constant stars shone as fragmentary neon in the sky and occasionally a piece of that same substance shot across that black overhead in the slightest of arcs. Water slapped quietly at the craft, the tide rolled easily under them, and the whole night took on the pallor of mystery and injustice. Twohig thought about his big blackjack game, Biggs shivered in the heat as he remembered Akins hung up on the bamboo rack, and Redmond entertained pictures of Twohig's wife alone in her bed, thinking of her not wasting any more time. The rest, Tozzi and Milano included, tried to envision a quiet retreat high in the mountains near Ledo where nobody died and nobody cared.

Diamond Harbor revealed little of eastern romance and Redmond thought it particularly dirty and mismanaged. Every conceivable size, shape and description of sea-going vessel was clustered in and around the harbor in immense confusion. Commercial and enterprising Calcutta was full of hunger and he had no idea how human bones with no flesh on them were able to stand together. The one night his command spent in Calcutta, and the one night Redmond dared not approach a woman for fear of disease, he stood under the arches of Chowringee. The abominable pageant before his eyes turned his stomach. Starvation was all around him; destitution, ulcerous and malodorous, was everywhere in every eye he saw. It was a slice from an unbelievable movie come for the taking. The war, somehow, seemed cleaner and more just, and he found himself anxious to get to it, to its fragmentation and incendiaries, to its riotously free blood and its depths of concussion, to its burial plots and impermanent markers.

The long trip from Newport News to North Africa, across the Mediterranean, down the Canal, across the Red Sea (bypassing Bombay where originally they were to have debarked but which had been changed by some big shot sitting at a desk) to Ceylon, up the Bay of Bengal and into Calcutta, had taken two months. For a long time it had seemed as if he did not have a command. Anxiety to get to Ledo and set up his post worked on him and he was excited and grateful when they left Calcutta after such a brief stay.

By wide gauge and narrow gauge railway they traveled inland. The country was rugged, and moving out of Bengal and into Assam it became more rugged as were the people of Khasi, Naga and Lushai Hills, looking as if they could wage a war on their own. At any minute, the dark eyes, the dark faces, the ready scabbards!

Box-boarded and nearly vacuumed of breathable air, the rickety trains moved on, perhaps to stay a day and a half in one place while repairs were being made, or stocking materials in another. It was a long journey and it brought them to the lap of the war with each unsure mile of travel. Biggs shivered. Twohig gambled. Redmond kept, at a distant seduction, the blond hair and flared hips and the white thighs at conjunction with his peripheral vision, her voice making itself heard in the deepest night beside the lake, the moon more than promise.

Twohig's luck had suddenly and dramatically changed with the big blackjack game in Ceylon. He could not lose. And those to whom he had previously lost much of his money could not keep themselves from playing. Only Biggs sat the games out, irritated by Twohig's luck, hoping it would end suddenly in one cut for the whole pie. Little did he realize that Twohig, when he was taunting him and taking his money, was the only one in the whole command who paid any attention to him. The bastard, he hoped, would die or go broke. In one hand, dead of cards. It would be worth the sight.

The intolerable heat of July in northern India sat in the cars of the old train like a curse and some of the troops slowly realized that the Red Sea really had not been too bad. What they did not know, of course, was that a march was in front of them, a long, back-breaking march when the tracks disappeared at the foot of a hill, an omen of the end of civilization.

Redmond spent his time talking to Tozzi and Milano, instructing them about Hindus and Moslems and the hill tribesmen they would be posted among. He wanted his command to work without incident among the native populace. Slowly blossoming in him was an inveterate fear of the wild and unspoiled hill tribesmen, some of whom he might have to exert authority over. That in such a diverse command of nearly one hundred men, two people should have the same basic fear was not implausible. Biggs hated Negroes, Indians, foreigners, immigrants, mulattos, Catholics and Jews. He hated them and he feared them, and in the eyes of the natives along their route of travel he suspected, with some cause, a smoldering hatred of himself. Even against the most decrepit looking amongst them, Biggs feared he might not be able to protect himself.

The -nth Graves Registration Company, cut in half, walked the last sixty-two miles to Ledo, the beginning of the Burma Road. During the long, agonizing march, Twohig continued to bet and continued to win. He flipped coins, he bet on the most ludicrous things that only chance governed, and he won. A provincial legend was growing in the ranks. He was becoming as big as the war.

All the while Redmond wanted to read Sara Twohig's letter again and again, but he was afraid to take it from his pocket, afraid it might fall into the gambler's hands. The return address on the top of the letter was burned into his brain: 8017 River Drive, Conneaut, Ohio. For a moment he could not recall if the address was really on the face of the envelope. That thought upset him. Surely the mail clerk would have noticed it. Redmond suddenly realized he knew Sara Twohig as well as any man and she could never be so stupid. So elated was he with this declaration that he was tempted sorely to pull out the letter and read it. But caution again denied him the opportunity. And Charlie Twohig continued to move among the ranks looking for something to gamble on, letting the legend grow.

From the time they left the train, Ledo proved to be four days away. They pitched camp at the first call of dusk each day and many of them fell exhausted to their sleep. Most slept, but Twohig dwelled in the luxury of his changed luck, Biggs thought about dying and getting stuck like Akins was, and Redmond went through a ritual of promising Sara Twohig all the help she needed. When he did sleep, the ugly, toadish-looking commander dreamed often about Ohio, a little town against the side of the lake, and a voice smoldering in the darkness.

The nights were wide and black without any light on the horizon and legions of stars moved majestically overhead. No less than the insensitive Biggs, who twice volunteered for interior guard duty because he was afraid of getting stabbed in his sleep, moaned under the imperial beauty.

It was in the midst of the tall darkness of the third night, when the company was pitched in the foothills of the Naga Hills, that Redmond found his answer for Sara's letter. It would take some doing on his part to set it up and it would also take, as the main ingredient of his scheme, a particular type of individual he had no doubt was on the roster of every outfit in this man's army. The next move was to find that man. Surely, without telling Tozzi and Milano any details, he could enlist them in this pursuit. Strangely, as if he had succeeded already, a surge of joy swam in his blood and he leaned back against a tree on the side of a hill and lit a cigarette. The night, with ease, he found particularly beautiful. It was high and wide and quiet, and he was alone. A fragrance of Ceylon twisted in his nostrils. The girl who had cried *Tai! Tai!* in his ear had been well worth the wait. Against the tree he slept without dreaming about Ohio.

They arrived at the bamboo city of Ledo near dusk on the fourth day of hiking. Twohig was seven hundred and twenty dollars richer than when they had hit Ceylon. Biggs was near complete exhaustion. His changeable green eyes were red and burning and he was thankful the sun had disappeared behind a hill. Tozzi and Milano, both whose feet were raw and blistered and who listened with odd attention to the captain's strange request, had special missions to perform. Redmond could hardly wait to have his command post set up. He hadn't worn his glasses since the company had left North Africa, except to sneak secret looks at Sara's letter.

Business as usual, he thought, was at hand.

That business was burials. Several times a day formality would be the key word, a touch of the civilized world that was otherwise non-existent about them. Formality meant full dress uniforms, bearers, firing squads and *Taps*. It was the saddest part of war, the departure, but, like the fighting and the dying, Redmond knew it would become routine. Familiarity, he thought, bred callousness, not contempt. Anyway, you hardly knew the man you had to bury.

At Ledo the accommodations were just as Redmond envisioned. They were assigned to a small compound of bamboo huts: one for the orderly room, one for officer's quarters, three for the men, and one for himself. Though there was no tap water and no air conditioning, he had read enough about India and the northern heat to have installed on his hut the thick mesh screens that were called *khus-khus tattie*. Woven from the fragrant *khus-khus* grass, the screens were placed over both door and window and kept moist by having water thrown over them. When the wind blew through the mesh, it would carry moisture into the room and sometimes reduce the temperature inside by as much as ten degrees. To perform the wetting-down operation Redmond hired a small native boy, Azard Phanitar, who looked strangely Mongolian and not unlike some American Indians he had seen. Azard was a scrawny but faithful twelve-year-old who performed similar duties for other officers. He liked the particularly ugly officer who had approached him and did not look as American as the others.

Lt. Peter Milano returned an hour after their arrival in Ledo. The man the captain wanted was in a nearby outfit. No contact had been made by Milano, but of the man's qualification there was no dispute. All along Redmond had known that Milano would find his man sooner than Tozzi. Hadn't Milano taken nine years to get his college degree? It was one of the reasons that Redmond liked Milano the better of the two. He was a plodder, not a flash in the pan as was Tozzi, and not a ninety-day wonder at that. Redmond knew he could trust him without question.

Redmond had his glasses on. He looked different and talked differently. "You're sure, aren't you, Pete?" It was the first time he had ever called the lieutenant *Pete.*

"No question about it, Captain. He's the kind of guy you're looking for. I could have checked him out more, sir, if I knew what you had in mind."

"Now, now, Pete, time enough for that. How about having a drink with me. I have a bottle right here. The office looks quite proper, doesn't it? It's about time we had a sense of uniformity around us. Kind of nice to get back to work, wouldn't you say?" His smile came over the full lips. The bottle was Ballantine Scotch.

While they talked the rest of the company was getting situated. Twohig, having dumped his gear in the farthest corner of a hut most distant from the orderly room, and escaping Biggs by doing so, set out to increase his capital. Lady Luck sat on his shoulder and he wanted her there for the long ride, trying not to let her change her fickle mind. Biggs, having lost his chance to bunk near the only man in the outfit who paid him any mind, sought out the newest man, Private Kranske, and bunked beside him. When Biggs dropped his gear, and said, "Mind?" Kranske only nodded. Biggs had no talent at all in wearing his corporal stripes. The outfit, down to the last man, often wondered in what kind of outfit Biggs's stripes had been earned.

Dawn kicked open the door of a furnace, but Twohig, as soon as he had set his section in motion, sat down to his first blackjack game since Ceylon. He won and he won big. No one could touch him. The aces fell on kings and queens, on tens and jacks; treys fell on nines paired. Invincible he felt and took great risks. But he continued to win. Even when his eyes became blurry and he was not sure sometimes what cards lay face down in front of him, he could not lose. Pain, the sole intruder, came like slivers or small arrows in the back of his neck. He thought it was anxiety and believed it to be a sign of the big streak. Fate or Lady Luck had kissed him a big French kiss and he dare not put it aside.

"Hit me again." A five to make it three of a kind. "Kick it once more." There couldn't be a face card in the whole deck. Trey for eighteen. "Again." The big one for nineteen. Not enough. "Kick." Big deuce. "All mine, man. All mine."

On and on he went for a whole week and walked like a banker from one game to the next. Redmond had tabs on him the whole time and even had an idea that Twohig's winnings were as astronomical as reputed to be. But Redmond, with incredible foresight and the great deal of knowledge gleaned from Sara's letter, sat and waited.

The one thing he did not know was Charlie Twohig was seriously ill. But not even Charlie Twohig knew that. Luck and hot blood, Twohig believed, went together like two fat people dancing, uncomfortable but together.

When at the end of the brutal days, Twohig lay soaking in his bunk and strange formations were working in his blood, Captain Redmond thought about Sara Twohig and how her mail would soon improve. Those first nights, when the demon of heat struck at him in wholesale measure, Redmond dreamed he stood over Sara Twohig and smiled down at her. There was no end to the good that a man could do for a woman.

Business came. The dead and the dying, like lost legions in a forest of night, called with frightening rapidity. The range of the –nth Graves Registration Company was far and wide and it was not uncommon to see one of their number climb into a jeep with a rubber bag, a shovel and a record book and set off for a long trip. At times it was a fighter pilot that had flown his craft into the side of a mountain. Other times it was the pilot and co-pilot of a larger craft that had crashed with a planeload of coolies when the engines failed over the hot Indian hills. The company dressed and undressed daily, served as bearers, marked records in triplicate, played *Taps*, lowered chilled bodies into permanent and semi-permanent graves, and otherwise found their roles in the global war that raged wildly around them.

But Charlie Twohig goldbricked.

"Captain," Lt. Tozzi said, his voice hardly masking his hatred of Twohig, "it's a friggin' shame if we let Twohig continue the way he is. Hasn't done a day's work since we hit this place. Everybody thinks he's got it made and we're a bunch of dummies."

Redmond sat back in his chair, heard the splash of water on the *khus-khus tattie*, waved his hand as if he were brushing off flies. "He's all mine, Lieutenant. Twohig's all mine! He's one problem in this company that I'll deal with in my own way." The mysterious grin was again on the ugly face and Tozzi thought he looked more like a sneak thief each day. Redmond was hiding something from him and it was not right. He was, after all, his right-hand man, as he considered himself.

Redmond saw the hurt-puppy look on Tozzi's face. "Rest easy, Lieutenant, Twohig's in the best possible hands," and his sly grin further agitated the young officer. All the young lieutenant needed was a parting word.

"Luck, Lieutenant, is not what makes the world go round. You remember that. Luck is for the birds, as they say." His large over-exposed eyes stared into his empty glass and a malicious joy swam in them. Again Tozzi thought Redmond the ugliest man in the world. On quick heels the young officer turned and left the orderly room.

Luck! Luck! Luck! Redmond could not hate any other word in the language as much as Luck. Luck did not bring the good pilots over the Hump. It was guts and ingenuity. And Luck did not bring his women to him. Far more important was his ability to discover what they really wanted from a man. What they wanted, he gave them, and he patted the letter in his breast pocket. Without ever meeting Sara Twohig, he knew what she wanted. He reminded himself to make a note that Tozzi should never be recommended for a command of his own.

In the middle of their third week in Ledo and when the heat was fiercer than ever before, Charlie Twohig's streak was still intact. GIs from all over came to see him play and went away with awe and disbelief riding on their faces. None of them noticed that the big winner Charlie Twohig was a pathological museum operating on the compulsion of sheer distress because time might be running out on him. None of them, or Charlie, knew the germs and microbes gathering force in him were bent on his annihilation. Infantrymen passing to or from the front lines through Ledo envied him and believed he of all men had it made. A legend was continuing to build and they carried it to the lap of the war with the usual hyperbolic descriptions. Neither did the nights and the impenetrable darkness swimming like dark thick webs cramp his style or his luck.

Merrill's Marauders, henchmen of intrigue and sudden hits and compelling bravery who passed between the two tea plantations where the company was located (in the darkness like Sicilian vespers being replayed, had their own challenger who dropped half his platoon's money into Twohig's hands, then passed silently on to a Burmese destiny.

And Redmond waited. Little disturbed him. The war floated around like a host of discernible balloons in a wind that did not touch him directly. Sara Twohig was in his blood as strong as the unseen enemies were in her husband's blood. Even the appearance of the legendary Doctor Gordon Seagraves, with his corps of nurses and native doctors, failed to attract his attention. Redmond just knew that the war was cleaner and more just than it appeared to eyes other than his.

In their sixth week in Ledo, Twohig lost his first game. The tall sergeant, a stranger to Graves Registration, announced himself to the gambler at dusk of the eventful day. His name was Paul Cask and he was thin as a weed with a potential of fibrous energy latent about him. He had a high forehead and the thin lines of his eyes almost merged above a sharp nose. Those who watched him play swore he hardly drew a breath, saw his lack of expression, saw the steady, quick hands at the cards.

Now it was that goldbricking Charlie Twohig, fully aware of the aliens in his body, did not allow himself a visit to the aid station. Fate needed such small impetus to alter her choices.

"How come you ain't been by before, Cask?"

"Busy." Cask had Biggs's habit, barely moving his lips when he spoke. Twohig had not liked him from the start.

"Been winning?"

"Some. We have turns." Cask was cold and emotionless. Twohig knew the contrast, for the fever was on him once more. The pain of it was in little digs at the back of his neck and thousands of pygmy spears pierced his skin. For the first time in a long while he thought about Ohio and being captured in Sara's arms. It all seemed so far away, so unreal, as if it had never existed at all. Azard Phanitar, the scrawny little houseboy, sat in a far corner and stared at him. In his young but knowing mind he was aware that Twohig was a battleground of unseen but powerful forces. Too often he had seen the eyes of the foreigners when the sickness came. He did not know how to tell the big money man. He was only a boy, after all, and this was a man's war.

Cask won steadily and a violent hatred toward him built in Twohig. "What's your job, Cask?"

"I'm in the motor pool."

"Know what my job is?" Twohig's eyes were burning and he thought he was back on the Red Sea.

"No."

"G.R., that's Graves Registration. We bury guys. Sometimes in just a raincoat when a bunch of guys get hit in one place and we can't get them to a cemetery in the rear. Know how we identify the bodies?"

"Dogtags." Cask's eyes had not even moved. He looked like an Aztec statue.

"How we use them is the trick. Know the one with the groove in the edge?"

"Yuh. Know it."

Twohig's eyes were redder and far more irritating. "That one's the clincher." He laughed forcibly. "We stick the groove between two of the top teeth, and then know what? We kick his damn jaw shut!"

Cask stood up. "I'll be back tomorrow when you feel like playing instead of talking." Spinning on his heels, he left quickly.

Twohig kicked the table over after he had gone. "Just who in the hell does he think he is!"

Biggs, on the sidelines, knew a moment of joy. "Tall and mean, Twig. Just tall and mean and cool as hell, all's he is."

"Just keep your damn mouth shut, Biggs. I'm going to spend the night planning your day tomorrow." Azard Phanitar, in the far corner, knew only too well how Twohig was going to spend his night.

A half dozen times Cask came back and he continued to win. The games went from blackjack to five-card draw to stud poker. Twohig went into a panic and the word spread and the infantry grinned and said, "When your number's up, you can't do much about it." Twohig was but another fatality of the war. His bankroll was being tapped by Cask. When he could, he got into other games and won, but Cask alone had the evil eye on him. Twohig was unable to refuse him a game.

Cask became the fulcrum, the point of balance, and when Twohig won, there came Cask quietly and coolly to take his money.

The sicker Twohig became, the harder he fought the disease. And the more he won from other hands, the more Cask took from him. Never a fist was raised at their table, but Twohig would scream at his opponent. "If you ever die out there, you son of a bitch, I hope you rot and never get a grave."

"Don't you want to kick my jaw shut, Twig?" The cold face without expression looked back at Twohig with complete disregard.

For nearly two months Twohig fought his disease and Cask. At times he had no knowledge of how he fared, so immense his hatred and the compulsion to win. Around him war was a great unknown that did not involve him, and Sara had long ceased to be. She had never been real. It was only a dream. Reality was a deck of cards and a man named Cask who never flinched and never held back.

And one night the war came for real. Lt. Tozzi, so often on the sidelines talking to Corporal Biggs, came into Twohig's hut, and said, "Sergeant, we just got a call. A man went over the rim in a jeep at Ketchi. I think it's about time you had a mission. You've been goldbricking enough."

"Hell, Lieutenant, I ain't feeling too good. I think I'll have to go on Sick Call in the morning."

"You'll take this trip, Sergeant, and that's an order." Tozzi was unable to mask his hatred of the sergeant.

"I'm sick, I tell you! I ought to go on Sick Call right now." Now it was he who knew the pain as a fierce and frightening enemy.

Tozzi could not hold it back. "You go out there and get him, Twohig, and bring him in. It's your friend Cask."

The gambler leaped from his bunk. "I ain't going nowhere on the face of this earth to get that bastard! He can rot for all I care." His face was in Tozzi's face and colored with hate. No one could make him go out there and bring in that rotten bastard.

Biggs broke the game wide open as he leaped off his bunk. Tozzi could not hold him back. The rat began to scream. "Big gambler! Big stupid gambler! Don't you know who the hell Cask is? He's a real pro. The old man sicced him on you! Your old lady's broke and the old man sicced him on you."

"Shut up, Biggs, before I kill you!" Now the pain came with weird intensities and fully known in his head. The needles behind his eyes began to jab! jab! jab!

Biggs had been target long enough. Hadn't he been played for a sucker as long as he could remember? "You got taken, big gambler. You got taken! Can't you see it? You got taken. Cask's all pro. The old man picked him out. Your old lady wrote to him."

Who wrote to who? What was he talking about? "Who wrote?"

"Your old lady. She wrote to Redmond." His old lady? Sara? How long ago was she...how far away? What was Biggs saying? Sara, Sara so good in bed, what's happening? His eyes were killing him and the rat Biggs stood in front of him staring into his eyes. The pain was shattering behind his eyes.

"She wouldn't do that to me... she wouldn't. I don't believe you. So help me, Biggs, I'm going to kill you." He stepped toward him and Tozzi saw murder in Twohig's eyes.

"It's true, Twohig. Your wife wrote to the captain and he arranged the whole thing. He knew you couldn't beat Cask all the time. He's been sending the money home to your wife, every dime that Cask won."

Charlie Twohig lay down in his bunk and the fever and the pain leaped at him and he thought he could never stand it through another night.

After midnight, with an insane idea in his mind, Charlie Twohig the gambler took a rubber bag and a shovel and climbed into a jeep. Next day a patrol found them, Cask and his retriever, on the side of a hill. Twohig had gotten the body halfway up the hill. The entrenching shovel was stuck in the ground and Cask's body was pushed against it so it couldn't roll down the hill. Twohig lay on top of the body and the fever and the dreams were gone.

Redmond at first was disturbed. He had no idea that Twohig was sick. Then he realized: it was his *piece de resistance*. He had *helped*. She would be grateful and receive him properly. He went to sleep dreaming about Ohio, the lake, the smoldering voice, only after he realized luck truly did exist.

BANJO

His stature, what there was of it, was the cause of it all. From a meek and mild beginning, barely making it into the world, to the inevitable and cataclysmic end.

Banjo. He was called Banjo, not because he was bow-legged (which he was and, at 5 feet 1 7/8 inches and stretching for all he was worth, quite pronounced); not because most of his life he could play without a single lesson any instrument that had strings and required picking or twanging (from balalaika to ukulele and zither); not because a lost testicle at the start of puberty had driven his voice two octaves up the scale, but because he was born of a blind mother, named by his hard-drinking, puzzle-playing, acronym-bedeviled father, raised at times of critical issues by a maiden aunt, all as Benjamin Arthur Norman Jobleski. *Banjo,* short for short.

His father, Joe Jobleski, pipe wrapper of the old school, a man of fists and thrust jaw, sitting at his favorite stool at the club, always remembered Banjo being born, how he came weak and wimpy into this world, the runt of the litter, scrawny, red as a tossed new penny, bony and near fleshless, fingers like Q-tips, toes like firecrackers in the gutter on the morning of the Fifth, a chicken lobster, a cull at the pound, and born of a blind woman who had not so sinned before.

"THE SMALLEST JOBLESKI in two centuries," he'd often said at the PAMVETS, an empty glass never in front of him for long, where two of his older sons had already found similar and lethal tastes. It was here where nights and weekends were spent away from home, where the eyeless scourge that was his wife Mary could not penetrate the leaden and stark sanctuary of peers.

"Came like a chip of wood on that salty water, did Banjo," he had exclaimed to his constant companion, Big Mike Shigalski. "Flushed out of the tube, riding the waves. Maybe he can go out in a blaze of glory. Huh! Maybe! Maybe not! Not enough fuel to light a lantern. A friggin' candle. Bless Mary, she can't see him. Held him like a doll, though, crinkly, like crepe paper. Afraid he'd break up right in her hands. His arms so puny, his legs, sticks and twigs. I was scared of holding him myself. Could lie like a pack of hamburger right in my palm. One of those special four pound jobs, and half it fat at that."

Mike knew the way to get additional rounds, how not to cut a night right in half, how Joe Jobleski turned on his bar stool to look around the room any time one of his four other sons or his daughter Aleksa were mentioned, always seeking approval, nodding in a strange self-centered way, waiting for the odd clap on the back, the soundless clap on the back, approbation, approval in the gesture, words held back as though all in attendance understood the non-speaker, the back-slapper. It was not an emptiness about his friend that was most pronounced to Mike, but the constant dread swirling about him, a threat swinging itself, a pendulum cutting through the air. Trouble or pain waiting to happen, sharp as a knife. The dark eyes under the mass of gray eyebrows, the jaw set as stiff as an anvil back at the shop, did not allow much expression on Joe's face. Stolid, rock-ribbed. Stubborn might have been said of him, but never to his face.

Mike looked at the hulking shoulders he knew were as powerful as his own, riding clean and confident like bareback riders on bones that would never break this side of collision.

"Can't win them all, Joe. You got yourself a handful of giants. The boys'll do you proud, you can bet on them, and Aleksa... well, no one's ever going to screw around with her, unless she wants them to, that's for sure." A small laugh was punctuation, an afterthought. "Paulie, he's going to be the best fullback this town has seen since Marion Motley. He's got a ton of you in him, Joe, a whole ton! It'll break out before you know it. And Andy looms like Bronco, only a freshman at that, lots to learn. Coach says he can hardly wait on him. Knees like triphammers. Puts his shoulders where they belong, squared away, downfield all the time, a real North-South runner. No East-West shit for him."

"Yah!" threw in Joe. "And his baby brother won't even be big enough to make the cheering squad."

"You can't win them all, Joe. You got to take something like this in stride. It's not the end of all things Polska."

He smiled a self-effacing smile, felt himself pandering, thought light of it, stared at the neon of the night light above the rear door blaring EXIT, the ring of redness becoming once again, as it did nightly, a mushroom of red, a blare of red that might otherwise be a trumpet of sound. He said, "Shit!" under his breath as if a decision had been made, though he knew he'd go through the same torture time and time again, *sucking up.*

Joe had thought about those things for a long time. Some days and evenings he would sit at the club, if Mike wasn't around to engage him in useless conversation that always turned on one thing, and think only of how he had been cheated of another robust son. *They* were his pride and joy, like medallions he could wear at a minute's notice, extensions of himself, his name now and then in print. Christ! He could feel them in his backbone. And Banjo, the tiny son, the aberration, the anomalous offspring, seeming never to leave the hands of his blind and now utterly sexless mother for the better part of five years, grew slowly and aching as the neighborhood target runt of all runts. Banjo was persecuted, dawn to dusk, hounded, driven, plagued by all those his age, and some even younger. Pinched. Kicked. Bitten. Cussed. Punched. Knocked down. Back pockets ripped wide apart so that the seam of his pants would snap and his drawers would show. No Jobleski ever came to his rescue. Never once. No Paulie or Mike or Andy or Stash. No Aleksa either. They barely abided him, not wanting to share any of his deformity. Touching surely was sharing. And Aleksa, secretly, down in her stolid, unyielding body, in her man-looking body, behind her deep eyes

136

and Jobleski jaw, behind the air of nonchalance she was able to evoke at will, hated her runty brother, and absolutely, positively hated her mother for mixing up their places in her womb. She had thought, from the early days when her breasts began to fill themselves, when strange things happened within her and odd delights came sliding and slipping through her, that her mother had placed her in the wrong niche in that dark cavern, on that hidden sea, carried her in the wrong place, gave to her brother Banjo the body that was supposed to be hers. "I hate the two of them!" she would mouth deeply while in the shower, her lips curling her testament, her hands finding secrets, sources of electricity, discovering that proportion and graceful symmetry were not to be her choice attributes.

So Banjo grew, unwanted, unloved, object of utter derision, nearly cast aside from the bosom of the family, held only by the arms of his blind mother, her fingers touching, measuring, finding in the dark silence some of the same pains that the rest of the family found, and held by Aunt Stacy only when men of the house were away or Banjo would slip over to her house for a visit, for cookies, to have her rub his feet and little legs for hours on end, as if the chilblains worked in him. Stories would fall from her red dialectal mouth until he fell sleep. Dreamed about her red mouth, he did, how it was wet but vise-like the way it held the bare tip of a cigarette for hours on end, dangling, bringing now and then of a smile the final curve to her lips.

Plague is a word and a condition that is long apart from us, long apart from Jobleski and the tenor of their times. Except for Banjo. Somewhere in his sixth year, the runt, the family failure, the blot on their fair horizon, tired of the pounding, tired of the smashing, tired of the soreness almost a permanent part of his body, began to hit back.

Oh, Lord! Banjo began to kick. Began to punch. Began to stand against the armory that gathered in all the other Jobleskis. He fought tooth and nail their fingers in his ribs, their knocking-rapping fists on his skull, their aimless but aggregate punishment, their name-calling and diatribes, the jokes about Tom Thumbs and little peckers and dwarfs and pygmies and midgets and half-grown jockeys, the incredible allusions to the blind woman who had carried and delivered him, the distances they tried to put between themselves and him, the endless assault against kin.

More than once he believed himself kinless, stray, urchin, orphan. But rising in his small and abject frame, like it did in cubs or pups coming eventually of age, predators at length at their appointed places, came courage and an ingenuity and a will to survive that belied such territory.

Paulie: The first time you put your dick in, kid, you're going to fall right through. Balls out you're going, right on through. They'll be looking for you for a month of Sundays and nobody in high heaven will be able to find you. Don't let go, Banjo. Don't ever let go the last cunt hair you grab onto because it might be the last lifesaver you'll ever know. If you go down that long tunnel, kid, you'll never come back. What the hell would we do without you? Why we'd be friggin' lost. That's where we'd be. No more friggin' punching bag, no more little shit of shits to make our days. You can count on that. We'd be lost without you. Can you imagine it, the runt adrift on a cunt hair and never seen again!

A rock the size of a baseball suddenly off Paulie's head. A knob just as big coming along shortly thereafter. Another rock and another hit and Banjo escaping under a fence, his route secret and sacred and plotted well in advance. He'd show them a thing or two. He'd bust balls or die trying. Pursuit would be over in minutes, he knew. They could never catch him, never go the places he went, never put themselves through the smallest slot or space where only light had gone before him. And under Aunt Stacy's rear porch, tight up against the decking, he slipped into and through the smallest fissure of all, letting himself into a sanctuary of stone that no man had entered since it was sealed for structural safety. A root cellar long passed over and forgotten, buried under the addition of the wide screened porch. His Shangri-La. His oasis. Twenty-one square feet of bliss and darkness.

When he slipped down to the familiar floor, felt his secrets and collectibles, touched the skins of their miniature bodies, inhaled their steep and lovely aromas he had refined with sprays and perfumes stolen from innumerable sources, when in that darkness he could almost see the eyes of each one of the dolls, he said his prayer, as if it were an entry code, curse of passwords: When the time comes, when the whole wide world knows the great Jobleski brothers are just doll collectors, they'll shit their Jobleski pants from one end of town to the other. I'll see to that. I'll show 'em!

Andy: Let me settle it right up front, kid. Something is out of whack here, way out of line, like the milkman coming up the steps when he should have been going out with the empties. Fell on the old dame on that friggin' couch and she never knew the difference, milkman or drunk at prongin', makes no never mind to the blind except in the final counting. Could probably tell the difference in your bone structure or fingerprints. If you ever get the red-eye, why, we'll know for damn sure! Christ, he used to look at me sometimes and I thought he was going to set me on fire. Hated empties that were dirty, cluttered with white sop and stinking with sour milk. Hated to stoop when any one of us was within fifty feet of him, the lazy bastard! Hated every goddamn one of us! Hated every Polack this side of Warsaw, and them there just as much. Just a shanty Irish bastard with the awful red eye who you might be looking back on one good day like you owe him special. Rootstock from the grand island of eternal sotted souls, and all that diminutive crap that goes with little people. For that's just what you are, one of the fuckin' little people only drunks own up to!

Andy's creamy white, almost delicate Ford hard-top, shiny, sun-catching, spit-polished like the elite in military circles, chromed grille sole residue of a Packard nobody had seen in thirty years, suddenly sitting on four flat tires, a dead chicken floating above the front seat with his neck still twisted in that final knot, a slowly running hose caught up by a rear window tight against the upper edge and yet pouring a second cubic yard of water into that yawning cavern.

Stash: You were probably adopted and she didn't have the heart to tell you, once you began to grow— or not grow, fact is. Never told one of us either. Was her painkiller, you were, her mighty small aspirin, killjoy, all in one. When you bleed, the blood's not the same. Take it from me!

Stash's Ted Williams card, the Splendid Splinter, Terrible Teddy, .406 and balls out for the batting title like nobody else in the whole world would have dared, went in one hurry to fifty pieces if one. Stan Musial and Red Schoendeinst, teammates, glued together upside down as if they had been having fun in the back of the locker room. Even in that pose, no longer of prime value. No longer pristine. No longer neutral in the Polish community all around the Jobleskis, mores forevermore different. Potato Man Yaz, Long Island Yaz's card split up the gut. Whitey Ford, rookie card, face of a newborn, gutted dead center.

Aleksa: She cheated you and she cheated me. You could have had these arms, these shoulders, these wrists born for swinging, for driving balls to dead center on a line. I could have been you and you could have been me, but no way was she going to do that, so we're stuck, me here in this weightlifter's garb and you there in your pygmy pants. We're going to be locked up here forever and she'll have a last dream of us as we might have been. If we count our blessings, we'll be in the minus column, and you know it as well as me. She played a rotten goddamn trick on us!

Run up on the flag pole, standing like a singular white birch of lonely beauty in the front yard of the Jobleskis's house of odd additions and strange angles, for all the world to see on the following morning, was just about every unmentionable Aleksa's chest of drawers would yield. Slapping in the breeze were assorted bras, black to flesh colored, pockets turned out to the wind, stringed, wired, strapped, all making as much noise as the underdrawers and panties and plain old fashioned snuggies that lay straight out on the taut rope. Body messages. They talked on the wind. They spilled secrets. Body remnants. Portions of her loose on the world. Cups filling now and then with masses of air. Bloomers for bare seconds stuffed with the shape of her more-than-ample ass, all the odors gone, all the aromas tossed freely to clouds and other spirits of the air, discolorations and other stains still hard in some crotches.

Burning clean out of her skin, cursing at the top of her lungs the language stolen from the backroom of the PAMVETS, pounding up and down stairs and in and out of each room of the house, she sought her runty brother. "I'll kill that goddamn runt, that little shit poke. I'll kill the little bastard! If anyone gets in my way, he gets it, too!"

Banjo, of course, had long since departed, slipping out of the house just before two a.m. as quietly as he had slipped into her room, rifling her secrets, and slipping just as noiselessly into Aunt Stacy's unknown sanctuary, hiding a pair of autographed panties, Aleksa indeed would kill for, in a pocket of fieldstone.

Banjo thought about his loot and his articles of revenge often enough, how to widen his collection, how to strike the most deadly blow. But he always stayed away from the football trophies of his brothers, a mass of gold and silver and mahogany wood adorned with running backs and stretching ends and bruising tackles at deadly mission. These mementos would, he knew, be the most fitting salute of all. None of his family could ever approach his thoughts, his calculations, his absolute deviltry. Every punch, every kick, every slap had its due. It was all coming around again. What goes around comes around. It made him smile a small smile. Disparity in life can be ennobled.

In the dark hideaway he slept peacefully.

He slept there many times over the next few years, there, or upstairs in the house with Aunt Stacy who loved to have him over. She couldn't stand the others, even Aleksa, at least not for very long. She found them too cruel and too boring and, in spite of their obvious strengths, to be too weak at will. The first ally of Banjo would have been this quiet woman who wore a little too much rouge, a lipstick perhaps two shades too dark for her face, the clothes of a woman who had no one man to live up to, to please, but delighted in many acquaintances.

That she loved Banjo was important to her and to her blind sister. One was a springboard and one was a sounding board, and at the core of their relationship they had made the puny little boy becoming a puny little man the secret of their existence. They did not live for each other, but for him. And when Mary died in her sleep one night as Banjo was approaching his sixteenth birthday, him still plagued, still persecuted, still a virgin and the lone one in the family, Aunt Stacy was impetuously proud of his survival, all the facets of it. "That little man of mine," she would say to herself, "will outlast all of them." And in the periphery of her hearing, at the edges of her memory, all the castigation and curses they had hurled down upon him came back to her with incredulous clarity. Too often the broad-shouldered, big-armed, thick-skulled hulks had centered their attacks on Banjo's male equipment: His dick's so small any chick'd say he had no visitation rights... even after he had been there! D'ja see the size of his balls? Like peas they are, or *it* is, the last ball remaining from the master set. Pea-Ball is what we shoulda called him, or Pea-Balls Minus One, or Pendulum Without Affair, or Who Gives A Shit Anyway!

They had all laughed and back-slapped and hoisted off another drink, and Stacy, in her cool aura, not batting an eyelash over her rouged cheeks, managed a slow interior laugh, and said under her breath, "Watch your ass, Stash. Remember what happened last time!"

Two days after Mary was buried, Banjo sat in front of the library thinking about his mother, how horrible the funeral had been, how much crap and derision was still tossed in the air by the whole family, as if she had been a simple hired hand, a maid servant, a ball of lint which had just blown through their lives. Her hands had been soft and warm and the tears on her cheeks were forever pearl full of special light, and none of them ever could tell him that his mother's eyes were lifeless. The pearled tears were special, jewels they'd never seen, but he would carry them always—he'd even carry them in the growing and continually fermenting hunger and desire to bring to his siblings the ultimate pain.

Inside the library he saw the tall blonde sitting off in a corner. She had been there before, at the same table, a little lax about how her dress rode up on her thighs, long and valley-like, a summons, the mystery of her crotch seeming to call out to him. He prayed she would not cross her legs, and took a seat with the surest tunnel of vision possible. Black or purple panties, he decided. Black or purple. His favorite colors. Now and forever. Every so often a squeeze of one thigh or the other, or both in concert, and the dark image would narrow, gap down, slink, like a wondrous eye winking at him. Back to him came a choice reading and some author he'd never remember, talking about The Seven Cities of Cibola, or The Mound of Venus, or the graffiti he'd seen on a wall once, *When you come right down to it, guys, there's nothing like cunt.* He lay the Atlas of the whole United States of America and all its territories over his lap to hide his erection, and liked himself at that particular moment because he'd never allow any of his brothers' or father's aspersions about penis or testicle, or lack of, or the small bunch of his ass to come back tauntingly upon him. He could now cast them over the side as if he were throwing out an anchor in the middle of the river.

Intent on that long vision, driving his eyes past the faint barrier that lay at the end, purple or black it didn't matter now, he flinched when her white thighs locked up completely, then opened slowly, oh ever so slowly, like the drawbridge over the river when a grand yacht was heading out to the lake. A pair of deep green-gray eyes was staring at him. In his chest he caught more than an ounce of breath. The erection might sound out a warning alarm. It came up so hard against, he guessed, South Dakota. That made him smile, and that smile, South Dakota and all, made its way across the room to the warmest reception this side of Aunt Stacy. She didn't move her legs again. The thighs stayed white. Her look was soft and appealing. His erection burned. The book in her hand was raised so that he could see the title, *Dreams We Don't Understand.* A light went on at the back of his head and it brought another dimension of smile to his face. A smile, a wider smile, came back to him.

He thought his pecker was going to explode; there'd be a Minuteman Missile going up from one of the silos near Bismarck or Lincoln, whichever one of those cities belonged in South Dakota. He could never remember. He'd never forget this smile coming across the silence of the library, across the deep red rugs, moving its aura on air already filled with aura. Nor would he ever forget the most personal signature ever sent his way.

Outside, in ten minutes, they found that their fathers had named each of them with some deviltry, or rancor, for unknown reasons. Banjo was explained, and she was Eloise Abelard, a joke of her father's, she was sure. "My mother cut him off at three months of her pregnancy and I think it was his way of getting back at her with sarcasm if nothing else. I don't think they ever slept together again, each going at the other in their own way. I didn't like growing up."

"So here you are talking to the smallest guy in the library, on the street, in the whole town practically, maybe even this side of South Dakota." With all that said, he looked at her with clear eyes.

"What's that mean?"

He told her. She laughed as he had heard no one ever laugh, throaty, honest, without any crap or flip in it, no phoniness, just plain laugh. It had fur on it. It warmed him. He told her. She said that she had seen him before, had seen him looking up her dress, had been warmed by it, flushed but warm.

"You have the whitest thighs in the whole world. I can play anything with strings." His eyes were so clear she could have been startled. She should have been startled. Clarity is precious, she thought. So much in her life had not been clear, but this was special. She had a vision of what his life must have been like. Pain came on her. It was in his aura and she felt it. But he didn't bring any of it to hurt her. He came at her clean and clear, out of crystal. The real pain was disparate, separate.

"Your eyes say you'll never lie to me." Her hand was in his. "You've music hands."

They saw each other just about every other day, at the library, at the edge of the river, back on the hill out behind the Evert's Florist Shop and flower gardens. He kept her away from the Jobleskis. She kept him by her side. They had their intentions. She was seventeen. He was sixteen. She was 5 feet 6 inches. He was 5 feet 1 7/8 inches stretched out, proud, not minding his height for the first time, not sworn to revenge, not filled with plans for coping and getting even for the constant transgressions.

One day, just about at the top of the hill after a slow meandering walk, a faint mist cutting across the sunset, a bird calling uphill, smell of new grass making them heady, she took his hand and put it on her breast. "I've been dying for you to touch me," she said. "I've been practicing on myself, but it's not like this. I like this. Here," she gestured, "go underneath. Touch my nipple." She took his hand with her hand, fire must have been at it, and slipped it inside her bra. "Be easy." Her lashes came down over her eyes. Mouth open. Lips red as a forgotten sunset. Moist. Shiny. A breath catching itself in her throat. If she told an absolute outright lie he'd believe her until the very end of the world came throbbing under them.

"I love you, Eloise." She laughed a little laugh, her chin shaking lightly. "Maybe tomorrow we'll get to Louisiana."

Both of them laughed long and loud, tears in their eyes. He saw his mother's tears on Eloise's cheeks. True crystal. Gems. Life! He took his hand away from her risen nipple, which had stayed against his palm as certain as a nail halfway through its job. The bird called back up the hill waiting for an answer. Grass continued to be cut somewhere over the hill. Any pain in the world he could stand. He had come this far in life and it had all been worth it. Clear across the library again he saw her white thighs. Perhaps he might tell Aunt Stacy about her. Maybe he wouldn't. Maybe she was just for him forever. A bird answered. More cut grass news came on the wind. Fuck Stash and Andy and Mike and Paulie! Even fuck Aleksa! Fuck the old man!

Now, his world was different.

A week later, all the Jobleskis but Banjo at the Flag Day picnic in the PAMVET's grove beside the river, Eloise and Banjo slipped through the back door of the house.

"They're all gone, Benjy?" She looked around and felt the pain flowing about her. An old wound rode about in the air, a cry. "Why did we come here, Benjy?"

"I wanted it to be here because of my mother. You remind me of my mother. Your hands are so warm." He took her down to the den. She saw shelves so heavy with trophies they made her eyes blink. Gold and silver and stained wood and colored enamels and plastic inserts and the family name repeated endlessly, and a great variety of athletes in poses cast in cheap metal. None of them, she knew, were Benjy's. There would be justice, she thought.

Laying back on the couch, almost giddy, loving the daring he placed them in, the idea of sharing consuming her, her legs out in front of her, longer than they had ever been, she said, "Benjy, put your hand under my panties. Go easy. I'll tell you what I like. You tell me what you like." His fingers felt the thick hair, then softness, then mystery, then depth, then more mystery, then a little knob she introduced him to, then more moisture than he had dreamed. He kissed her and her mouth opened like Ali Baba's cave. "We're going to call this *Going to Louisiana.* But don't laugh and don't stop what you're doing, and a little harder and a little faster if you want, and if you like it."

And his mind was going to explode and every pain he ever felt in his life was long gone and her legs opened wider and he saw all that whiteness and his mouth was dry and he couldn't swallow.

Then he heard the funny sound, from another room, and raised a finger to his lips, and moved away from her and slipped quietly from the room. The hand that clapped over his mouth, the arm that squeezed his body as hard as a vise, the other hand that slammed under his crotch and lifted him a meek feather into the air, had to be a Jobleski arm. He could not see, but he could smell a Jobleski. His voice was stuffed back into his mouth and he was carried from the house. "Old Pea-Balls, you're going under cover." It was Stash and a fist hit him on the side of the head. He was being carried over one hip like a frigging rag doll. Hatred surged and seethed in him. The whole coming scene ran through his mind in a mere second, then he was slammed into the trunk of Stash's car and the trunk door slammed down on top of him. Buzzing ran through his head. Darkness clawed its way into his eyeballs. "You, prick!" he screamed. "I'll kill you. I'll kill you, you rotten son of a bitch!" But he didn't scream for long or hate for long or waste his time for long because Eloise was out there with him. He had to get out.

Stash, with quickness, perhaps expertness, had surprised Eloise. Had pinned her down on the couch where her dress was still up over her hips. "So you were going to screw the midget, huh? I'll show you what a real piece is, honey baby. A real piece." He tore her pants off in one stroke. "You scream and I'll kill that little shrimp. You got it? And you're going to do some other tricks, too. Tricks I bet he never knew anything about."

"Please don't do this." She didn't want to scream. His hand was down there in Louisiana and a shudder went through her body. He began to explore slowly with *that* hand. His mouth came down over hers, yawning and wet and full of booze residue. She didn't know what it was but knew she would remember the smell of it all her life.

She didn't hear any sound. She only felt the abrupt and violent shudder that went through her attacker. Then he went limp on her, all his weight against her the way she had dreamed a thousand times, a thousand touches, a thousand reaches in classrooms, at the kitchen table, even in church. And Banjo stood over the two of them with a baseball bat in his hand and the ugly echo of provoked flesh and bone still sounding in the room.

They walked out of the house, past the car with one rear door open and the back of the rear seat pushed away from the clips that had held it in place. He did not say a word, just kept moving her away from the house, and the hatred and the seething and the mechanics of revenge fully operational in him.

That night, high on the hill, after he had entered her at her request, after she had argued with him for hours and moved his hands on her body and touched him as he had never been touched, they made plans to leave town. They'd go to a cousin of hers more than two hundred miles away. They'd never come back. They'd be together forever.

Later, Banjo thought long and hard down in his dark retreat, Aunt Stacy overhead telling company how much she liked her sex and what parts she liked the most. He thought about Eloise and then about a TV show on the wild dogs of Africa and how the runt of a litter had been given the hardest time of all and had finally walked away and died, the broad savanna flung out beyond the fallen body like space beyond a star. The image crushed him. The sadness of it all came over him with an extraordinary force, as whole episodes of his life came flooding back through the tight quarters of the old root cellar. And out of the clear blue sky came a vision of one of the old Minuteman Missiles deployed across the north Central States, their huge silos extending like inverted skyscrapers down into all of Mother Earth, peckers screwing the old dame for all she was worth.

The clarity Eloise had seen in his eyes was in his head; he saw everything he wanted to see, needed to see, how all of it would come to pass. And on the Fourth of July to boot! In salute of everything grand and beautiful and majestic from sea to shining sea.

Remaining out of sight while any Jobleski was at home, he came back to the house on days only when it was empty, all of them at work or at school or practice for one team or another. He loosened the metal cover that had been placed over the old well in the back yard, the well Paulie had fallen into one day and would have drowned if Aleksa had not screamed the alarm. Making trip after trip, he lowered his special equipment and supplies into the well, cans and other containers of every odd description, all without covers, supporting everything by ropes from the flanged bar across the opening and just under the metal cover. Working assiduously, without help from any quarter, much as his life had been spent except for his mother and Aunt Stacy in the occasional breach, Banjo Jobleski primed the engines of revenge.

They had all gone to the PAMVET's grove for the Fourth of July picnic and beer blast, Joe the father, stalwart daughter Aleksa and sons Paulie, Andy, Mike and Stash, still wearing from a mysterious source the ugliest of bruises and swelling. He could have been hit by a car or lightning. Nobody knew and Stash wasn't telling. Somehow, most everybody who had known the Jobleskis over the years realized that inexplicable causes and happenings could be attributed without failure to one Benjamin Arthur Norman Jobleski, shrimp, midget, pygmy, dwarf, Peckerless, Pea-Ball, Shit Poke, ad infinitum, though such attributes were not openly discussed near Jobleski muscle.

So while the beer flowed and prowess was being heaved on the air and broad backs were being clapped and slapped and a hundred hands would be run up under a hundred skirts even before dusk fell, Banjo came out of the vast savanna he had retreated to and went about his work.

All the trophies, every last one of them, collected from the den and sundry bedrooms and out of closets and eventually from the cellar, like a rich vein had been found, were placed in the living room. Every bra and pair of underpants that Aleksa owned, except those that she was wearing at the picnic, were draped over and around the aggregate trophies, as if a window decorator had been employed. Next came from hidden places about the house every smashed instrument from which he had once extracted music, the clutter of ruin, the remnants made by Jobleski boots, the denial of dreams. Finally, deferring to age and for no other reason, the old man's collection of anagrams and puzzles and acrostics and acronyms were placed across the front of the exhibit. Banjo looked down at odd papers and read the acronyms the old gent had come up with for a variety of causes: *ROMEO*'s, for the older guys who gathered each Tuesday morning for breakfast at Sarah's Diner, *Retired Old Men Eating Out; ABRACADABRA,* still a mystery, but not worth spending these last minutes on: *BANJO* in letters as broad and stolid as any he had ever seen, now faded and diminished on what was most likely the original paper, a memento of rancor saved for history. He thought of his mother's tears and how he'd never know the full extent of her pain, because all her pain must have been much more than his. After all, he had *survived*, hadn't he?

Outside, leaving the house for the very last time in his life, he walked all around the edge of the building, another one of the large cans tipped on his hip. He used a number of them, tossing the empties and near empties down in the well, careful not to hit any of his hidden assets still hanging by ropes. He took another piece of rope from another full can and laid it out from the house and played the other end down into the depths of the well. The crude metal cover was put back on top of the well and bolted down, drawing down the four nuts with a ratchet wrench. The wrench gleamed its stainless steel brilliance on the rust-colored cover when he placed it perfunctorily on top. It was odd how the wrench caught in gleaming silver the last of the sun, as if it meant to hold on to the day for as long as it could. He hummed to himself. Memorialized. Memorable day. Fourth of July. *Sea to shining sea.* The Fat Lady singing. Sousa. Cohan. Kelley. Cagney. Connaughton Kate. Benjamin Arthur Norman Jobleski. The world, amen.

From a pod of dolls, as if they were swimming atop one another in boxes, arms out, legs back, heads down, he took one at a time those he had long collected and hung them in trees and scattered them as shot residue on Jobleski ground for all the world to see: Barbie dolls and cry baby dolls and Ken dolls and wetting dolls and sucking dolls and balliky dolls, every one that had ever fallen under his hand for reasons he never knew and only now fully understood. Then, cool and collected and without any remorse at all, the tears gone, the pain gone, he knelt and flipped a switch on a device he had rigged and walked off into the broad savanna, off into that space beyond the star.

He was walking away from the whole brood!

On his own two legs, and walking away.

That other runt dog of the TV had walked a short ways into that endless space and staggered and finally fallen on his side. There had been no ceremony. No yapping. No sniffing or final licks from any of the others. But *he* was walking away, all the way across that broad savanna. The pearls on his mother's cheeks came back to him abruptly, then disappeared forever.

Benjy Jobleski and Eloise Abelard were two miles away, getting a ride from a salesman on his way to Harrisburg, when over the hill behind them, back toward town, a redness of fire filled the evening sky with a sudden clarity, and Banjo's wondrous collection of gasoline and cans and metals of every sort, and odd cases of shotgun shells and bullets and an uncounted number of stolen sticks of dynamite, and old powder wrappings and odd combustibles and exquisite fire and conflagration itself and dozens of the most special trophies of all that his brothers had been awarded, went absolutely haywire in his own Minuteman Missile silo and shot straight up from the precincts of hell.

FLESH OF AN UNWANTED FISH

Armand Tollbar remembered everything Clara said, on and off the pillow, in the bedroom and out of it. These days that had become a tough assignment for him, for while the memories were rich and repetitive, he now knew, deep down in his body, without a paucity of doubt, that the river was getting polluted. For the two of them there had always been a minor division: she loved the house; he loved the river. Nothing was inordinate about either love, except on both sides of the equation it was full and fulfilling. Now she was gone, that small, lively and ebullient body of hers ravaged suddenly by disease, and the river, a surface scum the first tell-tale sign, along with an indefinable aroma he was more apt to say in explanation was an odor, was changing. Life would gang up on him if he let it: the arguments and the happenings like railroad tracks coming up behind him out of his past, keeping time, matching hits.

"You'll die with your boots on," Clara had once said as she bade him goodbye from the wide porch she loved, his wading boots rubbing at inner thighs, the rod tip high, the empty creel hanging on a shoulder strap and swinging at one hip, and the river, downhill and in spring rapture, a prize for the taking, curving off into the shadows of trees.

"Outbound," he always said to himself as the river sought its way to the Atlantic a dozen or so miles off. They had talked about salutations and valedictions on many occasions, the ones said and those unsaid, or the whispered ones they knew were shared, fully understood. And when he uttered, "Outbound," even unto himself, he knew she heard. The sharing was as complete as two people could make it. Even as death made primal its division.

Now, on this day, Armand looked over his shoulder, rapt at the slight splashing sound sifting a music under the trees, the ripples coming downstream at his knees, waning at his boots, and heard in the limbs above the screech of a daylight owl slamming through the hunchback oaks and stately elms. All of it admittedly setting his bones at radical comfort. "I've seen you motionless for long moments," she had offered softly one late morning on his return, "as if you did not want to cast a shadow into the water, did not want to disturb the fish, lulling them into security, setting them up for the barb." She had, he agreed again, impeccable eyesight and knockdown reasoning.

On the river he was, fishing he was, with the sun slipping new needles down through the titter of morning leaves. Of course he loved the house (the argument almost coming aloud in him), every corner of it, the soft messages he'd find hidden in corners, in rooms, old smells coming at him he thought might have been forgotten (like the hint of morning cocoa in the kitchen), shadows playing games with his eyes. Oh, God, she could be anywhere! Anywhere!

Yet he had to get out every day so that he could go back to it, revel at arrival, almost expecting her to be there on the porch, the apron yellow as her Swan River daisies, hair neat even in that random way she wore it, as if meant for pillows forever; he'd never told her that because it was something she would know, could generate without trying. Fishing took him away and brought him back, the small sense of worms at his fingers, their survival's soft linking at work, working for the small freedoms. Understanding such a frail message as that was like knowing each room of the house could expel him if he lingered too long, absorbed too much, drew down from its walls the ideas and sounds and movements pasted there in some indelible function: Clara's hand prints, Clara's fingerprints, Clara's rush at things painted, open, western in message and color, the walls of the hall her bastion.

"This is my museum," she had offered another time, leaning back against the hall wall, her hair he noticed against the wall the same way it spread against her pillow, promise in it, supposed innocent portrayal, a language without words. "This is my great romance other than you," and that brought up without the slightest pause. Always she had a way of bringing him into everything important in her life. "The impact of words often lasts well beyond the sound of them," she said, not in qualification but as fact. "Words are irrefutable in that way. The energy of them is sometimes indestructible. They carry themselves. Mark that." The pause came, her eyes focused, and she added, "Remember that I love you always." Now, brought back in liquid memory, the words were present tense forever.

All of it so marked except the day she died; that day she had sent him on an errand. The last call by the doctor had been one of "some months now." And she had known the doctor was wrong again.

Days now he kept going back over his life. For such a prolonged part of it there had been the river, and not far from it, paramount as the flush of spring the river brought him, was the house. It was Clara's house. Down in a wholly formulary part of his body, in a wholly secretive but controlling place, he knew it would always be Clara's house. As children, as part of Mrs. Beckman's second grade class, and all up through those young years, until dates became real dates, until the idea of flesh sumptuously but slyly imposed itself, she had steadily said that the house one day would be her house, that she would live there in happiness for her entire life.

One of those days in particular came upon him fully; they were on a hay ride, snuggled form to form, frame to frame, chest to chest, against one side of the hay-filled wagon, noise and cluster and soft gaiety and whispers and new mysteries coupled around them. And the assault of a perfume he would remember forever and could never bring back, as if June nights would always hang around, teasing, on a piece of horizon.

The wagon was passing the house again, on the way back to the barn at Peterson's farm, the lights glowing in all the windows of the house, the porch lights on and glittering through the house-wide screening, bodies active on the porch, talk and music riding the night air incessant as bugs. His hand was dangerously close to one breast he had only recently noticed blossoming behind fabric. "One day I am going to live there and have nights like this on the porch, with music and friends, and my husband by my side." She had taken his hand and placed it on that breast and said, in words so faithful in his life he'd remember them perpetually, not caring if she might have measured and calculated them for that purpose, the way some women might want a man to remember special words forever, "Promise me that you'll love me every day of your life."

Those words echoed on every one of his days; he could not recall a day that he hadn't heard them coming at him, ringing in him their slow combustion of feelings, at work, driving, out on the slow part of the river when fall came and water started its trickling move towards winter, at her side drifting off to sleep, seeing her striped in the kitchen in the slanting rays of the sun.

Now the river, his once glorious river, was moving, oh so slowly but assuredly, into a polluted state, and the house, his house now but always Clara's house, was lonely and quiet. The mysteries abounding in each of those elements came at him continually, an elaborate and rich collection of yesteryears flooding him. He lived on the ripeness of memories, as if they were food; they sustained him, brought him push and shove, made dawns come up with expected elegance. There were days he was sorely convinced she was only off visiting, would appear over the bridge along with the sunset, both at revelation. More than once he had turned to look at the bridge for her, found just the sunset glinting off nail heads, losing itself in the trees. Some days he could be crushed down to his toes, and was only able to shake it off with stern concentration on something utterly physical about him, a jay at jangle, a quick squirrel at its scurry, a cloud like a blossom in the sky.

"Come to the senior center," some friends had urged. "Plenty of company. Lots of motion and commotion, people talking in your ear. The food is good and cheap. The women are lonely, ever so lonely. It's cheaper than shopping, you can bet."

He didn't have time for such a breakout, and he kept studying the river, seeing again the green-yellow scum that rode it some days, a filmy discoloration of all things loved, all things pure. The last few fish taken (how long ago was that last one?) had not the good flesh to them, not the near snow white flesh of holdovers he loved to sear fry, or place with cornmeal or bread crumbs and a bit of butter in an open pan on an open fire. Life could be so simple; but the river was different now, and it kept telling him so in many ways.

One day, he vowed, he would move all the way up the river, tour it, search it, make his own determinations as to the causes of the pollution. It would not be hard he assumed; she had said, "Most things are so evident. You have to find what is contained. Look at my paintings. They are so readily evident, but every single time I look, I see something else. Even though things appear evident, you never know them completely."

There was, for a sudden moment, as he stood up to his crotch in the river's water, a red wing blackbird uttering at disturbance, a fingertip tingle from the rod. The small charge rode his frame like a surge of glory. It must have been real, he thought, to be so electric. He had not dreamed it. Not this time. Not again. For months now there had been no bites, no suggestive nibbles, no electricity to send his heart pumping. The river was making its own statement. One leg ached in its stiffness, demanding he move it, shift his weight, ease that pain. Stock still he stood, in a contest, wagering himself in this battle. Again, slight as a tremor, a piece of Earth in movement, a touch came along his fingers.

"What is it that draws you back so often?" she had said another time, bringing him back to the river in a way only she could. "You have never explained that to me all the way through." She had placed the trout in the pan, and turned at the stove, the apron as yellow as he'd ever seen it, the sun slanting a new stripe across her bosom. "Is it like my other world, the cowboys, the Indians, the buttes and mesas standing like clocks in the face of time? Is fishing like that? Supposedly intricate but not." The words were whole. Her mouth formed them anew for him, her eyes lighting them up as apt as punctuation, the slight tilt of her head another punctuation mark. Behind her the butter in the pan made other small noises, the fish hissed along its flesh, cornmeal aroma rode the air.

He could not think of how he had answered. His own words would not come back, only hers. The one-way of memory could stun him at times; another time it might not be worth a single fret of worry.

If it was going to be uneven this way, he wondered how long it would last, how long he would last. In no manner did he want to start on the *Time* thing. It was so inappropriate, so disloyal. "Carry on," once came down the hallway to him, almost a tune, almost musical, but he could not bring back why she had said it, where they were in some distant conversation.

There! It came again! The nibble was alive, moving along the length of leader, the whole run of the floating flyline, the length of the rod, to his left index finger quivering like a tine of a tuning fork. To his toes he swore he knew it. Oh, she must have known all of this without his telling her. For the moment he convinced himself that he was never able to tell her, that she must have known as she knew everything else. "Everything is so evident, and so new." A jay screamed nearby. A leaf tittered in the air beside his ear. From the road he could hear the pounding of a heavy diesel engine, and a back-up alarm blaring. Everything usual and new at once.

Bang! The rod jumped in his hands. He leaned with it, pulled the rod tip up high, moved to regain his balance. The Earth fell away under him, under one foot, and only beckoned with a deep sense of nothing.

He weighed the water cresting over the top of one boot, knew the Earth under that boot, still in orbit, had moved away from him. The rod jerked upright as he tried to set the barb, keep the keeper on the hook. From a distance, in that thinness of voice making it across some great divide, he heard her say, "You'll die with your boots on. The cowboys said that."

HUMBOLDT HAVEN

The problems with the house project and a good stiff drink seem to go together. A good pair, Wiggles thinks. A half snicker comes up through his throat even as his stomach makes loud noises. Consciously Francis Pikethorn, known as Wiggles to everyone, licks his lower lip and his fingers roll against each other in an expression of suspense. There is, of course, the long wait and the dry throat. The hours since the last drink he quickly counts at the back of his mind. Brushing the thick sandy-colored hair out of his eyes with a flick of a thumb, he thinks that controls are easy this morning. Again he flicks the thumb and sees no momentary twitching, no delay in his commands. A day dried out sits well on him, as the saw would if he had wood to rip cut, a wall to erect.

Or if his wife Jennie had not gone off like that.

"It's got to be the house," offers his partner and brother-in-law Abel Damfort. "We have to create something provocative, interesting, damn different about that old house. Make the place shine if we can. Or spout ghosts or break out in a case of the crabs for all I care. It needs a transfusion. Hell, it could burn down in five minutes if we let it. Even most of the drunks have shied away from it over the years. Ever since the Carringtons, both of them, died in there."

He continues, his face showing concern for the old couple. "Oh, the shame of it all, the very damn shame. I hear they were nice folk, decent folk." When he says "decent" it sounds like "dacent."

Wiggles leans over the planning table. He nods at "dacent." He feels drawn and tired to his last bone but speaks more about their troubles. "If we don't get the loan and don't get the house, Abel, we might as well fold up this old two-man company and blow it away. I admit I've blown a few bucks. But I never missed a minute's work. Always gave it all I had. But we need this damn loan or we're history. There's nothing else out there for us."

Pressing his hands down on the tabletop, he stares at them for a long time. His hands are the tapering, long but gnarled hands of the laborer, as if a violinist has encountered other rude tools in life. Scars are as proud as badges on their backsides. One thumb has been found by a three-pound hammer in an errant swing. An arthritic-looking knuckle sits toad-like on the left hand. It has been a long time since the hand has made a tight fist. Not that Wiggles has gone without the need.

Blue-eyed, pasty-faced Wiggles looks at his partner Abel Damfort. Abel is early-forties neat, high forehead, green eyes under woolly dark brows, thick against the short sleeves of his shirt. He has a remnant brogue Wiggles thinks should have long disappeared.

166

Able listens closely as Wiggles continues. "Before we know it, we'll be as much history as the house. Something's tied to that place like a disease. That's all I can say. Almost cancerous. Something out of the past. Nobody lets on about it from where I sit, but it's there. Our future, for all we know, is tied up in that old house." He makes a half fist with each hand.

Wiggles again finds himself caught in a new kind of trap, can feel it squeezing on him. Words keep coming out of a dark tunnel. At times they come out of someplace he swears he does not know, has never been to. And then there is the little sense of pain that rides in him. He wants to say discomforts but knows he'd be lying to cover his ass. He keeps thinking: *That one harsh pain is a stupid little pain, though agonizing at times. It's kind of brittle, like chunks of metal or sparks behind my eyes, squinting now all the time, or thinking I'm squinting. I'm not sure. Jeezus, I must be some kind of mausoleum. A walking museum of crap and crap shoots, booze and broadsides. Jennie'd know. But she'd just say it was the booze again, being simple enough.*

"Think the bank is holding something back?" Abel's voice matches his face, somewhat masked, reserved, asking for surprises all the time, and not getting them. Not with Wiggles. Without doubt he thinks that he, Abel Damfort, is the rock in this tenuous partnership.

Wiggles Pikethorn shakes his head, thinking he is coming out of a fog. "Look, Abel, honest injun, I'm not hung over as usual. But I spent a sleepless night looking at things. Old reality has come a stop sign on my nightly reveries. I'm not sure if I was caught up in self-incrimination or lost opportunity.

Balancing one on the other gets a moment of ease. Doubts keep bugging me, too. Jennie haunts me, her gone off like that, without a true word it seems."

Abel Damfort says, offhandedly, "We don't mention her at home though we hope she's getting along. But no matter what we do, we don't get to change the mind of the bank. Against us since the start they've been, the lot of them. It ain't just your drinking, Wiggles, 'cause they know nobody with a saw and a day dried out is any better than you are. Hell, you about put all their houses together and in order, and all of them needing the mend to boot. Shankhill shitty enough of them were, right here in old Humboldt." He tosses his head in salute of a distant memory crossing his mind.

"What do we do?" Wiggles says, his face looking like the used end of a cork, his eyes in a state of sadness that people notice early about him. He adds, "I wish I had a cool one in my hands right now. Makes thinking so much easier. Finds real words for me I couldn't find otherwise. Not a hint of them."

WIGGLES, PARTLY MUSING, looks over Abel's head as if he were looking into a mirror back of a friendly bar. He says, "We have to keep it historical, even if it's over 150 years old. Them damn historical buffs keep saying that over and over. It's like they got the bank hypnotized, but hell, that's always been part of our plan. So what can we do to make that historical house more attractive? Make people sit up and look at it kind of different. The old couple, the Carringtons, going within a day of each other, carried it for a while, but the old die everyday. It wears off. Just crowds the cemetery."

Abel's face warms as if it has relaxed its guard. "It's marvelous that old man Carrington lived in the house all his ninety-three years. And her not much behind him at that. That's about all I know, 'cept the house has always had some mystery tied to it, like a tail on a lost kite. Must be something I don't know." Abel's brogue rolls in on itself. "What did his nibs Verikjon have to say at the bank? That one's an odd lot if I have the say on him." He looks down and studies his fingernails.

"Oh, Victor's okay in his own way," says Wiggles. "I tossed down a pint or two with him at the alleys a few times. Said it straight out to me: 'We know how good you are with the hammer and the saw, but you're always on the edge, Wiggles.' He's one of those always using the nicknames, warming your ass for you before they kick it, know what I mean? 'Some of us think when you fall we'll be left holding the bag. That's how simple some prospects can be looked at. There has to be another dimension besides you and your partner to make this house project at least seem bigger than what it is.' I appreciated he didn't dodge me like old man Shillings always did."

They talk and muse a while longer and Abel leaves to do errands. Wiggles Pikethorn, passing Calder Murphy's Bar, the day heavy on him, lets his thirst and dry throat have their way. Long before the day is over, Jennie floats in the mirror behind the bar. She floats beside the front elevation of the Carrington house. *She won't let go, no matter where she is, where she ends up, saying all the time it's just the booze. Who knows better than her?*

And he is damn sure he is not going to let go the opportunity with the Carrington house. He is on the griddle and he knows it.

IT IS AFTER MIDNIGHT, the stars hammered in place over Humboldt and the whole valley as if bright nails have been slammed with a six-pound peen onto the dark sky. Somehow, in a comfortable stupor, as he might call it, Wiggles finds his way to the house against the side of the hill. The two huge double-trunk maples out front are catching the breeze and bouncing it like chunks of sherbet. It had been said old man Carrington had split them as saplings with a keen knife in prospects of having four children. The idea of eternity strikes Wiggles, seeing an image of the young Carrington full of hope. *Life sucks,* Wiggles thinks, thinking about the Carringtons subsequently spending almost a century here without any kids. It makes him lonely, desperately lonely, and he can go no farther in thought than half-eyeing Jennie down the line someplace hosting someone else with her goodness. And minor retribution for his own lifestyle piles on its weight in its own way.

Through the leaf clusters and fractured-hand limbs of the maples, he sees a dozen stars in their nightly revolutions. A minor glimmer of a shooting star comes in sight and he hears himself say, "They always come back." It is his one stand in life. He is not sure he says it in response to the revolution of the nightly stars or his thinking about people nearing the point of no return. He further acknowledges that man and stars are in some mix of existence whose solution is a mere grasp away from him. It is a glare of light that fast retreats.

Myriad thoughts notwithstanding, before long he finds himself in the keeping room of the Carrington place, a room that runs the whole back end of the house. The huge walk-in fireplace is cold looking, monstrous, out of place, as if to say it will be the last surviving part of the structure. The house-wide landing above the fireplace, on the second floor level, still holds a worn rail with oddly thick balusters. No doubt it has prophesied children for years on end; company for the split maples out front, he affirms. But it is the silence of the keeping room that guns down Wiggles and he sits in a lone chair left in a corner, sweet as an afterthought, a condition of hope, and a place for at least one more visitor. Eternity bounces around him, with a sense of time that few men can measure. He is sure of this.

Within himself he is for a long time, bouncing ideas, himself being bounced around. What eventually drove him to such an odd errand he has no idea, but he is dynamically pushed and pulled by powers other than his own. In short order he is in the cellar of the old house.

In one corner of the vacant cellar that runs halfway under the house, the other half a sort of crawl space beneath one half of the keeping room, he finds a construction of wood. It is an immovable box of sorts. To it he takes an old pry bar that hangs on a wall remnant of an old coal bin. The air has kept its coal smell as sharp as ever, like a taste of kerosene touching his tongue. After much effort, some teasing of nail and wood, squeaks and screeches becoming part of night, he uncovers a deep-throated, fully constructed well.

He has no idea the well is there. No moisture smell comes to him and he goes back to his truck and grabs a strong flashlight and a drop-light. The lack of moisture bothers him. Has a well been dug, stone-throated down to nothing on the side of the hill? Is it a loss to match the split maple hopes? Is it another sign of hapless times? Another seed buried forever? *Watermarks should be everywhere,* he says to himself in rationalization.

Under the light Wiggles sees no residue or remnant of water signs. No ground water. No stains on fieldstone sides. No harsh alga dressage climbing the circular rock wall. Nothing down there but what looks like a clump of rope more than thirty feet down, piled like a long-dead hemp snake on the floor of the well. The flashlight shows little else. He lowers the drop-light and sees no more evidence of water. At length he notices a break in the wall under a large lintel-type stone more than halfway down the throat of the well. It all rushes at him, the mystery of the house, the clump of rope at the foot of the well, the lack of water evidence, and the break in the wall of the well.

Suddenly Jennie comes to him again. He wonders about her and then about the Carringtons. Finally he wonders about the strange pressures and powers working his poor soul. He imagines some stars in strange orbits.

Aloud, to the bare cellar, to the house in general and to no one in particular, he says, "A bit more suds in me and I'd be down there exploring." Then, all of it coming down on top of him, the house, the Carringtons, Jennie, himself, he goes back to his truck and gets the tow rope and a wheel of pulley ropes and a single construction pulley. Hanging the rope-fall from an overhead beam that was directly over the well, he notes how worn and round the beam is.

While his construction mind was trying to fathom the latest discovery, Francis Parkinson Pikethorn, known as Wiggles to a thousand people, lowers himself into the Carringtons's dry well. The drop-light, now connected to a long extension cord, goes down with him. There is, he keeps noting as he lowers himself into the earth, absolutely no signs of moisture. But he can feel the presence of time. With each release of his weight on the lead rope, with each foot captured in his descent into the well, he feels the presence of time. "Wiggles Pikethorn," he says loudly, his voice bouncing in the tight stone constriction, "is going back in time." There is no doubt about it. *Oh, now's the time for a cold one,* he thinks.

IN THE MORNING the banker Victor Verikjon looks out his window. To his associate he says, "Here comes that Wiggles Pikethorn again. Man, he looks like a load of crap this morning. Another night on the town, I suppose. But now he's got his damn lawyer, Garson Caruthers, with him. Slippery Lou they call him. What the hell have they got going this morning? This might give a kick start to our day." He puts away the paper he had been scanning, sips his coffee, and sits waiting for something new for the new day.

The outlandish pair, the seedy-looking part-time drunk and the carefully clad lawyer, in a suit an embalmer could be caught in, is ushered into the banker's office. The secretary, with a raise of her eyebrows, says, "Mr. Pikethorn and Mr. Caruthers to see you, Mr. Verikjon." When the door is closed behind her, Victor Verikjon thinks he can smell pure applejack floating on the air. It is as much signature as Wiggles Pikethorn usually could offer on either side of the dotted line.

"Good morning, gentlemen. I would assume this is a surprise visit to all parties." Verikjon says it directly to Caruthers who smiles back, understanding partners of commerce at two points of view.

Wiggles speaks to the banker even as Caruthers started to say something. "The last time we talked, you said we could move on with this deal if there was something new to add to the pie. You said we had to have an extra edge. I guess it is your way of saying I can't get done what I want to do unless I get help from someone or something besides you and the bank."

Wiggles has his hand up in front of Caruthers so he could not interrupt. "Hold on, Garson. I want to make sure we agree on the promise Victor made the other day." He pauses, looks at Verikjon and then at Caruthers. "I just want it squared away right up front so we know where we're starting from."

"Is there any specific requirement for it?" Wiggles continues. "Extra value? Greater promise? A matter of publicity for the bank? A conditional or promised buyer for the project once finished? Do they all fit or does any one fit more than another?"

Both Garson Caruthers and Victor Verikjon are somewhat caught by the force of Wiggles's introduction to the day and to the project. The part-time drunk seems, even in his evident misery, well in control of himself and the situation.

Verikjon replies, "Like I said, Wiggles, some aspect of any one of those would throw additional weight behind our decision and in your favor, but it must be something concrete and promising. We know you've done excellent work elsewhere, but the threat of your daily activities weighs on us. I am sure you can understand that. I know you're like a jackhammer when you work. It's the chances that bother us."

He pauses like all bankers pause, a mark of punctuation, and rises from his seat. His hair is thin, his eyes are deep, and he looks his age. "In banking we don't like chances that are not in our favor. It's the nature of the beast that we are. And we're always using other people's money. It's our role in life. That compounds our watchfulness. It controls us." He pauses, looks at Caruthers who shakes his head, and then says to Wiggles, "What have you got to add to the pie?"

"Well," Wiggles says, "if I told you we had a gold mine on the property, that would set you off, wouldn't it? But I won't say that, nor can I say we have a grip on something concrete." For a brief second Verikjon sees a smile on Wiggles's face. "But I can tell you that if you agree it's enough to get the deal done, with what I'll tell you, have we got an agreement? Have we got a deal? That's all I want to know, and Garson here is judge and witness."

Verikjon leans over his desk, his jowls hanging a bit, a bit of color now in his face, thick eyebrow hairs in varied directions. "How far do we have to extend ourselves, Wiggles? You speak a chunk of mystery here, far as I'm concerned. You haven't said anything yet I can hang my hat on. What's going on? Put yourself in my shoes, me with more than half the valley giving me their money to take care of. If you don't come up with something pretty quick, I'm afraid I'll have to go back to some real work." He smiles at Wiggles and then at Caruthers. "Not as hard as you guys work, but I still get tired at the end of my day." The full business pose is there for the banker: the locked fingers, the hardened eyes, the chameleon smile.

Wiggles knows it was coming down to the brass tacks. Put up or shut up. What if it all comes apart, all around him? Falls in a heap at his feet? Again? He wonders what Jennie is doing this morning. Is this the kind of thing that drove her off that morning in a fatal huff? Jeezus, is there any lingering justice in this world for a man who never wanted to hurt a soul in his entire life?

He wonders what Abel had gotten himself into this morning on his list of favors to do for people, taking up as much time as he himself did with the booze. All the ideas are popping up around him, all the balances and imbalances, all the just and unjust things. They come the way they do when he sits alone at a bar, the noise moving around him, doubts coming like the rounds of drinks, the slipping away of some element of resolve, of character. Jeez, he could write a book about it.

He has to bring it all back. He takes a breath and lets it go. "What if we, here in old quiet Humboldt, were one of fifty-eight or sixty particular sites in the country? Very special sites. Would it mean something to you? What if we could prove, without a doubt, that history had walked right under our goddamn feet, what would you say to that?" He lets it all go out of him, the energy coming from somewhere else. If he had a hammer in his hand he could drive a sixteen-penny nail with one smashing swing. He knows it in his sudden fists even as the arthritis answers back.

"What if we were on the golden path, not gold mines, but something else, what would you say?" The old-time energy is creeping and crawling at the back of his neck. Jennie once said to him, "There was a time you could be near lethal with that energy, with whole sides of houses and barns going up in a fantastic hurry, the adrenaline running at fever pitch for you." Jennie, oh Jennie, could be witness to all of this, if only if she were here.

He feels himself sliding off, running off at the mouth, breaking away from the target. How can he tell that what he has seen? What he has found? It had been so crystal clear last night and this morning when he first woke up, everything in bright focus, all the angles and the shadows coming alive. The whole scene had been at once almost exhilarating in its revelation. The whole breadth of it all, the marvelous extent of it all. Now, it has retreated to a small distance, some shambles of shadows falling with it. Would it up and leave him again? Has it already done so? *Oh, sweet Jeezus*, he thinks, *the hammer or the shot glass! What a choice! What a choice!*

Victor Verikjon saves him. The banker saves him! Of all people, it was the banker who pulls him up from that runaway he felt he was becoming. "What the hell are you talking about, Wiggles? Slow down, man, and tell us what you're at." To Caruthers, Verikjon sends a quick look of doubt or question. Perhaps he is not sure what it is. "What have you come up with now?" The long hairs in his eyebrows hang like obscuring lines over his eyes. He squints. His thin hair is thinner, but his eyes are darker, in a study.

Like the North Star, like the belt line at Orion's middle, like the cluster of the Seven Little Sisters weeping directly over his head last night, down through the clutter of the split maples, Wiggles knows Jennie will be back. She will revolve through him again. Like the stars, he knows she will come home again. It is the ultimate chance for him. The only chance. Chance plays its tune for him. But the stars, being forever, come back on him.

"Last night, late last night, I went back to the house. Down in the cellar there's a phony well." Victor Verikjon is staring at him. Caruthers is shaking his head. Out there, has Jennie stopped and turned around? "Halfway down the well I found an opening. I had a drop-light with me and a flashlight. It's a big opening, a big time opening. A chunk of it pushes in and you go through a wide tunnel and there's a huge room, a cave back in there. A big cave big as this room, I swear to God." His voice has deepened. At the back of his head the energy is recouping itself. The possibilities are back. Jennie will make that turnaround, they will have the loan, the project. Maybe he *has* taken his last drink.

"Is it a gold mine, Wiggles? An old gold mine?" Verikjon is standing beside his chair, his face a solid mark of interest. "My god, man, what is it?" He brushes the bushy hairs out of his eyes.

All the energy, all the possibilities, come back for Wiggles in one sweet surge. "It's going to be the new historical site for the Underground Railroad. Right here in our own backyard. There'll be a sign announcing it, in gold letters. Letters as bright as the sun. I looked on the Internet. I think there are only about fifty-some places listed now. This one will be different, I swear! This one has Harriet Tubman's mark all over it. There are a couple of letters there in perfect shape. They were written to her by some guy named Thomas Garrett from Wilmington, Delaware. He was part of the whole thing. And there's a map with some Safe Houses or Safe Stations marked on it. I tell you it's like the goddamn Freedom Trail itself."

He has to catch his breath. They are staring at him. "There's a small leather bag might prove to be hers. There's sleeping places and blankets and still some canisters of bread from the Army of the Republic during the Civil War. There's an old Johnny Reb uniform in a canvas bag. I swear to God you'd think they just left out of there last night and headed for Canada. All of them, whoever was there who knows how many nights. Harriet Tubman herself. Or Frederick Douglass. Old man Carrington's people must have dug that place up, built a house on it. Who knows. But now we have it. I tell you the shivers went popping through me like they never went through me before."

He pauses again, the rush still in place. "We're sitting here, in the Empire State, less than an hour out of Canada. Hell, freedom's ringing all around us. Can't you hear the damn echoes of it?"

And Wiggles Pikethorn thinks that out there somewhere, not too far, Jennie has halted under the morning star. She will be looking back this way over her shoulder, in the same, offhanded but loaded way that she could tease him with no end in the old days. It was as if every room she left the bedroom was next upcoming. He can also remember the energy that had been transferred to his body and brain as he lay down in Harriet Tubman's cave to get a nap in on history's deeply imbedded rack of memories. And an unknown voice, a faraway voice, comes to the back of his mind singing about going down to the river to pray.

Victor Verikjon, upright like a statue, the banker's smile frozen on his face, thrusts his hand across the desk toward Francis Parkinson Pikethorn, otherwise know as Wiggles. "You have your loan, Mr. Pikethorn. It'll be a distinct pleasure to do business with you." His brows go electric with expression.

IN THE COMPANY OF ANGELS, THE COMPANY OF MEN

W ith eight hundred miles of road under my butt in the last three days, my blood sugar barely holding the line, a couple of old wounds still talking sass to me, whatever else was bugging me besides my errand, fell off the face of the Earth when Disher Menkin's wife Elsie, the new widow, still somewhat of a knockout though she'd collected some flesh under her chin she'd never try to hide, a few other imperfections lost in a surprisingly good figure, hardly ever taciturn at best, said, "Where the hell have you been, Coop, when we needed you most?"

A kick in the ass if you ever had one. And she didn't bat an eyelash.

I'd made that long drive to bury a good buddy and comrade, Disher Menkin, whom I had not conversed with lucidly and face to face in more than thirty-five years. We'd sized up death before, me and Disher. Me, an old man now, Cooper Bothwaite, feeling the grenade rolling in my gut, road dust a new talcum on my teeth, the continual gray light coming off the hood of the car hurting my eyes, as if a mirror had sat on the dashboard the whole way. This is the way it is every day now, stuff coming in bunches, life a bit of companionable misery.

Normally that kind of jibe Elsie threw at me will knock the hell out of any type of gathering, but in a funeral home, the body on display like sleep was unbroken from the night before, it's as strident as bugle calls. But I always hated reveille and the others, for that matter. The only one I liked was *Call to the Colors*. It still gets me, right where it hurts the most. But here's this hard-line new widow giving it to me who's been out of the picture more or less for those long thirty-five years, and her, I know, with a chain saw tearing up her heart and loneliness and doubt hitting her right in the face with the reality of five-card draw.

It's not new. I've been there, and it is an odd lot.

God, even being trim and shapely outside of the neck thing, she looked tough, bags under her eyes, tunnels leaning backwards out of them as if she had been there and back in a hurry, large dark spots on her arms as if they were badges of some sort not to be hidden. I know what those oversize freckles are saying out loud to the whole world. But there's no long sleeve cover-up for Disher Menkin's lady. She was front and center as she had always been, as memory served me. Truth is, she had scared the hell out of Disher right from the start. Thing was, he could not stand fakers. The claptrap of bullshitters really bothered the man. With Disher you had to be up front, and not piecemeal. No phonies ever made it with him, so the straight-out talking lady from Brunswick, Maine impressed him the first time she opened her mouth: "You know, soldier, your uniform looks like frigging hell. Why didn't you have it pressed?" I think Disher fell in love with her right then. Must have been something, because it went on for more than forty-five years, her speaking her mind, Disher hearing every word.

Whether he believed it all is something else. Even foxhole buddies like we were don't tell all, even when the Grim Reaper sits atop the hole with his dark visage and terrible eyes and the edge of the scythe keen as a new bayonet.

"Coop," she said, not at all backing off, as if nothing else had happened in the way of the curt introduction, "this is my daughter MayBelle and her husband Nicholas." I could remember Disher saying, on that old gray bucket going toward Europe in 1943, the Atlantic in its own turmoil, rank odors like real characters aboard every corner and stairwell of the ship, "My first-born, if it's a girl, will be called MayBelle. Was my mother's sister's name, and she drowned in the Amicalola River down in topper Ca'lina looking for frogs when she was a kid."

I swear MayBelle looked a bit like her father, eyes as serious as one can make them, like measurement is always going on, and blue-green as if not sure which way to lead. I measured her at the forty years of age I knew her to be. Her skin was nice, and there was no tiredness coming off her face. The ease of one good child can do that for you, and she had but the one boy. I bet she was more like her father than her mother. Her husband Nicholas, somewhat uncomfortable in a dark suit, was another case. On one hand there was but a finger and a thumb, and the thumb oversize to begin with. Immediately I wondered about their lovemaking; did he make special use of that odd hand? I had heard others' stories of such graceful impairment. A man's gotta do what a man's gotta do. But Nicholas was of good size, perhaps a shade over six feet, a full head of blond hair, dark brown eyes rather at acceptance than measurement. I was pretty sure that he was unaware of all the other people in the room. Something in him, in his handshake, in those dark eyes, said he seriously wanted to talk to me. A crisp impatience kept touching at his person, like a loose ignition wire.

"So you're Coop!" he said, shaking my hand with that odd hand, the grip almost malevolently hard, like handcuffs in operation, but he released the grip quickly. If I didn't have a thumb to counter its slide, he could have manacled me in a hurry. "I've always wanted to meet you. Knew it would come sometime, but never thought it would be this way. Disher loved you, Coop. I can say that without a bit of reservation. We used to sit down in the cellar summers, cooling off from the hot sun, sipping on beer he made in a big porcelain crock, like dipping in a well with a ladle, stories falling by the wayside on occasion. Those were good times. I think he liked them too, as much as me." The smile on his face was a full and bright smile loaded with memory. I decided, on the spot, I trusted him. The ladies looked surprised at the quick revelations he spun off. I truly believed he had not spoken of such things with them, had not shared Disher with them, at least not that way, but he could readily share with me.

"He said I'd get to see you sometime if you were still alive, Coop. I guess he was thinking about this." Around the room he looked, a long while at Disher's face over the edge of the casket, then shrugged his shoulders. "He was positive that I'd meet you. I guess what he was saying is that he knew you'd be here if this happened." He went through the survey with his eyes again. Not once did he look at his wife or his mother-in-law, but kept his eyes on mine. I knew he had something else to say; it was there, just off the edge of his voice, behind a small screen in his eyes. His mouth seemed to hold back other words. I felt the impatience again, the distraction of it almost electrical.

Disher's widow said, "Why didn't you come earlier, Cooper? He was ranting and raving at the end. Said your name a hundred times. I sure thought you'd be here earlier. Your buddy, huh?" When MayBelle put her hand on her arm, she continued, "Disher must have been hiding something all the time. Never once ever said anything to me about a fire, or kids. Never once. But I thank you for making the long trip. They don't get any easier."

Even with that the edge was ax-sharp in her voice. MayBelle jumped in. "I'm sure Nicholas would like to talk to you away from all this." She took her mother by the arm and was about to lead her toward a couple that had just come into the viewing room. With that move I knew she was Disher's daughter.

Disher's widow Elsie said, "I tried to call you for the last four days. There was no answer. Why don't you have an answering machine? Everybody has one of those contraptions these days. How did you find out about Disher?"

I said, "They called me from the vets' hospital."

"How'd they get your number?" There was a jiggle to the flesh under her chin, and her head was cocked at an angle, the measuring mode still in place.

"I gave it to them four or five weeks ago when I was there to see him."

The bare bones of surprise came up lightly on her face. "He didn't tell me. Why didn't you call me?"

"He couldn't tell anybody anything. And I came to see Disher, not to socialize." It was a slice of her own cake and she ate it easily. We had made a small peace, if that's what it can be called. I knew that I had been between her and Disher forever. It's like that sometimes, but we never exploited it.

NICHOLAS, THAT LARGE THUMB hooked onto his pants pocket and partially hidden, and the single finger sitting like a curse along the edge of his pocket, though somewhat undisturbed by any of it, walked me to an anteroom. It was quite evident that he wanted to talk out of earshot of the two women, that he had broached the possibility in front of them and it seemed he had depended on his wife to carry off his subtle need. Her response was, I thought, expected.

Nicholas's shoulders were a good span, his head shapely in an angular and regal manner and the blond head near full of curly tresses cresting the back of his neck. Though there was no other hippie look about him, no beard, no mustache, no heavy growth over the ears, a bit of the rebel mark sat on him, sort of an invisible tattoo. I was not sure if it was the hand that made him different or his locks. With faint stripes that may have been a tint of orange, the dark suit he wore fit him well, saying he was somewhat comfortable in such dress, but not fully at ease. I'd bet he'd get out of it quickly.

The anteroom *No Smoking* sign was small and almost unobtrusively noticeable, the law now a matter of fact, and three elderly gents, sure to be older than my seventy-eight years, had gathered their almost three centuries of experience in a small huddle. It appeared as if they did much of their talking with their hands, their eyes, the almost casual shrug of a shoulder. They could have been marionettes. It reminded me of the ward in the vets' hospital where I last saw my buddy Disher breathing, rolling his eyes at some unknown and past sight, mumbles buried and barreled deep in his throat. I remember thinking then that if this was down the road for me, I'd make sure the road had a bridge that was washed out and I'd drive like hell heading for it.

With that solitary and awful finger, showing an ordinary use, Nicholas pointed to two big easy chairs sitting in a far corner of the second anteroom. "Those ought do us." Over his shoulder he looked, and said, "There are times when I have to stay out of earshot of that woman. She does take aim when she wants. Never bothered Disher, that I know of."

I just had to ask. "What was all that about back there, other than Elsie being her curt self? She hasn't changed a bit though I haven't seen her practically since ever. You and MayBelle must keep a good chunk of Disher handy." Nicholas had made himself comfortable in one of the chairs, though sitting near the edge, and he let the awful hand sit in his lap like a bone remnant on an empty plate. Looking at me, his eyes were locked on a sadness I could only guess at. His blond eyebrows, close to a gray snow left over from plowing, aged him slightly but with a kindness.

He would have been, I assessed quickly, a welcome companion, a comrade, dependable, durable, on for the long ride wherever it went, Grim Reaper and all.

"I wanted to talk to you about that," Nicholas said. "It's been bugging me. Hell, it's been bugging Elsie like a burr under her bonnet. I guess she suspects that whatever was going on with Disher at the end, down there at the vets' hospital where they took such damned good care of him, like a baby, I swear, you somehow have privy to and she doesn't. It was not something he was letting go of, perhaps repressed and trying to come out of him at the end. And it looks like she can't let go of it either, her not knowing. She's one tough woman, fair as hell, but tough. The shot's there to be fired. Take it, or take the one coming back at you."

"You mean Disher was talking at the end? I was with him for four hours one day, just weeks ago, and he never uttered a sound. He looked at me a few times, like he knew who I was. I suspect he did, his eyes settling on me an old look, a glance of sorts I might have seen before in him, but never said my name once, nor anybody's name. None of the old outfit. Not a one." I twisted around in the chair as Nicholas's awful hand settled in his good hand, peace settling down in place like ashes. "What happened? What did Disher say that's got to Elsie so hard?" I wanted to ask if it was the French girl he had spent the night with in an old farmhouse one Christmas Eve. It hung on him for a long while afterward, but I kept it all back where it belonged, in the past.

Nicholas looked over his shoulder, back at the viewing room, and the ladies out of sight, the first nervous strain he'd shown to me, a new side of him under some import I am sure. "He was kind of noisy at the end, old Disher, the last couple of weeks, on the downhill run if you want to know, getting so thin, like he was melting away. I'd swear to God his face was like the side of a cereal box, pushed in, his dentures big as lumps in his face, oversize like. Lots of crying, calling out some strange names, ones I'd never heard, then kept crying more and yelling out, "The babies! The babies! He did that loudest. I mean, that's when he got real loud, and then wailed like a lost kid himself, shaking in the bed. Jeezus, his arms were going crazy, his legs kicking, his head jerking around like he's looking for somebody or something. We had to tie him in a few times, get restraints from the ward nurse. I don't mind telling you, Coop, he scared the hell out of me." Again he looked back at the other room. "I know some of the names were French girls' names, at least they sounded that way to me. Elsie never heard or never said anything. I figured she didn't hear or recognize them because, knowing her, she sure would have had a few things to say about it. Wouldn't be like her to let something like that get by her, I don't care how long ago it was."

AT FIRST NOTHING came to me, as if a silence had been etched, a darkness convened. Being notoriously drunk for some period of your life locks away lots of memories. For a drunken rifleman, a footslogger, soldier of the earth, being a stranger in a strange land, loss of some kind is guaranteed. So it was not surprising that nothing immediately in that anteroom, near the visible death of my old comrade and fellow warrior, his widow's tongue tart and afoot, made a connection for me: not Nicholas, not any picture on the walls, not the ladies in the other room whose voices were barely audible in turning that corner between us. To me there is such a thing as horizon-peeking, a cyclical break in the clouds, an opening. Perhaps it's a light down a narrow tunnel or through an old casement window of sorts, and, at best, ephemeral. Slowly but surely the face of a French girl came to me, pale but pretty, eyes set up with a haunting deep as caves, the half globes of her cheeks tarnished by something I could not read other than war. Perhaps, I surmised, she came out of a cloud, certainly she was cloud-like, just as if she was lit up, neoned, her face in a sunny glow, the softness of her lips her sole and most animate prize.

She had spent the night in a barn with Disher, a barn leaning every which way to ruin: the doors missing so that you could see out the back end, but not see the stalls or the haymow, or where the dusk coming in took them. They were like kids in love for one night. Next morning a German .88 took her and a kid brother at the well. She was standing there in a blue dress with the ladle in her hand, leaning against the rock wall like sex personified and perfected, the thrust of her stomach arched and tormenting, the little brother waiting to take his turn, and *wham!* they're gone. Just like that! I heard the stuff coming in but didn't even have time to duck. You couldn't pick them up with a blotter, neither one of them. Of course, I'd been on that royal drunk and didn't know how much it hit Disher until later. But we were all screwed up. We'd pillaged a small village. Brandy and cognac were like water around us, coming up out of cellars and dim recesses and who knows where else. Some was given to us, some was taken, retribution for time spent, wounds received, hell paying out its dues. I drank the stuff like I drink beer sometimes, guzzling it. Lord, I could have washed in it. I was thinking that a whole bunch of some of those days had passed me by, lost for years. Now here's my buddy, gone from me, gone from all of us, bringing me back, waking me up. I can smell the day, the village, the liquor, the hay, the barn, the smoke, can see them at the well and then gone from the well. In the back of my head, at some point where it seemed I had been raking the compost of that mind, scenes and images are breaking down, coming apart, falling out of the darkness like a pile of dominoes being spilled. Pictures. Pictures. Pictures.

Then it all came back to me, came clear to me. Over the long years the whole scene came back to me over half a century of my life, and I wanted to unload it on Nicholas, needed to unload it on him or somebody, this scene coming through darkness and uncertainty, through turmoil, to this newest death. There was another barn and a German trooper, half dressed, we'd cut down in a small farmyard, a hail of bullets going in there, raking him, a gray tunic in one hand and his rifle in the other, not quite ready for the rest of the war. I saw smoke, and the barn is burning and tossing off clouds of black smoke and a woman's screaming and we see her at the haymow window. She's holding a baby. There's another kid at her elbows, standing right beside her. Disher runs up to the barn. "Throw the baby down! Throw the baby down!" he yells. She doesn't know what to do I guess, Disher probably no different from the German we'd just shot, the one not dressed all the way like he'd been taking his own liberties. Then Disher says, back over his shoulder, after trying to get the door open, "There's a lock on the door. The Kraut locked her in!" Disher doesn't use his rifle to shoot the lock off. He runs back to get an ax or something from the farmhouse porch and a Six-by drives into the yard. Disher jumps up in the seat and pushes the driver over. I heard him yell, "There's kids in there."

He drives the Six-by over to the barn and points to the canvas top. "Throw the baby down," he says, and makes gestures to the mother. She throws the baby down and it lands on the canvas top. Christ, it almost bounced off the canvas, the baby. Another GI grabs the kid. Disher yells at her again. "Throw the other one down." She doesn't move. He backs the truck up and rams the locked door. The building shakes and the woman disappears. Puff she's gone! And the other kid disappears and the roof comes down on the whole goddamn barn. Flames come shooting like only dust is burning, or gases. Lots of it. Like acetylene. Like a frigging torch and Disher goes batty. Loses it, he does. The whole thing. Thinks he knocked her deeper into the fire, was the cause of her death, who knows how many kids might have been in there. You think I'd been drunk on that toot, man? You ought to see Disher after that, fucking hoot-owl drunk for nearly three days, and we kept moving and I kept him out of the limelight and out of serious trouble. Pulled a detail or two for him. When he woke up one morning, rank but sober, he never mentioned it again. Hell, I had forgotten it too. But it looks like Disher never let go of it, him being with that other girl too, like he had been punished for the little fun he had. Like he worried about Elsie coming at him the way she can, all mouth and hellfire, and I swear the end of the world in it. But he loved her. Old Disher never let go of that either. He loved her right to the bitter end.

I couldn't unload all of that on Nicholas, so much coming at me all at once, and the voices are rising in the other room, as if they were on the way to invade our privacy. I looked at Nick, and said, trying to poke it all together for him, "They're going to say in the funeral service that he'll soon be in the company of angels. I knew him in the company of men. And he was the best of them, old Disher was."

"There they are, locked up in some more damn secrets, I'll bet." I didn't even have to look up to see who was talking. And Disher was probably totally deaf by then.

LAST CALL FOR A LONER

He had never belonged anyplace, and that realization was slowly dawning on him. Of all the places he had been in this whole land, East Coast to West Coast, border to border, foothills or river's edge, none came charging up in his memory rugged with warmth, none touched longingly at him: no village, no harbor, no vast plain running off to the far horizon, no collection of people near such places.

This time out of the barn he had been moving for close to two months, hitching rides generally north, new stars and the wash of pine trees in April's breath calling him on. The contradiction came at him again as harsh as a fist: of all the places he had been, he had been no place. His mind kept telling him the same thing the way a canyon echo sounds, distant, muted, out of a deep solace, hollow, near metallic. It was, he was ready to say, as if he had never stopped long enough to listen.

Now, near the foot of this day, the tidal flats wide and enormous, the sun at odds with itself on Earth edges, he could hear something. It was universal. It bore intelligence. It caught his attention.

As usual he was alone and swore he was the only one attentive to that *thing* and seeing all this around him, the late sun splattering gold on every surface, moving or still, for as far as his eyes could see. Though he was not unkempt, he was not headed for the boardroom either. A worn but decent dark blue jacket hung on his slight frame, over a red plaid lumberjack shirt buttoned at the collar. The pants were brown corduroy and shiny at the knees and at the thighs. Brown ankle-high boots dipped up under his pant legs. A roadman he obviously was, a hitchhiker, but one apparently who spent his nights abed under cover, his clothes not covered with strange bed residue. This day a shave had been accomplished at some place back down the line. Under his arm he carried his baggy Matilda of sorts, and a vast marshy area spread before him, just a few miles up-river from the ocean. The sea salt and reed grass of the brackish land were stiff as knuckles at his nostrils.

Where he had paused, at the side of Route 107, along the mile-wide marshes, a sign stood its ground as heavy metal. *Cast iron most likely,* he was thinking as the last of the sun flung itself in reflection. It had a gray field and black letters about two inches high that simply said, "SAUGUS," and some part of its beating called upon him. *An Indian name,* he was convinced in his own reflections, thinking some names have importance, some do not. His name, for that matter, was Chug and he was a loner, acknowledged, as he often said, the loneliest feeling a man could have. For him there were no roots, no wispy grasp at footholds, no family beachheads he could remember. A loner. It might have been that he had not been long enough in one place, or had never let his past catch up to him. No such determination as yet had fully surfaced on that account.

But now, in the late afternoon, the name Saugus drew him on. It stuck in his mouth. What else was there? Where else? What place could he belong? A trucker's horn suddenly startled him. "How far you going, pal?" The rig was a Diamond-T, a monstrous breed of new redness and shiny chrome sitting beside him on the marsh road, and a hum under that giant hood as deep as a cement mixer. The driver, leaning at him from behind the wheel, half filling the cab, presented red hair and big eyes with shaggy brows and a smile as wide as the window. Chug looked again at the cast iron sign. "Saugus," he said, quixotically, and then with serious conviction added, "To the middle of Saugus, wherever that is."

"What's your tag?" the trucker said, re-adjusting the sun visor, shifting gears from the dead start, clutching, gassing, leaning back in his seat. Artistic, thought Chug. "Mine's O'Malley Fighorn, and ain't that some moniker." He laughed. "My mother sure as hell wasn't letting go her last bit of Irish. My brother's name is Sullivan, Sullivan Fighorn, Mal and Sully, that's us." Deep from his chest rose a laugh as though he was remembering something special, someplace special.

Chug said, "Chug," like it was a simple flake of rock falling off a cliff face. "Chug it's been forever. Plain Chug."

"What's your real tag?" Mal Fighorn bowed his head and looked at Chug as if something else special was waiting on him. Crows' feet almost crinkled with sound at his eyes. A bump sat prominently on his nose, proud badge of badges. Looking ahead at the stoplight now green in the distance, he downshifted the rig, then looked again at his rider. He had shared his name and expected, it seemed, his rider to do the same thing for him.

"Tylen," Chug said, caught by that charge, the depth in the driver's eyes, the fan of crinkles friendly in its marking. Then he added, his breath coming out of his chest like it had been saved up for a long time, "Tylen Chacone."

The two grown men looked into each other's eyes and began to laugh. They laughed all the way up to the red light with an arrow saying "Saugus" beside it. The arrow pointed north. The tears rolled south on Mal Fighorn's cheeks, and on the cheeks of Chug Chacone.

"Ain't we the friggin' pair!" Mal Fighorn said, as he swung the rig into the northbound road, a huge hand pawing the shift lever with adroitness, his feet tap dancing on clutch pedal and gas pedal. "Tylen Chug Chacone, you and me, pal, are having dinner with my dad. Lives here in Saugus, loves his company. And get this," he added uproariously, shifting again, tap dancing again, his brows heavy over bright eyes, "his name is Montcalm Fighorn. He's friendly, he likes his beer and wears twenty years of beard." They laughed all the way into the Fighorn driveway on the far edge of town, near the Lynnfield line. Laughter had taken them right through Saugus Center, past a veterans' monument at a green rotary, past a stately old Town Hall bearing late traffic, past a handful of quiet churches.

Tylen Chug Chacone, loner, felt again that unknown sweep of energy come across his chest or across his mind. He could not be sure which avenue, but it swept at him and by him in the long driveway, making him think he was in a kind of wind tunnel. Once, long ago, someplace in his travels, that sweeping might have been known. He could not remember where. Out back of the house was a barn and another truck, looking like its last mile had been run, sat beside the barn. Painted sign letters on the body of the truck had faded to an unreadable point, pale as old scars. Its tires were flat. Chug thought about old elephants going off alone to die. His mind, he thought, could never compute how many miles of service the truck must have delivered. Now it did not seem so important; it was just rusting away as much as the barn was decaying, though not seen the same way.

A bit later a delicate spring evening hovered around them as they sat on the porch, long and screened-in with at least a dozen chairs scattered its length. He'd bet that some evenings every chair was occupied; it was that kind of house and that kind of porch. In the distance clusters of fireflies dominated the dark landscape. Across the road and up a steep hill, in the growing darkness, an owl called out. Chug thought it to be a place called home.

"So you got a name thing, too," Montcalm Fighorn said, pouring beer from a quart bottle into three frosted mugs still wearing shadowy clouds. "They've been calling me Monty since I can remember. Never by my real name. Hell, I never called this boy by his real name. Enda, my good Enda, never called him anything but O'Malley. And Sully had it the same way." Toward a bit of darkness off the side of the porch, adroitly, in modest ceremony, he tipped his drink, and the tipping was understood by those who saw it done.

Chug drank slowly and deliberately, and the bearded Monty Fighorn watched his guest drink with dainty sips after the healthy meal. "Don't be bashful, Chug. End of the day's the time for a good swallow. Have at it." He raised his mug and drained off the contents. "Best damn part of the day," he vouched with certainty, poured another full round, and then raised his eyebrows at his son who went to the small icebox at the end of the porch and brought back another imperial quart. "I'm not the real curious type, Chug, but wonder where you've been, what you've seen. Mal says you spend the winter in Florida. That so?"

"Two or three places down there. Sometimes they put up with me and sometimes they don't. I have a special delivery box and they hold all my mail. Usually it's just a few retirement checks from Uncle I use to try to get through the winter."

"You in the service, Chug?" Even as he asked the question, Monty knew the answer. The signs were there. Besides the bracelet Chug wore, it was written on the man. His clothes might have been second-line, but he was shaved that very day, and his hairline cut half moons high over the ears. The boots, beat up as they were by the road, were not long from a spit shine. He'd bet there was a pair of dry socks in his small bag if not pinned to the inside of his jacket.

"Twenty-six years in the Army."

"I got me one of those," Monty said, pointing at the bracelet on Chug's wrist. "Where'd you get yours?" The wreathed Combat Infantryman's Badge, its blue field long since faded, curved loosely on Chug's wrist. A small chain kept it in place. A circular stain was on his wrist.

"Couple of places were good enough. But first with the Thirty-first in Viet Nam. Then in the desert in the Eighties. You?"

"Nam, too. Four oh first. Caught a bit of hell and was rolled out of there in a hurry. Think I was pinned down for two months, then on my way home, on evac. Had one friend, talking about nicknames, who was transferred to first battalion of your outfit. We called him Grunt before we had grunts."

Perhaps from the dark hill or out of a field now gone into the night, the sweeping energy came on Chug again. Almost electricity, it ran right over the porch as if the fireflies had let everything go. Chug knew a rustling at the screening, a possession of sorts, at the very spot Monty had tipped his mug. "Talking about names, his wasn't Billy Pigg, was it?" He could not bring back a face, but a piece of it, a nose.

The energy, the sweeping, told him the answer even before Monty Fighorn came up out of his chair. "Damn it, guy, don't tell me you knew Billy Pigg! Hot damn! Thought about him a thousand times. Old Kentucky Billy Pigg. Great boy he was. Marksman of all marksmen, I tell you. Often wondered about him. Often." The plea was in his voice and he nodded again at his son sitting there, the son's mouth agape, his eyes wide in the darkness, wondering what the hell had made him stop and pick up a hitchhiker off the marsh road, the end of the world itself. From the corner of the porch Mal brought back two more imperial quarts of beer and poured the round himself.

"Hate to tell you, Monty," Chug said, setting down his mug, as if his right to drink had been suddenly halted, perhaps his welcome stopped in place. "Died in my arms, not quick, not slow, but long enough to ask me to bless him with water. I did, from a canteen, and him leaking badly, one of them old sucking chest wounds that'll never let go. Said his daddy picked him up one day, about to walk into the river with him and do it up proper, when his daddy keeled over from a heart attack and never got him wet. All that time, it seems, it was all he could remember, being on the grass and not wet. But I got it done for him. Boy had a nose been smashed all to hell before he even got in the army. That your Billy Pigg, Monty? That the one you knew as Grunt, nose broke up all to hell?"

Chug was aware again of the spot Monty had tipped his mug to. The unknown sweeping was coming through the same place, the rustling, the net of screen separating sounds and energies, paying them due respects. And he and Monty Fighorn, old soldiers at the pair, had a sharing of lasting memories coming at them in pieces.

Chug said, "Tell me about that old truck out back. Looks like an old soldier in the Old Soldiers' Home, just waiting to go the last mile. Serve you that good, did it, not letting it go?"

"You're right on that account, Tylen Chacone," Monty said, and laughed loudly, his laugh ranging the porch and out into the night. "Was a hell of a rig in its day. Brought us a little freedom, worked so long and good. It ain't going no place before me, and that's a given." Turning to Mal, he said, "Tell him that's so, son."

"It'll turn to rust in that spot long as I'm around. Bet on it." He tipped his mug, but it was not at the dark space just off the porch. It was more at an idea.

All of it, Chug thought, was measurable.

Monty swung around in his dark red Adirondack chair. Chug heard it creak. "I got an idea I want to run by you, Chug," Monty said. "No strings attached, as they say. Got lots of room here, most of it going to waste. Boys here got business I don't want to get into. They do their thing and I do mine. I'm willing to let you have a room for the summer, go and come as you please, go off as you like when you like, doing your road thing if you have to, and head back down to see your friends come fall or late summer. It's no charity farm nor the Old Soldiers' Home. You cut some grass, you do some dishes, make your own bed and do your own laundry, and you got a place to drop your head come of a night. And you don't plan to drink all my beer. Can't lose anything from where I sit." The chair creaked again as he stood up and said, "Want to show you something." He went into the house and toward the back of the house.

Mal said, "He's going to show you his," pointing to Chug's bracelet. "We had it mounted on a piece of cherry wood a lot of years ago. Sets some store by it, he does. Makes me think you should think real serious about his offer. Doesn't do something like that very often."

"I'm just a guy barely out of the tank, Mal. Doesn't know me from a hole in the wall. Why make me out so special?"

"He knows you a lot better than you think, Chug. You and him, you're like blood brothers maybe. I'm sure you share something I might never know, though it might be like Sully and me. He's a good man and he finds stock in you. Hell, man, there must be some of that in me, too. I picked you off the side of the road, could have gone right by. Usually do, these days. I have no idea why I stopped. Something in the air, I guess. Would you believe it?"

Only Chug Chacone heard the rustle at the screen, the promise of sound in a small shrub, with a host of fireflies coming closer to the porch.

And so it was, practically for the first time in his life off a post or station, for more than four months of belonging, Tylen Chug Chacone sat on the porch at night with Monty Fighorn. They listened to the fireflies almost, to the owls on the hill, to the old truck turning to honored rust, and every now and then, from a distance, like down a one-way street, to the limitless, endless charge of energy finding its way to a couple of old souls.

In the dread heat of late August, the heavens at rampage, electricity beating about the skies like a thousand cannons at battle, one bolt of lightning followed another bolt through two aged hearts.

Mal told Sully over the phone, "Damned won't believe it, Sull. Neither one of them spilled a drop of their beer. It just sat there beside them, waiting to get sipped up like it was last call."

THE OLD MAN
OF THE RIVER

There were times, Musket Jack Magran swore, he could hear a dog pissing in the night, another drunk pissing in another alley, a moth touching down on a lighted globe or, between his ears and his fingertips, humming and vibrating, the vast platelets of the Pacific Rim moving on each other their endless rhythms. In tune with the universe was he, had been forever, and tonight was no different. He had his booze, he had his sack for the night, he was in touch.

Pieces of a broken moon splashed on the dark blue waters of the river and shot off the ripples of a late wake, a small craft having passed by minutes earlier against the other bank, a craft without night lights, dark, sly, faintly noisy, like a ferret in the rushes. It had been down river, possibly out to sea. Musket Jack Magran, groggy from sleep yet ears cocked, bones still bearing an ache in his old body, could hear the fading engine's hum from upstream darkness, where trees on the curved banking and a small copse of birches gave off vertical neon, slim arrows in a quiver, catching moon traces.

Skullduggery without lights, he whispered as darkness swallowed up sound, as night crawled back to its place of keeping, the gathering of silence and darkness.

On the deck of someone's lobster boat tied up to the T-shaped pier at the Lobster Co-op's landing, Musket Jack Magran had begun another night free of rent. His old canvas shelter-half, infantry issue, its Army legend imprint long faded, not mated for thirty-odd years, edges frayed and stringy, the sheen gone to lively abrasions, still kept the dew and late dampness off his single blanket. He knew the odd stars; on five continents he had slept out in the night, and on islands and territories too numerous to mention.

Now and then he'd swear the water lapping at the dock or the sides of the boat was hypnotizing him, melodies lingering in the sweep and ripple, old station or post songs mostly without words, the wide world at call and command... *China Night... Japanese Rumba... Manila Moon... The Maids of Mandalay...* and, for brief catches, *Lily Marlene, underneath the lamplight by the garden gate.* It was better sleeping on an odd lobster boat on the river than under the steel bridge or up above the pier on a park bench, old ladies too nosy or too solicitous, or old men looking for company or a voice in the darkness. Side benefits came easier on strange boats: general silence within darkness, the long and rhythmic inland reach of the sea, time passing off its melancholy and letting him handle it on his own terms. In another five or six weeks he'd think about hitching a ride south from a gypsy truck driver. On this night, like the others on numerous occasions, came back the old promise he'd made to himself in too many dry and arid infantry posts that some good part of his life later on would be spent on the water, the obverse life of a sailor, the eternal hum coming off that span about him. These lobster boat nights were part of that promise.

The last burp of the boat whispered to him from the bend of the river, beyond the silvery copse. His large ears, derided by many for years, were keen for sounds and had saved him and comrades in numberless firefights or skirmishes. For the bracing of comrades, being called "Wingsy" by some, "Elephant Ears" by others, he readily absorbed and accepted the ability to hear the click of a rifle in the mountain or jungle darkness, or on the wide sands of the Sahara Desert.

Then, for a lucid moment, another piece of the moon falling across his eyes, he heard again his father on the porch back in Vermilion, Ohio talking about Black Jack Pershing, a perfume of cool sweet breath coming off Lake Erie, Canadian air at its best. In another moment, as if in a movie, he saw himself caught in his tracks on a distant post at distant years as *Call to the Colors* came to him, hauntingly clear and infallible. All this time the tune was still riveting, making shivers at his spine, making dictates, driving his mind for known or unknown reaches. What post it was he could not remember, some place off in the vast world of his adventure, but he heard the bugle as clearly as that same revered moment, and then came the command in his father's voice. He flirted with an argument about memory's structure but quickly gave it up. The last ghostly purr of the faint motor sound brought him back. Two nights earlier, just after midnight, the same boat, or one sounding just like it, and without night-lights, had crawled by his night bed, the deck of another lobster boat.

Not only a free sleep brought him to the river, or the toss of the sea, but also an occasional beer found in a cockpit or cooler, forgotten with a good day's catch. Tonight he'd found a six-pack and drank two cans, putting the empties back in place, draping the plastic loop around the cans. And a half pack of butts with a lighter, quick treasure. Yet his mouth was sour for the find, his palate sassy. The low hum of the dark boat having faded completely, he whispered half aloud through that sour mouth: *Tomorrow night, from the other side, from the Lynn side, I'll watch for that boat. Something tricky in the wind, I'll bet. What moves in darkness sure isn't light.* From the other shore, eastward under the moon, from a distance on the Lynn side, came the closing of a door, a faint yap of a dog at relief, a hushed command, the door closing again on the night.

Well before dawn he slipped off the boat and made his way around the lobster shack and up the road heading into town. Few cars moved on the road, but their lights danced on his face as he moved towards a morning of washing dishes at Smokey's Diner, where lobster boat crews swallowed breakfast like a Lenten fast was over. Their breakfasts were mountainous, as if they'd be at sea for a week. And they talked as they ate, part of the ingestion process, noisy and garrulous like someone gargling and getting rid of a bad night. He loved to listen to them, their gripes as timeless as the tides, sea stories like barracks' stories with characters rising from their oratories like people off-stage in a play, not seen but heard from. "Friggin' line was cut by knife, ain't shittin'me none, them assholes from Bev'ly!" "Swear she's got these humungous tits you can tie knots in!" "When she straddles, man, you fucking disappear from the face of this here good earth."

Often they were subject to poor fortune and seas that turned savage in eye flashes. But they were a vibrant bunch in spite of their lot in life, hard drinking and hard swearing, riding at times the crest, at times not. Jack had seen hands and fingers mangled by sudden ropes or arthritis or the curses of salt water, arms laced with scars so deep they could make you wince. He'd seen storms that sat in some men's eyes long after the wind had faded on-shore. Like watching a late movie, he said to himself.

Dud Whelmsly of all of them intrigued him the most. Dud, to Musket Jack's eyes, was built like a Budweiser keg with short arms and short legs, the lord of the realm perhaps, perhaps of the river and the fleet itself, but a voice with a threat of music in it. "Goddamit, Smokey, repeating this all the time just about spoils my day... don't break the yolk in my egg sandwiches. Let 'em break themselves and sop in, the way I like 'em. Let 'em sop into them there bulkie rolls, goddamit!" Jack almost broke a gut the night Smokey came out of the men's room right behind the counter zipping his fly, the hopper flushing, and started to mold two hamburger patties for Dud. "How'd you want them hamburgers, Dud?" he had said. Dud had looked up from his newspaper spread across the counter, looked around the room, caught a few eyes, bent his head in the way he had of doing it and said, "Well, Smokey, might's well cook the piss out of them two little fuckers."

Now this morning, the sea out there for the moment calm, the noise here intense as the day loomed in front of them, there was talk among the lobstermen of thievery, missing lobster traps, lines cut. Some unknown force, out and about the good earth, was lining up against them. There was talk of a night watch and Coast Guard involvement. The small diner hummed with a loose vengeance and anger. It was a recent activity obviously grown out of hand. Eyes often spoke as loud as words, layers of cigarette smoke cut by their stares, revenge working the horizon.

"He comes under my knife he's chum bait," burly fisher Fall Dixon said, patting the near-Bowie blade sheathed at his belt line. That patting hand was enormous in its spread, and bulbous as though an arthritic warrior had lodged there. The years of seawater and salt, hawsers and traps, inured skin and bone and callus with a quick identity. Fall, like Dud, would be known hands-down in a crowd, *lobsterman.*

"I'm suspecting he must sure know his way around what he's at," Dud offered, half pivoting on the counter stool, a page of the paper twisting with him.

"What the hell does that mean, Dud?" The voice was from behind a newspaper in the corner.

"Simple," Dud said. "One a us or knows us too good. The price down, what a small catch does to a man's day. Anyone know anyone wants a boat real bad?" He stared out the diner window, not letting his gaze rest on any man, effecting neutral for what it was worth, yet it was like slipping a knifepoint into the clasp of a sea clam or quahog. It was harsh intrusion, the room itself being cut.

Musket Jack saw rather than heard the silence. Heads lifted, eyes aimed like pistol sights, jaws froze on words. Union and divinity and brotherhood were once again at the forefront. Musket Jack, for all his downhill slide through a whole lifetime, knew what was happening there on the line. He could feel its net, had lived within it, depended on it; Hug Scroggins's dive on top of the grenade seemed a hundred years since came back with ferocity; and followed Little Davie Davenport's sucking up pieces of his own grenade. They had made and broken many a day. The elitism of fragmentation, its hunger and global dissemination, leaped at him. These lobstermen all about him were certainly now in the throes of some kind of war. Hostilities had begun in part, he was sure.

The corner speaker spoke. "You'se first hit, Dud. Seen nothin' that day you went out? You was early enough, I know."

"Nothing but my lines cut. Lost thirty traps and whatever was caught. Nothing on the horizon. No oil spills. No markers of any kind, but what he loosed from me. Rat-ass bastard'll get chummed, that's for sure. I guess nobody here knows anything or they'd be speaking up about now. Never too late, even if it's your brother or your son or your son-in-law or your old daddy."

"You swearing to that, Dud, that it's one us or close to? That's powerful stuff for breakfast." It was Napoleon LeMars who Dud had fished out of the Atlantic two years earlier, after twenty-two hours in the water. "I'm going to take an early look. Over by Hatty's Run, then I'll come back by the Pines Light."

"You not fishing today, Nap?" Dud said.

"I'm giving my day up for looking. Somebody else can do it tomorrow. No kids sitting to my table." He snickered. "Least not so's I know." The ladies' man of their group basked in a moment's glow, not one hair of his thick crop out of place, pleasant crinkles at his eyes, his Roman nose as clean as the day he was born. "If'n I see anything I'll let you know. Tomorrow's somebody else's day. But, hell, Dud, I don't know what the hell to look for even."

Dud was not imperious, but a bit lordly in his advice. "Keep a sharp eye, Nap, for what ain't supposed to be where you see it. If it's not in among us, it's sure like us. That skirmish they had in Beverly back a few years, when they were losing boats and traps and lines galore, it was outside but inside, if you know what I mean. Someone wanted the riverfront or the harbor for commercial stuff the guys of the fleet couldn't touch in a hundred years. If anybody hears about that kind of thing coming here, we got to sit up right away."

Fall Dixon came off his stool. "There ain't been a whisper about someone new trying to get the river cleaned up, and us out of it. Not for a few years now, but it's always there. That ain't anything new, but it's sure been quiet. No snoopers I know of. No real estate guys walking around with little notebooks in their hands or talking into small recorders, getting so frigging lazy at it now. You heard anything, Dud?"

Musket Jack loved to watch Dud Whelmsly operate. He'd seen a hundred company clerks over the years running the whole show of an infantry outfit, and Dud was not unlike them, letting innuendoes and side remarks do the work of order and command. Mere suggestions built slowly on themselves, became laws unto themselves. Questions, posed the right way, in the right tone of voice at the right time, in some measure became fact. It was an art form. Dud's head lowered on his massive body like a turtle retracting, then he scrunched his eyebrows and looked deeply into Fall's eyes as he let his baritone voice float across the diner. "What's a stranger among us, if he's not a brother?" At an angle he held his suppressed head, for a moment breathless on stage. Musket Jack shook a little in admiration. "What's a visitor in our midst, if he's not a brother? Who are we, being alone, but brothers?" It was part of the art form, as if he had gone down into his body to find those words and then *shared* them.

And it was as if an edict had been posted in Smokey's Diner, an imperial edict. In the kitchen, looking out through the serving window, the old soldier almost pissed his pants having a good laugh. Dud Whelmsly had said nothing at all, not a damn thing, and here was rapt silence stunning the room as if some ages-old philosopher had made a pronouncement. He could remember no beliefs or espousals except names. Dud could be like Locke or Kant or Descartes or a hundred others floating at the back end of libraries, dust coming down atop their words, dead a hundred years and still making waves just off the river. Dud's head was still at that most confidential angle, that sharing pose.

"You oughta be in the movies, Dud." The voice was still behind the newspaper, like a small bell tinkling a few stray cows home.

Dud pretended he didn't hear that pronouncement. "If there are people who want us off the river, they'll come at us any way they can. But the pocketbook's the best way. That's my traps and your traps. My boat and your boat. My catch and your catch. No boubt adout it!"

Now, Musket Jack also realized, Dud Whelmsly was coming at them with the real ammunition, Topkick stuff. He suddenly realized that Dud knew there was an enemy within and about. Was damn sure about it. And Musket Jack himself had been witness to some piece of it. The fading sound of the midnight engine came back to him, even as dishes rattled and glasses tinkled against one another and silverware was in minor crescendo. The idea of energy came at him, the spurt of it, his blood moving. First it was heat from his task, the water scalding and steamy. Then it was an old convoy climbing the long slight grade of a hill he thought perhaps was outside Wonson on the way out of the Pusan Perimeter. Then it was a flotilla of craft as they crossed Lake Hwachon, a whole battalion of infantry. Then it was the men of the lobster fleet sitting out there in the little stuffed diner, the smoke hanging in the air like old rifle residue and burning cosmoline and spent gunpowder going on a day old and the hurt still in place.

"All I can say is that it'll probably start at the town bank if that's what it is. But I'm telling one and all, something's up and about and it pays us to look close to anything odd. From the landing, and both river banks all the way out to the Big Daddy."

MUSKET JACK MAGRAN was a listener. He kept his ears cocked for every piece of input. Washed out, but fed well by Smokey, an old soldier himself, the small mountain of morning dishes washed and put away, Jack walked away from the diner at ten of the morning with two fried egg bulkie roll sandwiches in his pockets. Way ahead of time he had planned his move to the other side of the river. If that boat came again, in the slip of darkness, he'd be watching.

After midnight, cloudy, the moon off someplace, the old soldier felt the disturbance in the air before he heard any sound. On the other side of the river, from the Lynn side, after passing through the small yard of boat gear, he had slipped aboard another lobster boat. He had spread his blanket and shelter-half, found two beers in a cooler, had a few nips picked up earlier, strictly for his late watch. Darkness invaded his thoughts. The river, like every river he had ever known, was alive even if mute, from the Pukhan to the Mekong to the Saugus. From deep in his past he remembered a perimeter outpost, two ration cans tinkling on a strand of commo wire as the Chinese infiltrator tried to come up his hill just beyond Lake Hwachon at three in the morning, to try to toss a grenade into the listening post bunker. He felt anew the chill slipping up his spine as he remembered that slight tinkle of cans, and now, under dark clouds on a dark night on somebody's boat, the small vibrations came to him from the body of the river. The supposedly mute river, its waters trying in vain to catch another tune.

Musket Jack Magran sat up slowly, the shelter-half sliding off his form with the soft grating sound of canvas. That old sourness was in his mouth and a new ache at his shoulders. He cursed a sleeping foot yet caught with tingles. Commiseration was his until the *purr* and *put-put* of an engine brought him to attention. There was no moon, no offshore lights falling on the body of the river, but there were shadows. Shadows, in spite of their being, give measurement, and he peered over the low gunnels, giving least mark to the given contour. Other lobster boats rose dark in the darkness, small radar and radio equipment slim atop their shapes. The water slapped almost in silent applause against his bed boat, the small boat coming up the river sending tremors ahead of its passing. The slow roll of his craft was sensual, the rivers of the world never letting go. He saw a girl on a bed of straw reaching for him, that too had been beside a river whose name was now gone, as was her name. The boat rolled again, slowly, the sound of an outboard came like a whisper. He saw a shadow moving. Then he saw two men on a small dinghy. He heard the splash of liquids. One of the men was spilling liquid from a five-gallon can as they circled around each lobster boat. He recognized the dinghy with the phony spar out front. It was Dud Whelmsly's dinghy, but neither of the two lank and lean men on the boat was Dud Whelmsly.

Then Musket Jack caught the unmistakable odor, the rich purifying odor, the nostrils-cleaning odor of raw gasoline. They were going to torch the river! They were going to torch the fleet. Tag! He was it! Tag! He was the sole guardian of life and limb and liberty. Scroggins came back, his dive through the air on top of the loose grenade. Little Davie Davenport had carelessly dropped his grenade at his feet. His eyes had gone wild as he looked around at the squad, and then fell down on top of it. They were faces in his night, Scrog and Davie. He saw their eyes, their mouths, their chins. He knew them again, knew that they would never leave him. Had never left him. *I'm half drunk*, he said to himself, as the dingy circled around another boat, and another five-gallon can spilled against the side of a boat and splashed on its deck. *I am the last night guard,* he whispered. They were forty feet from him. He was sure he did not know them, sure they were not part of the crews at Smokey's Diner. That thought sat well with him. What could an old drunk soldier, years past his last hitch, do in such a situation?

Musket Jack Magran let the shelter-half and thin blanket fall away from his body as he stood in the shadows of the cockpit. "Halt!" he yelled out. "Hold it right there. I've got a wild-ass Forty-five aimed at your last can of gasoline. You so much as move a muscle this little cannon of a sidearm's going to go off with a bigger bang than you ever heard! Now you tie off onto that boat and sit in your little dinghy until I rouse some help or so help me you're nothing but flames."

He yelled, loud and hard, for help. Upriver a light went on, and then another. Behind him he heard a door slam. There was a pounding of feet, booted feet, on the Saugus side. He kept on yelling. "They're pouring gasoline on the lobster boats. Watch your ass! Don't light anything near a boat."

"Who's that over there?" one voice said, throwing a torchlight onto the river, letting the light ray fish around.

Jack recognized Fall Dixon's voice. "This here's Musket Jack. There's two skinny gents who were dousing gasoline onto the boats. They're tied off to Gunther's boat here, the Maryanne Kay. I got a Forty-five aimed somewhere near their balls and their last can of gas. Call the fire department if you want these boats saved. They been using Dud's dingy. Better get his ass down here."

One of the men in Dud's dinghy moved. "You move again, feller, and you're flame. I swear to God you're flame." Back across the river he yelled to Fall Dixon, "Better hurry, Fall, my goddam finger is getting tired on this here trigger. These Forty-fives were never any good. I couldn't hit a bull in the ass with one, but the round'll go someplace close."

The night watch of Musket Jack Magran was over. The scramble came: firemen and hoses and decks washed down, police going out to the dingy and bringing the two tall strangers ashore, Dud finding his dingy chain snapped through at one of the lower links against the dock. The smell of gasoline slowly dissipated in the morning air as the dew came down and the tide went out.

One policeman, coming across the river in a small dinghy, said to Musket Jack, "I'll take that Forty-five now, mister."

"Shit, man," Musket Jack said, "I wouldn't own one of them little cannons for all the tea in China. Never was any frigging good at all, them things, 'cept you carry it you didn't have to shoulder a rifle. And that was pretty good unless you had to use a rifle." He held up his empty hands. He smiled at the policeman.

At Smokey's Diner, the air thick with cigarette smoke, a brand new pack at his elbow, a pile of scrambled eggs and bacon and a pot of coffee in front of him, the new god of the river told his story over and over again. And the identities of the two men and their connections were swiftly known and more arrests promised. "They must have been casing the river the night before, trying to see who or what was round, what the lay of the land was, what they could get away with."

The voice behind the newspaper said, "They never counted you being on guard, Jack, no boubt adout that."

Dud Whelmsly said it at last, his head in that confidence-sharing angle, his voice dramatic but honest, "The Staties've been onto something for a long while. Some development company from out of Providence, and you know what that means, wants the river for something big. Maybe gambling or a casino-boat kind of thing. Who knows but them who wanted to put us out of the river. Hell, taking traps never did it, or cutting lines. We've been through enough of that crap. This was going to get us big time. Me and Fall's been keeping an eye for a long spell, but I was too quick to sleep the night before and Fall was out of it last night. Took the old soldier here, half in the wrapper I bet, to stand guard for us, like he's always done."

Another spill of Jim Beam went into Musket Jack's coffee cup. "You got a day of it coming, Jack, and then we dry you out and get you a ride south. No more dishes for you, soldier."

Musket Jack Magran, an aura of cigarette smoke swirling around his head, his eyes beginning to fish once more, the alcohol putting the quiet down in place, old scars getting buried bone-deep in his body, vaguely remembered a boat ride on a river flowing away from the hills above Leyte. A girl's dark skin he could recall and the light of stars in her eyes, but could not see her face. The way the Earth shifted under him, quietly but dramatically, came back, the whole range of it. A tune from down a wide river came at him as if night were finally taking leave of itself, a post soldier out on the edge of darkness playing his guitar, while overhead the Manila moon went sailing wherever its voyage took it.

And for long hours no person had called him "Wingsy" or "Elephant Ears." Not a one.

SACRIFICE FLY

Twenty-one-year-old Corporal Durvin Broadmoor of the 28th Massachusetts of the Irish Brigade woke with a start from a dream on a hill in far off Virginia. War had come again with the false dawn of a June day in 1864. His mouth felt muddy, constrictive, and someplace as yet untouched a bone ached. The narrow red scar on his face reared its thin but ugly edge, as if the initial wound's cause for a moment was known again. An itch was at his neck without stop. The imprint of the wagon wheel, against which he had slept fitfully, was surely etched on his back, but the dream, as always, was elusive. Crowd noise had sounded there in the dream, he remembered piecemeal, hawkers and criers loose among massed people each time, but all other elements of the phantasm faded as quickly as clarity came to him. And just as quickly, the crowd dissipated and fled ethereally. Only the diamond shape of the grass surface stayed with him, and a ball in flight, a ragged, not quite round ball working its way in the air, gyrating, pulsating. At length, the sky gray, shadows starting, the ball disappeared, but there was a magic in the disappearance. And that magic lay under his skin.

A state of mind, he knew, had been created, had character to it if not a body of its own. Days, events, life itself, often begin at opposite ends of a wide spectrum. But there comes at times to such beginnings the strangest connection. Some call it fate or karma or chance. Some call it odds. In war, in battle, it doesn't need a name. It does its own thing, as it does in baseball.

Once he had been a striker in front of four thousand people, and some part of that day had found its way under his skin as sure as a tic had done its dowser work. A love had burrowed deeply; baseball has such a shovel, he believed. But New York, where he had played his last game, as well as his home in Massachusetts, was months and miles in the past.

Images, all related to the ball, to the flight of a ball, struggled for windows or doors at the back of his mind, looking for a way in or a way out. When he was hit this way, caught up in a feverish wash, he was never sure of the route or the portico. Everything round or nearly round leaped through him in a hardware of imagery, of like correspondence... at once came the end of the hand-crafted bat sitting on the mantel at home, then the driven orb of another ball his swing had powered over the head of Shannon, that center outfielder in the New York game, and, blue and untamed like late night small campfires, Beth's eyes watching him as the chief striker in the last game he had played. He could feel the continuity of her stare.

At that same moment of Durvin's reverie, a replica intensity of watchfulness was being exerted down across the field from a gathering of cottonwoods and a few straggly birch trees on the far reaches of the now-peaceful meadow. There, the lead scout of a southern infantry group, a Georgian named Sgt. Elwood Plunker, crawled a few feet closer from his lookout position in the copse. The Yankee defense line, ragged he was sure, was somewhere off at the other edge of the wide meadow, under cover of any sort, masqueraded, camouflaged, counting their wounds. Plunker, head down, prone as tight to the ground as he could get in an attempt at cover, laid his weapon against a blow-down. The rifle musket, of which he was extremely proud, had been made in Richmond from equipment confiscated from the armory at Harpers Ferry under the very nose of the enemy. And he was a dead shot with it, as deadly as one could get.

Sergeant Plunker saw a Yankee soldier, a tall lanky fellow alone at the edge of the meadow, turn and urinate directly onto southern ground. From a mere two hundred yards he noted the man's corporal stripes. Plunker was infuriated by the urination. He had been three years from home in Georgia, with the prospects of getting back there being lessened every day now. The taste of his grandmother's peanut spread was alive at the back of his throat, and thick and sticky. His throat was dry and felt as if it would crack or open up on him. Breathing came with some difficulty, as if moving past sharp edges. At the back of his head he could see fields of peas and corn waving in a late morning breeze. The fields crawled and undulated, waving crop tops like the thousand hands of a huge gathering. And he could taste the well water taken from the deep throat of rocks with a bucket he had made himself. Inwardly a groan mounted and was silenced. He had much earlier learned to control many bodily functions. He was a soldier, bred for rigors, but his mind held onto a longing and a hatred he could neither dislodge nor forget. And here was a bluecoat pissing on good southern soil. The hackles rose again with their decided edges and he wondered what the enemy's day would bring. He would surmise while at rest. He would watch, he would signal back any information that came to him visually, and he would bide his time. Time being the only thing he had plenty of.

At the same moment of Plunker's recollection, atop a nearby hill, in the announced meshing of fateful lives, Nancy Petticot of Nanticoke, Virginia had planned her day. She had risen from an irregular sleep also filled with dreams. Nancy was a listener, it was easily said. When she spun about and swept a dangling spider out the window, she might well have heard it descending on that silvery thread. Chickens spoke early to her, guinea hens roosted in the trees chattered like backyard gossips and could have been telling her of their night, and the one last piglet made its own noisy contribution. At seventeen she was the lady of the house, her mother Anstrice dead from a runaway wagon only six months past, her father Desmond off three years now with the Army of the South; and not a word from him in more than a year. Her three younger brothers lived by her hand and off her wits. Threats to their existence had bounced around them for a few years, but she held the reins firmly.

Nancy was a dark-haired beauty of a girl, with deep eyes of an unknown color as if caught up in the rotation of emotions. Perhaps she oscillated, but she never flagged in her push. She wore a complexion worthy of any good habit, and was graced with a startling carriage. Like temptresses her lashes floated, full of messages, full of promise, and yet she appeared ragged with a kind of despair few might notice while she was about her work. Men had noticed her at least three years earlier, and that included most of the soldiers that had passed by their rough house, passing on to their savage destinies, and taking some of the chickens and all but the last piglet.

Yet character floated about that house of hers. Three of its walls were made of logs. The fourth wall was constructed of old barn boards that Desmond had reclaimed from a barn that had burned at the end of the valley. She remembered the day he had come home all sweated up, the wagon piled high with wide boards. Two days later, hammer and saw irrepressible, the house was completed. Now, cozy inside its walls, old coffee talked to her almost as loud as the guinea hens. The smoldering late fire, holding its breath in the fireplace, showed the comfort of many embers gone gray and white. Shadows in the house were subtle and cool and the bare breath of a breeze rustled the flour-sack curtains at the end of the room. The faint rustling of fabric gave the room a sense of depth and the cool quality of a tossed mantle. Wide boards of the floor were rugged but noiseless spans, and did not echo an ounce of her weight on them. She thought an army could walk on them and not give that army away. And she harbored no thoughts of ghosts or specters.

In the darkness not yet fully letting go she yelled down the hallway to Daniel, the young voice fading with her short measure at authority.

"Get hitched up to the day, Dan'l. Today we will picnic under the high trees and watch the war. We can count cannon volley or count horses, whatever. You can have your choice today." She paused, took a breath, measured the oncoming dawn still at a distance down the Chawkenauga Valley, saw gray holding back in all the corners. Remnant mule smells, tired barn and old leather odors and the dust of chickens crept through the house. A stale pickle in some corner of the house gave evidence of itself. "Today will be a solemn day. Shake the others from dreams."

Daniel, fourteen, blond, just beginning to broaden at his shoulders and through his chest, a bit surprised at the morning call, leaped from bed, tore off his night shirt, pulled the covers off Micah and Judah clustered like the last two bananas in the bunch. He admired their blond heads, and the sleep rolling out of their blue eyes suddenly wide. He knew where they had been in their run at sleep. It was not the war that would excite them this day; it was the game they hoped to see.

Baseball rather than death had visited their dreams. A week earlier, down on the valley floor, they had watched a slim Yankee soldier drive the ball high over the head of a far fielder. They had whooped it up even for the Yankee running the square circle of the bases. That night they had spoken deep into the darkness about the game's exploits, wondered what the striker's name was, where he came from before the war grabbed him in its lethal grasp. Micah had dubbed him *Hammer*.

Now the name-dropper sat up and rubbed his eyes. "Think they'll play today, Dan'l? No game yesterday. Think Pa plays it wherever he is? How could he do that?" He shrugged his shoulders and shook his head. "He never did see a game that I know of. What kind of a striker could he be, never swung a bat afore?" From his dropped head, almost talking into his own lap, he said, "Think Pa's awright, Dan'l? Think he's coming home?"

Daniel leveled a finger at him. "You ask more questions than a suitor, Micah. Always looking to see what road's been traveled, I swear."

From the depth of the kitchen they could hear the new mother at pots and pans. The sizzle of bacon crept to their ears. Then the smell of bacon, toes turning up in the skillet, sauntered into the room.

On a nearby hill, perhaps a mile distant, Capt. Miles Murtaugh slapped Cpl. Durvin Broadmoor on the back.

"Well, old Knickerbocker hisself, think we have a game at hand today, Johnny Reb don't make a perfect mess of this day?

"Well, Captain," Broadmoor offered, "they need a break much as we do. Certainly makes war look damn foolish when we play baseball. I'd love to play a game against them, and knock the skin of that tater, as they might say. Play their artillery, the big gun boys and teach them a lesson. Joy of joys that'd be."

"How good was that team of yours, Durv?" Murtaugh wore a warm smile on his face as he looked down the sweep of the valley and across the low spread of scrub and meadow between their position and Johnny Reb's. Three mad charges in three days he had been in and his army time measured but in weeks.

Pride rippled and showed itself in the young corporal's face. He too passed his gaze across the open land that drew warriors in desperate turns. Trees, those that were left, were stripped of limbs, leaves, lives. Brush and bush in the rough turmoil of battle had been uprooted and tossed together. In the morning light they looked like breakwaters at some wide harbor, ready to hold off the waves of men poised on either side.

"We could have been a dynasty, sir, I swear. We had capability at every position, had players not always in the game could have played for all the other teams we played against. Yes, sir, we were that good. Makes a commanding prospect walking up to your turn as striker, like the whole park knows what you're at. That's a kind of excitement I never had in anything else I ever did try. Makes the neck stiff with joy, ripples your arms."

"If it's so blasted good, as you say, there must be a bad side to it. A counterbalance. A twist of the blade, if you must. What might that be?"

As if called for, down the Chawkenauga Valley came the single report of a canon, then a tearing, rending sound at another distance, and utter silence as if Time itself was at attention, waiting to see what had happened.

Durvin looked over his shoulder at the canon's sound. His shoulders flinched once, his eyes blinked. "Oh, it's not the losing, sir, but being the ultimate out for the other side's win. That can stick in the craw at least until the next game." His snicker told another story. "Teammates usually don't come back to it. They let it go. There's always another day, another game, when the war's not in the way, when you can make it up to them... strike one for the total bases." The echo of the artillery round came up the valley as if it had shot off a stone wall. "As Alexander Cartwright himself said, 'Take the game seriously, but not yourself in it.'"

Behind them, on a high hill, Nancy Petticot and her brothers had come out to watch either the war or a baseball game. All of them hoped for the ball game. The ground they chose was somewhat level though interspersed with tree roots that appeared to have crawled into place. Nancy put down a piece of canvas and placed their day's rations on it. Thin slices of pork and thick slabs of bread were the main course. A few dill pickles sat in a container, and another tin contained a drink their father had called *berrywash*. It was close to sweet but not quite there. They had heard a single and distant canon shot, but the echo died quickly. A bird-broken silence came into place, catching them at attention.

Micah said, "Look, over there in that field. There's room for a game there. Looks like it drops off on the far side only a little, towards those cottonwoods. Oh, I hope they play. I hope the striker bangs it out like a shot and races all around. I hope they play today." His voice had climbed up a rung or two on the ladder.

Both Nancy and Daniel saw the excitement in Micah's eyes, and nodded at each other. Judah, sitting on a log, pointed across the broad width of Chawkenauga Valley, his finger stiff and arrow-straight. "Johnny Reb's over there, at that end, hundreds of them. If Pa's there, I'd bet he'd be here. They're having breakfast or lunch I bet. See the smoke coming out of that deep spot in the woods way way off?"

Micah said, "The Blue's eating too, a picnic like we have. They ought to make their minds up to play a game today. It'd be better than that other stuff, taking our chickens, the piglets like they belonged to them."

Close in against the hill they were on, Union troops, some cavalry and some artillery, had seized the moment. The Petticot family saw the start of a baseball game in the shadow of the hill, in the shadow of the war. Three men trotted out to the far side of the meadow and spaced themselves equally apart, as if a fan was spread out.

Nancy saw the blond boy in the middle as he raced out to his position.

Daniel said, "He's a center outfielder, Sis, the middle one. He's the one we saw the other day, the one who ran the whole circuit of bases so fast."

"I remember him," Nancy said, her eyes on the slim sprinter bouncing lightly on his feet in the distant part of the field.

Cpl. Nathan Brewers was chiding teammate Durvin Broadmoor from his position in left field. "Durvy, you mess up out here that old captain gonna get you sent up to infantry quick as a wink. No sense bringing your glove you go up there." He pounded his fist into his own glove, a small, sewn collection of fingered canvas, worn to the thinness of comfort. Like Broadmoor, he was tall and lean and quick of hand and foot. The pair could have passed for twins.

"Get all the outs out here and make none at the striker's box." Durvin Broadmoor announced his game plan. "If you make the final out, do it here with the glove." He held up a triple sheath of canvas, also cut in the shape of the hand. Out of use, it would fold easily and fit in his pocket.

Back and forth the game went, beneath quiet skies, in the middle of a war, and at a clearly visible point from the picnicking family of siblings on the top of a Virginia hill.

Nancy Petticot could not take her eyes off the loping center outfielder who had caught five high fly balls, one of them on the dead run the way her father once chased a runaway horse and wagon. Micah and Judah and Daniel marveled at the play of some ballplayers, in the field and at the batting box.

"See, there's that big fellow again, Daniel," Micah said, pointing out an opponent of Durvin Broadmoor's team. "He's the one whacked it like the fire bell and that other fellow, the one Sis remembers, caught it on the run. He's at striker again. What's the score now, Daniel?"

"I figure it is eleven to nine for Sis's team, her favoring that lanky guy so much. We'll see what the big guy can do. But it looks like we're getting close to the end of it. May be decided pretty quick."

Two strikers from one artillery team had earned their way onto the bases while two others had failed. The big batter, announced by Micah, was advancing to the plate, his bat ominously large, like a blunderbuss among weapons.

Sgt. Plunker, in the distance, studied the game from the blow-down, mesmerized at first. The lanky corporal had smashed the ball twice deeply to the other team. Justice seemed distant, a complete stranger.

This was a game they were playing out in front of him! Deep down inside, where all kinds of engines make themselves known to a man in turmoil of any kind, Sgt. Elwood Plunker suddenly knew he was never going to get home. At the back of his head he saw old Joseph Kava Kava, the old black man who had been nothing but kindness in his life and he shuddered inward when he remembered the ankle and wrist scars the old man wore for most of his grown life. Now the deadly sharpshooter Elwood Plunker knew truthfully that old Joseph Kava Kava should never have been a slave to any man.

The awful engines moaned in the universe, as the big striker swung at a thrown ball and drove it outward, toward the man who had urinated, with incredible speed in its flight. Plunker saw the outfielder turn and race toward his own spot in the copse, his legs pumping swift as a runaway horse's, arms matching his enormous stride. Like some god truly in flight, the player raced across the meadow, for the moment as totally free as an arrow from its quiver, and from its bow. The ball seemed unreachable, the player's speed incomprehensible, the war an abomination to all and for all.

The eternally sad songs that Joseph Kava Kava had sung all his life were heard again. Then, as the awful engines sounded down inside him, homebody Elwood Plunker, dead-shot and marksman of the first order from Georgia, laid his rifle across the soft moss on the blow down, knowing the distance was in his favor, took aim and fired at the sprinter coming at him, just as the sprinter leaped in the air and caught the ball over his head.

In that small piece of heaven in the middle of the Chawkenauga Valley in far off Virginia, all the pertinent entities collided, as called for since the beginning of time.

Nancy Petticot's sudden but short dream fell into the defilade portion of the meadow when ball and player came together. To her eyes the puff of smoke from the edge of the copse was merely a quick piece of punctuation. The baseball and the player were together for eternity. Not Nancy Petticot or her brothers or Durvin Broadmoor or Nathan Brewers or Capt. Miles Murtaugh or Sgt. Elwood Plunker knew at that moment of collision that a half inch, .58 caliber Minie Ball was also in a place of rest, in the last game of baseball Durvin Broadmoor would ever play, the line drive still in his glove for the final out.

The last man standing in the Grand Army of the Republic (GAR) post in my hometown of Saugus, MA was Doctor George W. Gale. The post was Gen. E. W. Hinks Post 95, Grand Army of the Republic. Dr. Gale died in 1936 at the age of ninety-nine. He had seven years of military service. The charter of the post was surrendered on June 8, 1936. Over the years I had seen pictures of him at Memorial Day parades and other civic ceremonies. Older citizens around our local ballparks, prodding their own bits of legend, often told stories of his love and interest in baseball. Also, it was said, he told many stories of the war to patients and friends alike, and on many occasions took himself and others to see major league baseball games in Boston, about a dozen miles away. So it was, years after his death, amongst his papers were found the skeletal elements of this story, which I have scratched together from those papers gifted to me, and for the first time in 140 years replay it here as if it were a throwback piece of television, history with attendant drama: our country, our war, our game.

All of it strives to include the graceful therapeutic panacea that baseball is, to player and fan alike, oh the diamond's elixir, the catholicon of it all! I bring it here from the edge of the battlefield, to what it has become, as indeed Alexander Pope might have said of it when he wrote, "the physic of the field." And it all comes along with a further fitting salute from new Commander Abraham Lincoln's words about the fallen, including the rangy striker and center outfielder Durvin Broadmoor, as they were often heard during the span of those years after his first inaugural address on March 4, 1861: When again touched, as surely they will be, by the better angels of our nature.

THE CANOEIST

F rankie Plegger got the idea looking at a travelogue on TV, three men and one woman in an oversized dugout canoe on a small river aiming itself for the Amazon, the water around them burgeoning with flesh eaters of all kinds. All kinds. Crocks or 'gators or caiman, or whatever they had down there that grew tails long as houses, and then the piranha like an army of friggin' fire ants. Bet they could get her to screw all day, he thought, if they threatened to throw her over the side, and her big enough, proud enough, all woman right down to her goddamn toes. In a pair of beat-up and ragged denim shorts she had hips that caught onto his eyes like his own personal clamps, as if they had his name on them: *Frankie's stuff,* they said. Her secrets were fingers away. Oh, he could smell her, the bends in her, the dips, the fadeaways to you-know-what. The aroma was magic and he remembered someone saying once a long time ago it was the essence of life itself, that *down-in* aroma, that *not-ever-letting-go* smell. And he bet she couldn't even swim, not a stroke. That's all it would take, a non-swimming non-fucker who suddenly meets life head on, right where she couldn't walk away from it.

He wouldn't even have to practice at all, just trigger the ultimatum out in the middle of the lake, a full mile if an inch: fuck or swim, baby. *Bang!*

Shake the canoe. *Bang! Bang!* Make her take her clothes off and neatly fold them and hand them to him as evidence legal enough for even a *NOW*-biased court. *Bang! Bang! Bang!* Make her peel her sweet little panties off like she was slowly stripping the skin off a banana, and the moonlight playing her golden as a goddess, knowing what shadow is and what shadow does. If she threatened to scream, he'd tip the canoe over, letting her have her way, down in the lily weeds thick and strong as webs of wire. *Steel spiders*, he thought, and loved the image he had created for himself, feeling the magic of it spinning wildly out of hand. *Steel spiders. Goddamn!*

Bang! Bang! Bang! Bang!

Get a chick old enough and it would be a lot safer than screwing around with kids and hoping they'd keep their mouths shut afterwards and not having to tell them his phony made-up buddy had taken pictures of them pulling down their jeans or taking it in their mouths down in the vacant foundation where he'd promised them model planes like a camouflaged Spitfire with real spent .22 shells for exhaust ports or an original set of old Lionels from a great collector "who died just last week and left them to me and loved doing what you do only now he's dead and can't do it any more." *Stroke 'em any way you can, Frankie.* Like that Havendarp kid. He could be a winner for a long while if he kept his mouth shut. And the Brinkley kid who had no fears, it seemed, down behind the old vacant house and again right under the porch with Frankie's mother hanging out the laundry right above them and the kid waiting for his model planes. *Tough luck, kid!*

Leeanna was her name, he found out from Hazel, the woman working the diner counter, who liked the come-on look in Frankie's eyes, the way it used to be for her.

Frankie had seen this piece at the diner. "She lives back of the fire station, Frankie. I guess she's twenty or twenty-one and works for the doctors in that medical center on Garrison."

Her smile was wider. "She looks hot, don't she, Frankie? That's the way I used to look." Hazel had a way of moving that said age didn't want to take hold of her, not really. She was as live as an open socket, her lips red and wet, nipples near black under a thin yellow blouse, the clutch of black hair alive under her arms he'd seen just that one time and it still made him shiver. She was a monument to something only women had. That thought made him shake his head and think on it.

"You're not done yet, Hazel." Said it, he did, like a hot fudge sundae being propped on the counter, sugar and all the old goodies, the old cherry right up on top. "You got lots of rocks in your crib. You ain't shot off all your rocks, not by a long shot." The old bitch, came another thought, would grasp at any promise and he hung it out there like dangling a fat worm for a hungry trout heading upstream.

"I'll point you out to her real cozy, Frankie. Real cozy. That's what friends are for, ain't it the truth. She's Eddie Brinkley's cousin. He has that little plumbing place off the square." His hand fell across her wrist as warm as a promise. Frankie knew about Eddie Brinkley and it made him think about Brinkley's kids, Bobby, smooth as peaches, behind the vacant house, under the porch more than once.

Leeanna came into the diner late one night, ordered a hamburger trilby and a coffee.

"Gee, Leeanna, that's what Frankie over there just had." Hazel's nod was at Frankie who had heard every word, who kept his eyes on Leeanna's eyes, who didn't let them wander much as he wanted to. "Frankie, this is Leeanna. She works at the medical place on Garrison. Leeanna, this is Frankie, an old friend of mine. Say hi."

"Didn't I see you down at the beach one day," Frankie said. Right on it, baby.

"I don't have much time for the beach." Her voice was smooth and her jugs were good-sized jugs, that he could tell, and her skin was juice cool. It made him tremble. He wondered if she could detect it.

"Maybe it was on the lake, down by Simmons's boathouse where they have the rentals. I go down there a lot." No sense wasting any time, he thought. Get right to it. If she didn't pick it up, he'd give her another try.

"Not the lake either. I don't swim very well. A little. But not too well." One small dimple rode at the corner of her mouth. He swore she was winking at him straight on.

"I tell you, Leeanna, there's nothing like a canoe ride out there on a quiet night, the moon bouncing off your soul, the loons at the far end crying as if they've lost their mother or their best friend, the lake sheer as a pane of glass. Once, out in the middle, about as far away as you can get from everything, I smelled the lilies from the cove way over by the old icehouse." The old shovel felt good in his hands. *Goddamn!*

It was enough. First there was a walk one night, holding hands eventually, his hard-on crabbing his walk half the time, her saying little. He kissed her once, lightly, when he really wanted to toss his whole tongue right down her throat, and he knew she felt his rod against her. It was handing her a compliment, he figured. She'd understand, he was sure. It was in her nature to understand such things. All women knew. Hazel, even in her spending days, knew.

The third time they were in the canoe, in the middle of the lake, the moon barely rising in a crescent out over the hill. He was thinking her legs were absolutely friggin' fabulous stretched out in front of her, sitting in the middle of the canoe and facing him, her short shorts creased where they ought to be creased, like they were molded in place alive. She had great tits. He couldn't wait.

"Leeanna," he said, "I'm trying to be a gentleman, bet your ass I am, but I can't make it. I got to have you tonight. Tonight you do it for me or I'll throw you right over the side of this goddamn boat. It's easy, kid. All you got to do is fuck or swim, and you ain't too good at swimming, but I bet you're a great piece. Am I right?" For her he was all ready; she was luminous in the faint light, and the long elegant legs were so fabulous he couldn't take his eyes off them.

"You'd really do that, Frankie, throw me in if I didn't do it for you. It didn't have to be like this, you know." Those eyes of hers were enormous, and full of expressions he couldn't read, but like they were going to go right through him. Her jugs, he swore were going to pop right out. "Maybe we could have done it in a few months, when I got to know you better. I was just waiting for the right guy."

"That's the way it is, kid. Fuck or swim." He was thinking of the piranha again and the big chick in the canoe with the guys. What did they do when they camped for a night?

Her voice didn't come oozing out of fright, but it wasn't folded over on itself either. "Frankie, I told you, I don't swim. I'm terrified of the water. I almost drowned once." On the sides of the canoe her hands and arms had stiffened. Her eyes were bigger. Her jugs were bigger. A button, he knew, had popped off her shirt. The moon was working on her face; the lips so edible, ajar and beautifully breathless.

"You can start by taking them shorts off, kid. I got to get a look at you." Those legs were the highway to heaven and back.

"What if I don't, Frankie? Will you really let me drown? What'll people say?" She was a cool kid. You had to see that.

"Nobody knows you're here with me, kid. It's fuck or swim, simple as that." As a handy bit of inducement, he aimed the paddle at her.

"Right here in the canoe? Out in the open?" In the middle of the canoe, balancing herself perfectly, she stood up.

"Right here, kid, or over you go. Now get them shorts off. And don't rock the boat or you'll be in over your head before you know it. There's no bottom out here, that's what they tell me."

In the pale light of a crescent moon and a sky yet faintly blue, she stripped her shorts off, slipped them down her thighs. Her panties, nothing more than a shoelace it seemed, came off next. At her crotch the darkness grabbed him with a mythic loveliness and want. His mouth began to water. The breeze touched him faintly, the moon froze in place on the hilltop, and her breasts came out of her bra as if they had unfolded from heaven itself.

For that split moment, out in the middle of the lake, the moon giving up all its secrets, she was the most fantastic creature he had ever seen.

"Come up here real careful," he said, his voice getting heavy and husky. "We got some pre-game stuff we're gonna do." He started to unbuckle his pants, when Leeanna Brookson, non-swimmer, apparent virgin, slipped over the side of the canoe and was gone. A faint ripple was all that was left, like from a full 10-rated dive off the low board. The small handful of clothes had gone with her.

She'd have to break surface soon, he thought, hoping she wouldn't be screaming at him, waking up the lakeside. No other boats were around. No lights on the shore. No more ripples in the water.

Five minutes later he knew she wasn't coming up. The woman in the dugout canoe, the one with the great hips, came back to him again. Piranha and crocks and 'gators teemed in the darkness below the surface of the lake. In his chest came the ultimate pounding of his heart. This he hadn't bargained for.

Later, cautiously, he beached the canoe just below Simmons's Boathouse from where he had earlier slid it loose of a line of chain. The partly opened link of chain he replaced on the same bracket he had taken it from. Then, with no one in sight, he slipped off into the darkness. Maybe it was better with the kids, he thought. They never came off this way, didn't have the guts she had. What the hell, she might stay down for a year if caught in the weeds.

First thing in the morning the knock at the front door was loud, official, frightening.

"Frankie," his mother yelled from the kitchen, "will you see what that racket is?"

Frankie Plegger opened the door to three policemen, two uniformed and one in civilian clothes. They walked into the front hall. Frankie could feel his heart thumping.

The plain-clothes cop said, "You Frankie Plegger?"

"Yeah, sure. What's going on?"

"That's what we'd like to know," the guy in plain clothes said. "You mind telling us where you were last night?"

They couldn't have found her already, he thought, unless some goddamned fisherman had spotted her in the weeds. "Just hanging around, that's all. I hang around a lot."

"Yuh, we know *that*, Frankie. Were you down at the lake at all last night?"

How should he handle this? Nobody had seen them, he was sure. Nobody at all. No boats or canoes had been out on the pond. His ass was covered. He'd only known her for a few days. What the hell.

"You know a girl named Leeanna Brookson, Frankie?" The plainclothes guy was a hard looker. A spot of black sat on one corner of his mouth like a cigar had sat there half its life and had just spun loose of itself. The wrinkles in his face were harsh as an old washboard, and just as deep. "You know her, don't you, Frankie?" His eyes were like searchlights, not moving but boring at him.

"Sure I do. Had a couple of dates with her." Keep the tenses right, he thought, in line with everything. "Nothing real serious. Seems like a great kid. I was with her two nights ago. We were walking. Something happen I don't know about?" That's it, be cool, he thought. They probably spend most of their time in traffic court.

"You ever go out on the lake in them canoes down there at Simmons's?" The black spot was still on the cop's lip. Frankie prayed it was cancer just beginning to show itself.

"I been out a few times. Maybe a couple of weeks ago the last time. Why, what's happened?" Frankie was thinking if he stared at the black spot the cop might notice it and move on. He thinks he's making *me* uncomfortable, the shithead.

"Well, Frankie," the cop said, "I'm Detective Hardy, and Hazel at the diner says you've been dating Leeanna recently, trying to get in her pants. Is that a fact?" The black spot actually moved when he asked a question.

"You saying there's something wrong with that, Mr. Hardy? You saying you never tried? That ain't your thing?" Give it back to them, cool, don't give 'em a bone. He could feel his mother standing in the doorway to the kitchen and Hardy had nodded at her. The top lip covered the black spot when he pursed his lips.

The eternal white apron, he figured, was wrung in her hands. "What's the matter, Frankie? What's going on?"

"Beats me, Mom. They haven't exactly said a thing, 'cept I've been dating a girl they know." One thing he was sure of, he couldn't turn around and look at her and that way she had of looking right down through him to the soles of his feet. Since he was a kid.

"Frankie," she said, the way she had said it a thousand times, something crawling in her voice with arms and legs on it and hands that went searching through his body, pulling at him, always pulling at him.

"Jeezus, Mom, I don't know. I don't know!" Don't turn around, he said to himself. Do not turn around! He knew she'd be leaning against the doorjamb, like a laundry bag ready to crumple, all wrinkled and empty. Done it a thousand times, she had. Now it was in her voice.

The cop Hardy, the cop with cancer on his lip, the cop with an ugly black spot that'd make any girl throw up, was staring at him again. "When's the last time you saw Leeanna, Frankie? The very last time?"

"A couple of days, I guess. Yuh, a couple of days. What the hell is going on?" Behind him he knew his mother was laundry again.

"Well, the trash pick-up was going on this morning in the parks and one of the summer help found some clothes at the edge of the lake, might have floated up on the beach. They were wet, sopping wet. Leeanna's clothes. Her library card was in a pocket of a pair of dungarees, and a couple of bucks."

"What the hell does that mean to me?" What the hell is going on, he said to himself, seeing again the short shorts tight in her crotch, coming down off those hips, the black bush of her crotch? Immediately he saw Hazel's arm pits the way he last caught sight of them. What the hell, this had nothing to do with him. Relax, he said to himself. Relax.

Black Spot came right back at him. "Know a kid named Bobby Brinkley, Frankie?"

Oh, shit, he thought, that kid behind the vacant house, the kid who loved model planes, got his pants down so damn easy he was sure he'd come back for more.

"Don't think I know him, Mr. Hardy. What's he got to do with finding Leeanna's clothes by the lake?"

"Funny thing about that, Frankie. He's Leeanna's godchild, says you abused him one day behind the old Stott place, and under your porch. Says he told Leeanna a few weeks ago, the only one, and now she's missing and her clothes have been found at the lake and we figure something's happened to her. She did not come home last night and the kid told his mother what happened and she came down to see us. Someone said they saw you with Leeanna last night, going down toward the lake."

Frankie heard his mother gasp and saw one uniformed cop rush to her side.

"Frankie, you didn't," she said, as she folded empty and wrinkled into the arms of the policeman.

This is crazy, Frankie thought. "I might have seen her for a minute, but she was wearing a pair of short shorts."

"You have to come down to the station, Frankie. We've got to do a lot of talking. Find out a few things. Where you hang out. What you do when you hang out. Who's with you when you hang out." For the first time Frankie noticed the thick eyebrows on the man and then realized the wrinkles in his face were deep as ruts and how every now and then he bit at the black spot.

"I didn't do anything to her."

His mother was out of it behind him and the cop was fanning her face. Frankie could feel her eyes on the soles of his feet. Something was coming all apart but he didn't know what it was.

"Well, Frankie, there's the kid and his story, and Leeanna's missing. Doesn't look too good from where I'm standing."

The goddamn black spot was out there on his lip big as an ace of spades. If it ain't cancer, it's got to be something, Frankie was thinking. Would serve him right.

One cop was still fanning his mother as the other cop put a pair of handcuffs on Frankie's wrists. The detective with the black spot was walking out the door, across the porch, pointing his finger over one shoulder, pointing toward the street and the cruiser parked at the curb, motioning them away from the house.

Three days later, in a motel room more than fifty miles away, looking at the news for the third day in a row on television, the swimmer nonpareil, splendid diver, possible virgin, schemer and plotter, vengeful godmother Leeanna Brookson finally figured Frankie Plegger, child abuser, womanizer, terrorist, had stewed just about enough in learning his lesson under a genuine threat of homicide, and then some. Maybe this was just the beginning for him. There was a lot of catching up to do, for sure.

She decided it was time to go home.

THE RIVER THIEF

English Wells fought the Pumquich River for forty years, moving his will ever by degrees at it. "By God, Miriam," he often said to his wife, "I'll go at it until I drop, most likely. What you work for, you get. You get what you work for." English, lacking funds or worldly promise, wanted to steal more land from this side of the river, to push his *small estate* out over the river's run, to claim energy's due.

"The two of us," she'd say, partners to the end, the crochet needle at a small and quick twist in her hand, or a sewing needle making code against her fingers. At such watch her nose would announce when the pie in the oven was ready, or a roast in its own rank of juice. English always noted her almost inert actions, the messages driven home by them, and said the best things said were often unsaid. These days, he thought, she had become, for whatever, rounder and more content.

On the same hand, by its gifts, the Pumquich was magnanimous, an opulent river, a river that slipped unheralded out of the far country in various disguises. Furtive, escapee, melodious in turns it was, twisting or dancing on the face of Earth. At first a placid no-nonsense runner, gaited by life, it never ran out of normal breath. Then for a hectic bit it came a robust galavanter in those wild, wild places where hideaways gleamed their darkness among harshest rocks and vertical cliffs old as time itself. And now, decoded and broken into a lesser tributary by Earth's curves, sleepily at times under alder-branched archways where fishermen lurked, near breathless but ongoing in the way of rivers, it came past English Wells. For those forty years he had gone without pause in his evening labors, after a regular day's work as a truck driver. And Miriam watched him from the window or the porch of their small bungalow, no children ever at her feet or at beck and call, saying, "You go about your work, English. We have no call on us otherwise."

There, for the nonce, in this one man, the Pumquich seemed to have met a match.

Miriam dwelled on him from odd angles, saw him broad, thick-browed, his deep brown eyes often at repose even when he was at labor, his energy seeming to leap from a reservoir she thought had no end. She'd see him at the very edge of the riverbank he was always moving, or attempting to move. English would look back on his property, at the peach and pear and apple trees marching in ranks down to the river with him, and random but deep green clutches of grapevines that joined the slow march outward, his invasion. She mused he was a mathematician at a problem's resolution.

The measurement, his own planning with fruits of geometric concentration, almost overpowered him.

Stabbed with accomplishment, Miriam heard, time and again, his confidential but tempering aside: "Them peaches keep pushing me, Miriam. Damned if they don't." He'd look outward, and continue, "On the other side, over there by them muddy spots, it's too damn low for any use. If I can stretch our piece of land a foot at a time, we just plain get bigger. It's really that simple. And them at the town hall can't plot the river's line, but just obey every turn it makes."

To his liking, she phrased her comments or replies in a turn at formality and a bit of elegance. "You carry on, English, early when the sun leaps like a jumper. Or the moon later on, tired of repose or isolation in darkness, breaks loose of the horizon. Oh, like a prisoner from his cell, my river thief." The roundness hugged him.

With a new neighbor at a kaffeklatsch, English off on his regular job, Miriam said, "At first English makes a small dent in the Pumquich's passage to the sea six miles down, hoping always by some miracle to bend its course forever in one night. He'll build a wall of sorts against the river's flow, backfill it, and start anew, all by a measured degree... rock by rock, stone by stone, shovelful by shovelful, or eventually by the third generation of his new wheelbarrow. Granite, big or small, in all its beauty, is moved with a loving care. Sandstone and mica are nursed into place as well. Boulders beget him, I swear, fused by some old glacier hereabouts. English, in this trade-off, never knows how much sweat his body gives back." She paused, sipped her coffee, and added, "And he never counts."

It was simply one of his old saws that came repeated in another voice: "Hell, Miriam, all it takes is energy, and I got a ton of that." She knew all of them, the one full page.

The weight of the statement, fully defined and worldly, fell off his shoulders, like a slab of rock off a Pumquich cliff far up the river. His thumb was as green as ever, but he wanted a wider orchard, a bigger claim. "My sweat demands it," he would say, "and that force pounding in me, needing to move the very Earth itself."

"English," she would say, "you're more than ever at your significant work." Her blue eyes shone their lamps on him, the needle in her fingers working that tactile code.

At the same time Miriam loved the slight smile at the corners of his mouth when he made his honest pronouncement, as if he thought he was sharing a secret she had not known. Her needle, or the crochet hook, would go its merry way, which English saw and took for an abiding message.

Pointing out a rock or boulder he was hustling, he'd yell up at Miriam at her favorite window or at her favorite chair on the porch. "This rock might become a keystone, or this boulder the base of a pillar." There was reality in his proposition. Sunset glazed his sweaty forehead.

Then he'd shove his shoulder against the monster or wedge a bar beneath what only a glacier might last have moved, the glacier long ago calving the rock and the land into a lake of deposits, it seemed. Never had he been a serious student of Earth's history, but nevertheless felt it tremor through his arms every day with his efforts: the shiver, the shunt, the movement, Earth on the slow prowl, reforming.

Miriam could not count the hours English had spent *down there* at the back of the house, with pick and shovel and barrow, nor did she count his trips of donated fill dumped practically at their door; he had his own designs on what should go where. It was not that he was an engineer, she had convinced herself as well as he had, but certain things would last longer than others in the continual wash the river exerted and the drainage plying storm after storm across the land. Over the years he had developed his own laboratory for tests, calculated the results, planned the future moves.

Neighbors dropped their excess fill at the rear end of his driveway. Rocks, old stone walls, parts of foundations. Rock gardens, suddenly flattened out to choicer lawns, came trundled onto his property. English would accept only that which was natural: no junk, no plastic, nothing that would take a thousand years to get back to its original properties. He could have accepted Hank Patterson's old Ford, because Hank had proposed its use. English could have loaded it with brick and stone that it would keep in place for years, a miniature chunk of breakwater, until it rusted out. He did not take it.

"Hank, I know you're trying to do what you can, but this move of mine is for keeps, and I won't really try to screw up the river or the land, other than just letting it mosey a bit. I know iron was here ever before I started, but I'll not add it, or any plastic either. None of that new stuff that never lets go."

"English," Miriam argued, "you could start a new wall with that car sunk in place. You could roll it over and drop it right where you need it most. It's a sure way to make a bottle cap." She felt she was trying to shorten his task, to see his dream done sooner, his place in the physical world marked off forever.

And so it went on for those years. English would handle shovel or barrow; she would cook or sew or bring a book of poems beside the window. She was content with him; life was sure, smooth, promised tomorrow on the plate. He'd wave the shovel at her, or the huge, rock-ribbed pick ax, with the shades of evening coming down on them. She'd wave back, in that gentle way she had, a book or the invisible needle in her fingers. Either was enough for English. She'd be there after the day's last shovelful was flung or the last rock dropped into place. As rich as the Pumquich, she was. No other man could be so lucky.

From her spot at the window, she believed the span of his shoulders could support the world, and she knew the promising shadow those shoulders threw coming into the bedroom at night, his labors done, the next drive at hand. Never had she said welcome, though she could have, but threw the covers back for him every time, the white shank of her thigh like an exclamation mark. She thought it not lascivious, but part of her total need for him. And he thought she was beautiful at cover tossing, poetry in motion. English could have said so, but he didn't. They had always passed on the pillow small talk, their energies matched and compensated. Morning was often the next thing they knew.

Shadows, though, as in all of life, were like hands reaching to grasp one another, or take them in; though these mates knew the distance between shadows was covered with good ground.

The one dark shadow in all of it that came at Miriam, out of context or kilter, was who would, in the end of it all, come into ownership of all his labor. Even with no children of their own, it still would not be fair for the town to end up with forty years or more of English's work.

That shadow, though, lingered for her. Often she thought it like a forgotten meal reinventing itself on the palate at the strangest hour, a gourmet roast, a dry and irresponsibly memorable red wine. The taste was there, even if phantom.

The Fourth of July bomb came into their lives, bursting from the shadow. Miriam's sister Georgette and her husband Paul Linkard were obliterated in a head-on crash with a gas tanker truck in a night rain storm as they came from the wake of a neighbor woman. Georgette had ironically serviced the woman through a difficult health issue. The sole child of the Linkard union was five-year-old Paul Linkard, Jr. Shortly he was the responsibility of his Auntie Miriam, or, as his mother used to say, *Auntie Em.*

Now Miriam had her own task: at her age to get this child to some kind of maturity so that he could function in the world. English had his river; she had this child. And, as with all things emanating from shadows, the changes came. Exhaustion came early at her in her new days, the day full of running, doing, getting done, chasing down the child. And taking care of her man.

The first night the covers were not thrown back on the bed, and Miriam deep into a demanding sleep, English Wells knew, even with the river still running, that life had changed.

Paulie drew at him as well, the towheaded smiler locking up a new place in his heart. Nights Miriam's hand flopped innocently against English, and fell away. He thought of the river again, as a kind of lover, making demands, giving parts away, taking them back. He tried to think of some line of poetry she had read during one of the *other* days, days before Paulie. As always, he could not bring it back, knowing each verse was but momentary in him. Sleep, in its stead, came in reward.

And it was Paulie who came screaming out of the deeper yard one evening when English was pinned in the water by a boulder. Miriam screamed at neighbors. Two men leaped down the yard in bounds to find English caught between the boulder and the last wall he had built and the river washing over him. One of them, Patterson himself, wedged the long crowbar in place and freed English from certain death. Waskovitch pressed on English's stomach to push the river free of its claimant. English gagged and gasped and gave mouthfuls of water back.

Neighbors thought English would give up his quest, and Miriam for a few nights was back to her cover-tossing, but the river continued, and so did English Wells until the night, beside her man in a sudden stillness, him cool as the river, Miriam Wells knew one journey was over.

Evenings occasionally, Paulie leaping upwards and off to another school, Miriam Wells waves an invisible needle or a twig-like crochet needle out the window or from the depths of the porch. One night, nearly inaudible, she read a line of poetry into a small patch of darkness at the edge of the river: *Once, near thirteen, we shared/a cigarette under cover of*

*the mist/and the alewives passed us, upstreaming./
That's the night we forgot to listen./That's the night
we began.*

It was the only secret she had kept from English,
her own poem, and that night in the soft darkness
she let go of it forever.

TYLEN BRACKUS

I will tell you at the outset that I have seen some puzzling and imponderable events or situations in my life. That life is now halfway through its eighth decade. Some of the circumstances were believable, some not; some I wanted to believe, some I didn't. All of them, each instance whether believable or not, had been caused or created or somehow set into motion by the attitude or action of generally distinctive and memorable men and women, whether for what they were or what they did, or, in some circumstances, what they did not do. Believe me, the chance of something not happening is oftentimes as much a story as that which happens. My wife Agnes was a woman such as I have spoken, and old acquaintance Tylen Brackus was such a man. As Agnes did things at her own swift command, Tylen also did things; he moved things at appropriate rate, though he was born into this life with but one fully useful arm, the other a mere shaft with a mere hand. His deformity was, as one might say of him, in miniature.

No god was he, nor was he supernatural in talent. Tylen, to say the least, as can be said of most of us even on our best days, was vulnerable or suspect of vulnerability. Yet the man was equipped with an inordinate amount of energy, an energy that he simply had to call on. All he had to say was *Giddy-up* and it was there. And he was a loner by most standards.

Tylen, I was quite sure at this time, was in the morning's mix. It was that kind of a day, and the October clouds were raggy and less than unique, filled with promise of the ominous sort, darker than usual, inertia buried in them, as if they were hanging there for a definite purpose. Out over Pressburn Hill the hidden sun presented a slightly silver edge on one long cloud that seemed to hover with a timid grace.

This is how it all happened: for the third day in a row, from my own little house out beyond the old woodworking plant, long closed and boarded up, I noted a plume of smoke, a feathery wisp of it tall and slender, rising flue-like above the trees. I was as far out of town as you can go before you are someplace else. I knew that there was nothing either civic or habitable over that way to demand what could be considered a hearth flue, but nevertheless I ran my mind about the ground that crawled off slowly through trees to the top of Pressburn Hill, plotting the ascendant geography of the area. The small stream in there was very quiet, the near-silent way it lurked at tree roots, ambling along until deep winter took hold of it, which it usually did. The old abandoned rail line that once had brought material to the plant by the carload or took away products, now had sparsely visible portions turning to rust. And again I reminded myself: Nothing much out that way. There was only, suddenly coming to mind, that small cave in the hillside ledge, like a hole in the wall for a minor abode. Perhaps a fire might be there. It was not known as a hangout area for a night, with no place in there for cover. But perhaps the smoke signaled a morning breakfast fire for a hungry itinerant passing through. Or a hunter lost of a night. I thought the nights had become quite chill of late for any extended stay. I promised myself I'd check next time I went out there for mushrooms or on my constitutional.

I put the consideration to my Agnes, for fifty years a sounding board, a definitive conscience, and the tremble of a daily tuning fork of all things noisy or noticeable about us. "What do you make of that, Agnes?" I said, pointing from the porch out over the bank of trees to the narrow lift of smoke, now as thin as cigarette smoke above the thickness of trees. Its blue tint, as well, was fading against the backdrop of Pressburn Hill.

Round and pleasant Agnes, whom on one occasion, and one only, I had called Aggie, and that occasion a full fifty years earlier, turned to me and said, with her soft mouth pursed in certainty, "That's breakfast, Dewey. I can smell it." Her smile was the morning edition and her yellow apron was still tied at her ample waist, herself but the matter of half an hour from our own breakfast. It went with her blue eyes, the yellow apron, for somewhere between the two they melded in a pleasantness that had wholly shaped my life. Colors became her, my Agnes, as well as did being ample and being direct. Warmth, the length of her body, as if bundled, had long been my night's certainty.

On this late October morning Lyle Agersea had come up on my porch roughly at that moment, bringing his last vegetable gift of the year, a small squash out of his garden. And we talked about it, that thin thread of smoke, though we both knew he had come to see Agnes firsthand for the day. In his own way he highly favored Agnes, once having taken her to a picture show a half-century earlier. You'd have to say there was no quit in Lyle Agersea. He was as sturdy and as straight and as durable as his denim trousers, the both of them with patches, with worn spots, proud of their long and sure delivery, and time left in each. His smile was direct as he said, "I swear, Agnes, your coffee travels two acres of crusty ground quick as a boar down a rifle bead. It is memorable."

Smooth and friendly Lyle could also have been the history teacher at the school, knowing a story or two about our neighbors. He could knock off a story the way some men could knock off shots of rye or bourbon, the bottle as handy as the grip of it, as well as the weekend. "Only thing out in that direction'd be the old freight car they left behind," he said, pointing with his full arm and the cup of coffee at the end of it, and not a tinkle of sound from his steady hand in illustration of his good health. He thought about his words for a moment and then added, "When the mill closed, the tracks, at least most of them, were torn up for scrap metal. For the war, you know. Trees growed all around it now, like as can't see it unless right up close. Them doors was welded shut. Some of the boys a few times tried to burn it down, that old boxcar, but never got it full caught. How long since you been out there, Dewey?" Lyle had a way with questions, as well as storytelling.

I know objects, large or small, at times even huge ones, which are inactive for long periods of time, seem to sift or disappear into background. Inertia itself might take them out of a visible realm. They fade, lose their contours and identities, become patchwork on the near horizon. Deserted, forgotten, out of touch, they become like old grave sites where family lines at last falter and die out. For me, the abandoned freight car was such a thing.

Lyle didn't wait my answer. His face was lively as ever: clean-shaved, a pinkness on the high cheek-bones and wide brow, his eyes bouncing like aggies in a game, popping here and there. "What I'm thinking about this morning, Dewey," he said, putting that old smile up for Agnes's second cup of coffee, "is that Tylen's due in town pretty damn soon. First good snow does it. Don't nobody know where he hurries off to in the spring, ever since Comerford Mabel up and died on him. What, been ten years now? Lonely is what gets you lonely. Sure can say that about Tylen. And clockwork too. First good snow brings him in. It might be a month of cold running up before it, but it's the first snow does it."

"Ever think about that?" My curiosity had spoken.

"Hell, it's like he's leaving no footprints behind him. Always comes in during the storm, takes up a place with old Betty Marlin or Elder John, whom-soever's got a spare room. And no trail back into wherever he come from."

"He never looks none the worse for wear," I said, remembering how Tylen climbed up out of the grade one or two years earlier, waved as he walked past the house and into town, the little bundle of his Matilda wagging off his shoulder like some Aussie going down the road, casual is as casual does.

"What's that man do of a summer, you think, the way he finally comes into town, gets his room, showers, changes clothes like he don't want any trail dust falling from him, giving away his long-hidden abode? He don't waste any time finding a woman spend time with, go to a picture show, have a meal. Saw him get drunk only once and was the first night he was without Comerford Mabel. Man has a different clock and a different paddle, far as I can see. Bill Barley at the gas station said he once stayed inside Elder John's house without coming outside the whole month of December. That's as near hibernating as any of us can get."

Lyle kept lighting up when Agnes poured, and kept talking. "He gets his grub every week or so at Molly's store, when he comes to town, looking none the worse for wear. He don't look much beat up or worn down for being out there in the woods. Would think he'd show some of that. But just slips away at night like he wasn't here in the first place, that neat pack on his back, the good hand holding his cudgel, the other tucked in his armpit like always. None of the youngsters ever come across him while hunting or fishing. Never see an old fire or any kind of sign. Like he might just keep going off into the next county, halfway out being halfway in someplace else. I'd almost pay to know." He stared hard into the cup like he were reading the remnants of coffee grounds.

When the pot was empty and the squash set on the kitchen counter, as if a promise had been made it would sure to be used before the day was over, Lyle cut off his visit. In his mottled dungarees and heavy denim patchwork jacket he crossed the field the way he had come, the same way to and fro as every one of his frequent visits, turning once at the big tree to wave back at Agnes, who would always wait to wave back. Now that's what I call a fifty-year romance, Lyle having no quit in him.

So later that morning, menial chores done, I told Agnes I'd be taking a spin off through the trees and would be home by lunchtime. My own good old denim jacket was snug and stood well against the small breeze coming down the way from Pressburn Hill, and I carried a good stick for balance and for knocking at things.

Fifteen minutes later I came across the old freight car nearly buried under the overhang of leaves and limbs from a cluster of willows and an occasional pine tree. Long ago, after the car was abandoned, the locks on the doors were welded shut and up one side I could see where the young arsonists had tried to torch it; the black scars of that fated attempt lay a dull patina on the surface of the wooden car, which, in its younger days, must have been a sour-looking maroon; the drab remnants of that color showed in corners less touched by the weather, dabs of maroon an artist had left.

The name of the rail line the car was originally birthed to, no longer visible, came out of my memory; I could hear the steam whistle, feel the ground chug and tremble, see the old legend saunter past the crossing in its spastic fashion near my youthful home, humping, banging, out on the road, out on the free road: *The Nickel Plate Road*. It sang out that name, that tune; *The Nickel Plate Road! The Nickel Plate Road!* Long ago I had savored its adventurous title, tossed it through my teeth again and again, day after day, night after dreams, and heard it in the back of my mind, along with the quickened menu of *The Route of the Phoebe Snow, The Old Lackawanna, The Mississippi and the Yazoo Valley, The Boston & Maine, Grand Trunk Western, Delaware Lackawanna and Western, New York, New Haven and Hartford, Rock Island* (oh, good old *Rock Island), Bangor and Aroostock* (potato cars for a mile, it seemed), and the singing again, the *Atchison, Topeka and Santa Fe.*

As a youngster I had been mesmerized, hypnotized, sent off on dreamy adventures by the names posted in great letters on the sides of freight cars and coal cars, and those little houses like shanties on wheels riding the end of trains sometimes two hundred cars long, where railroad men ate and slept and spent much of their lives crisscrossing America, watching America grow. Freight cars on the move. Tankers and coal gondolas on the move. Great steam engines, puffing, shaking, and beating it down the rails. The joy of seeing other places used to fluster me with its richness, the sudden flare of its warmth totally numbing me to the bones. Not yet subsided, the call of the open road, I swear still making its call on me with the fact of this abandoned boxcar.

Now, before me, dreams gone down the road, the old boxcar seemed to sag; rust had touched its great wheels and mild but honest decay crawled about its face, inertia having painted it anew. About it too, as much a part of its identity as the old legend, a slight acidic smell, that of ash or old fire, as if the light flames the boys had introduced to its sides had permanently touched the air. The thin memories of smoke I smelled—my grandfather's pipe filled with cut Edgeworth tobacco, an orange campfire into which my friends and I had tossed potatoes waiting the delicious blackness, the iron monger's stove at the dump where my grandfather worked—even as the wind began to blow, leaves at temperament beginning their endless and haphazard flights into the wind and with the wind, and then a very fine snow started to fall. The ground, quickly, with sudden charm and celerity, accepted whiteness and wind and my homeward path.

For three long and interminable days, clouds permanently in place above us, it snowed. It snowed that finely particled snow so easy in its promise, so dreadful in its fate, that had driven me home from the side of the old *Nickel Plate Road* freight car. And we did not see Lyle for a week, until he and the sun showed up one morning, both frisky, bright, boding chatter as he walked up the road.

"Agnes," he said, the lightness on his face and in his eyes, him brimming with a week's worth of news and no-news, "I swear I could smell your coffee clean acrost the field, clean as gunshot on opening day. I swear, Agnes, it was that clean."

The bowl of his hand accepted her cup as he added his choice bit of news, him practically jumpy all the time with wanting to tell it: "And Tylen not yet showed his face. Not showed a minute's worth! Down to Molly's they been talking 'bout a search party going out there, wherever the hell he be, and hauling his bottom back in here before he freezes himself altogether."

A week later Tylen Brackus still had not showed up at Molly's store or at Elder's place.

You have to hand it to Lyle. He got the energy going in them, pulled the crowd of men together, the sheriff but a paid hand at that and a little put back in his place by Lyle's energy, got them pushing at themselves. "Think of being out there, the snow putting you in your place, freezing your little ass off, and only one hand to help yourself. If he needs us, old Tylen must be sitting beside himself with worry and we have to get out there."

So we went, some only as far as they dared to go. Some only as far as the tree line on Pressburn Hill, the snow too much to contend with. Some not being such good friends to the one-armed man. The younger guys cutting away on skis, snowmobiles, one or two on horseback. Rag tag as you can imagine a small town muster.

And there, under the willows, under the remnant pines, out along the backside of the closed wood-working plant, the slight and slender file of smoke issued from one corner of the *Nickel Plate Road* boxcar. The small army halted as they eyed the smoky residue patina left over from the young arsonists. The welded joints still secured the doors, each great span easily seen as not having been moved in this recent lifetime.

Molly's husband Clocker said it must be on fire and none too soon as far as he was concerned, everybody knowing his boy Charlie was one of the group which had set that last match. "No way in or out of that car, boys," he said. "It'll burn for sure this time."

The snow was drifted high against one side of the freight car, and we were about to pass by, leaving it to smolder or whatever it was at, when I knocked at the side of the car with my cudgel.

A weak knock came back.

"What the hell!" Lyle said, as I knocked again. The weak knock came back.

"Someone's in there, boys. Must be old Tylen."

"How in hell could he get in?" said Clocker, trying to push against the huge door. "Didn't go this way. Try the other side." A few of the boys trudged to the other side and came back. "Didn't get in that way either."

They buzzed a spell, the lot of them, snowmobile engines shut down, two horses mouth-clasped, and in a moment, when wonder and concern was hitting at them, the weak knock came again.

"Jeezus, God!" Albert Binworthy, the old submarine sailor let out. "Sounds like the Squalus out there off Portsmouth, down a couple a hundred feet and the boys banging out the last message. Jeezus, God!" A chill hit the back of my neck like the edge of a blade.

The weak tapping came again. It hit me suddenly that if it was Tylen, there was a way in. I slipped under the end of the car, snow going up my sleeves, down my neck, my eyes searching for an opening, a way in.

I saw a twist of black conductor wire tight up against one of the great axles, and saw where it went through a hole drilled in the bottom of the car. It was electrified I knew. It looked like Tylen's work more and more. I crawled a bit further. I heard Lyle yell out, "You all right down under there, Dewey? You all right?"

The weak tapping came again for a moment. Then all I could hear was the whisper of wind as it tried my neck for openers, as it came the length of the freight car and brought the total chill with it. "Dewey," Lyle yelled again, "Agnes be well pissed off at you if you mess up down there." The silence came then as all paid attention again to what Lyle was saying.

It was the shape of it that caught my eye. The squareness of it. The right angles of it. The lines of it. A trap door of sorts cut up into the floor of the car. I pushed at it. At first there was minimal resistance, then a wisp of air hit at my face, and the whole section slowly lifted away heavy as a slab of granite. I stood up, my head and shoulders passing up into the body of the abandoned freight car. Light hit me. A bulb glowed. The tapping came again. I saw the small rosy redness of an iron stove. I saw two chairs. I saw a radio dial. I saw a cord of wood piled against one end of the boxcar. I saw a full-size bed in the other end of the freight car, and the crude and deformed hand of Tylen Brackus pointing his stick at me, and him saying, "Is that you, Dewey? Damn it, boy, I knew you'd get here. Got myself in a poke of trouble. Broke my arm week or more ago I guess. Couldn't lift the trap door to get out of here once I got in here, seems like it's been a long haul for me now." He fell back on the bed, finally letting himself go, knowing that help was now at hand. I think he fell asleep.

With some difficulty we got him out of the car and onto Nate Murphy's snowmobile for a quick ride to Doc Fenton's office beside Molly's store.

It was all reconstruction after that. How he dismantled each unit that would not pass through the trap door, all of it done under the car itself. The bed. The stove. The crates he used for books and storing stuff. We'd found a radio. A fan. Knew how he tapped into the old electric wire circuit by the mill and laid a line all down the old track bed. Wonder hit us at how we had not seen anything amiss, had not a clue, and piece by piece little insights, forgotten little twists, began to come to light as the whole episode brought itself together. Misplaced or lost or junked articles came back into memory. The radio was Bit Murray's, thrown out at the landfill, as well as Fred Lewis's old Franklin stove. Paul Lavelle swore the bed was his honeymoon bed last seen at the backside of his barn. He'd completely forgotten it under weed and brush. Everybody had a take about one or more of the furnishings.

To this day, long after Tylen, one snowy night at Elder John's, chased Comerford Mabel all the way home, it's always been the picture of him with the one good arm and that one twisted little arm and the twisted little hand, perhaps in darkness under the freight car but hardly in distress, taking things apart for their last transport, for there was the night, later on, that the car went up in flames, the fire fully caught and naught but the wheels and axles and steel framework left.

And I was seeing it all, all the marvelously imponderable things of life in all its makeup: Lyle hit by lightning one day crossing the field, just after his old girlfriend set the last cup of coffee in the cup of his hands; and Molly's husband Clocker breaking his neck after falling down the stairs with his arms loaded with dishes; and Doc Fenton lost in a snowstorm and found frozen after a tough delivery of a newborn; and that utterly silent morning when my ample and round and direct Agnes was not warm against me for the first time in our lives together. Just like I had seen Tylen Brackus, at night, under the freight car, working at those terrible odds he always faced up to.

THE GOLD DEN
REVISITED

From nowhere, it seemed, a voice startled him, the voice deep, heavily male, demanding. "What the hell you doing on my property, bud?" The query came downhill as if in a landslide. "That's a couple times I seen you out here this week alone." There was another level of demand and insistence in the delivery. "You a goddamn surveyor? We got more trouble wid you guys?" From a cresting guard rail he was pointing a stubby finger at him. Burt Morpin could imagine the fist that might be behind the stubby finger.

Burt felt silly if he were to counter with, "I'm writing a book." At any rate, the words seemed to stick in his mouth. He looked uphill and saw wearing tan shorts a squat man even squatter as he propped one leg up on a guardrail type fence. The man's calf muscle was enormous, with Burt thinking he'd be more comfortable in a New England Patriot's uniform than a tuxedo. Indeed, he gave the impression of being able to battle it out on the line as an offensive guard. His chin was solid and wide, his nose battered

271

from some long-gone street battle, and even at a distance the scar tissue on each brow was salient, discriminating, much as a badge worn.

"C'mon, bud, break it loose! What ya up to?"

Trying to match details, Burt believed there'd be a couple of Mercedes out of sight behind the man and the rise, a rock-hard man who must have hit it big... the lottery, the numbers, something like that. The house was proof enough. A slant of sunlight gleamed off a bald head and a New York Yankees T-shirt was dark with sweat. The way the stain showed, Burt thought of the map of South America.

"You ain't answered yet, bud! What you up to?" With hands on his hips he was a stone structure on the old Maginot Line, a Fordham Block of Granite, one of The Seven Mules.

From deep in Burt's throat the words broke loose, almost falsetto, trilled, full of apology. "I'm writing a book about Vinegar Hill. I sent everybody up here a letter saying I'd be doing some looking around. Did you get one of my letters? What's your name?"

"Oh," the Yankee fan said, "so that's who y'are. C'mon up. I'm Cliff Martignetti. I got your letter. You the history guy, huh? Nice touch." Staccato, machinegun style, he continued, his voice rough but sure, a man who'd gotten his way many times over. "C'mon, I'll show you my house. This monster here over my shoulder. My wife loves company, but don't get too much up here. Couple of nasty turns getting here on that goddamn hill. Hope we never get burned out, the fire kit'd never make it in time. Might as well come all the way from Eastie. Want a beer?"

IT SEEMED TO BURT it was always going to come to this kind of confrontation... the whole history of him and his cave, long hidden, now exposed to a newcomer, undoubtedly a usurper. With the challenge, he leaped back over the years carrying him to this confrontation, and it came to him in an immediate sense:

For a few years, as a youngster, he sneaked by the cave on needed occasions, in the dusk of late evening or an early fog, the path visible to some of his senses, dreams taking on his nights, at times usurping them completely. His mind was abounding with one thought: All he needed was a moment to seize the opportunity. Burt Morphin initially saw the shine on the walls of the cave when he was ten years old, and slim enough for that slim entrance. It was in a small, hardly accessible cave on Vinegar Hill on the Saugus-Lynn line of Massachusetts's North Shore. It had to be pure gold! Without doubt, pure gold! Walls covered with it! The first thrill of amazement overpowered him as he thought of the things he could do for his family, ease his father's six days of labor every week, and plot his mother's lifeline.

In one quick oath, he had sworn it was the only way he'd share his find.

And then, luck and fate working its strange ways, he was in an accident, hit by a motorcycle at thirteen while chasing a foul ball in a pick-up baseball game at nearby Stackpole Field. That young mind was rattled no end. Hospitalized off and on for months, he lost all memory of the shine, and the place. It went away from him like one might think of a UFO or an apparition or a once-strong face seen along the wayside and deteriorated by time. Distance, even in the mind, draws shades, closes curtains.

Then, on an afternoon of swimming at Nahant Beach more than a dozen years later, robust and strong yet pulled under by a maddening undertow, he saw the shine again in a complete but panic recall. All was a tease, coming back from the abject: the walls lighting up, the bright clusters leaping, the magic abounding, all as if bidding him adieu. Bodily alarms were going off through his frame and his mind. All would be lost now! The devil himself was shaking hands with him!

The mere glimpse of the cave came in one of those bodily alarms, but it was enough to solidify its being, coming back from the darkness of his mind. And coming back to him also was the dream that he'd get all that gold for his family. No doubts in all the arguments; he had been convinced the shiny substance imbedded in the cave walls was nothing but pure gold. He remembered that implant in his mind. Getting his father out of a poor position, paying off the family mortgage, setting things straight for his mother's easement into old age, had once crowded his dreams. Was it possible that chance had come again, and he'd drown in the middle of it? He wondered, perhaps it was pure irony stretching its hand.

There, off the sands of Nahant, dragged, pulled, life on the edge, he saw colored fish by the dozens, schools of them, darting, wiggling in and out in their dance, going off like fans waving goodbye. Coming past his eyes were rolling quahogs and sea clams bouncing their way in the tide change. An old bottle appeared as his last breath was about to leave him. But, in one of the pictures of life, gray as at most beginnings, for one moment neutral, he saw the hand of a lifeguard reach for him and a sure arm encircle his torso. At length his left foot found the sandy bottom. Up from the sea he came breathing deeply, his legs still thrashing, and the regained picture of the gold den squarely locked in his mind.

The dream, the chance, still lived. Irony's and the devil's hands dried in the sun, in the warm sand. Resurrection without the fanfare, a part of his mind said.

And then the voice of reality: "C'mon, bud," Martignetti yelled, "get your ass in gear! It don't hafta look that bad."

This day of encounter, of potential dream-burst, was to be an uneventful climb up Vinegar Hill, no longer as exhausting as it had been as a kid. Houses, huge houses, had been built across the peak and down into the swift rises from each town. They leaped two and three floors atop deep basement foundations clasped against hillsides, and changed forever the skyline of the hill. Though old paths had been obliterated, newer ones had found new ways, edged property lines.

He had heard a man at the post office say, "They don't build small houses any more, do they? Have to have in-law apartments to pay mortgages stretched out longer than you can think, and wider." Land once simply sitting idly by as town property was now scooped up by speculators. The cave, if he could ever find it again, would most likely belong to somebody now, somebody with designs on further development, somebody like this guy calling him on from the top of the hill, this Yankee lover.

In the beginning, the obstacles and threats had festered their realities in his mind. Every action would have to be secretive, under cover of darkness; it would be totally stupid to give the gold away to someone who had no idea of the cave's existence, or its potential.

Thinking had earlier crowded his mind: *It will have to be night work or posed work, work under some kind of cover, surreptitious at best, and painstakingly slow. The last sane thing in the world would be to give it away to someone who does not deserve it. After all, I'm the one who found its plenty. Carefully I'll plan my surveillance about the hill, delusively search out the cave if it in fact still exists. A blast might have hidden the entrance. It might have collapsed in on itself. The foundation of a new house might be constructed right across the front of the cave. Oh, hell... it could have been filled with cement from Wakefield Readi-Mix, the gold walls smothered in a caisson forevermore.*

The small mound of rocks he had long ago collected at one point in the trail might still be there, the rocks left over from the mad scramble of the Ice Age that passed through Saugus a million or so years before. When he once hefted each of those rocks he swore the energy of that awful push still vibrated at the rock's core. The tingle up his arm, he had been convinced, was the real thing. That too had been exciting, adrenalin gone wild, his head spinning.

He had wondered how many people felt that kind of message, the excitement and the awful power of it. Maybe, as far as he knew, only the man at the Brunswick, Maine restaurant one day who had mentioned he was originally from Saugus and had told him "what happened down there once, how the ice sleds moved an inch at a time, calved themselves into valleys, abruptly made hills and made the valleys." Or the maple tree, stunted and ugly as a menacing oak, in which he had carved his initials on one snappy fall day, might still have its roots in place, might still be scrambling for life on the edge of the path. He could hear again in recall the wind in its crooked and ungainly limbs, hear the slow whistle of it, basso from the orchestra pit, music fit for the spheres.

Yet houses now leaped into the sky on the hill's crest. History being taken down by rising up. Oh, he could be pummeled by it if he let go. The same man in the post office had said, his voice coming as from a lectern, "Our parapets are breached." The words were spoken as if part of a history lesson. They had come as fact. Ben remembered his ingestion of that moment, that knowledge. Now he knew. Where he at first decided on a camera as the best prop, to pass himself off either as an animal lover, or a geographer or a geologist collecting the data on land changes, another idea leaped to fruition. Perhaps, he said aloud, I'd best be an historian.

In one of those rare moments when his mind worked to its full capacity, he had decided to write a book about the town. A text book. A picture book. A history book. A book of nostalgia. The heroes. The semi-heroes. The demi-heroes. Life on the run the way some townsfolk lived it. Some so memorable and for imperfect reasons. The purple jokesters. The yellow journalist studies. The town workers he remembered so vividly, their years bent on shovels, in ditches, sweat burning them, the sun an enemy, time an enemy. Their cool drink of an evening clogging their minds. Balm of the territory, of their passions. It would be a cross section of life, the whole gamut.

It was perfect. He'd write a book; find a fortune!

"C'mon, bud. You climb like a girl. The suds'll get warm, way my old lady's looking at 'em."

Oh, he had been thinking, people would flock to him with their material, and his cover would be certain and certified. All he'd ask for would be the evolution of Vinegar Hill as his project, his take on the hill that leaped up from the Saugus River, where he believed all his young life that Captain Kidd or some such pirate had buried plunder from the seven seas. He had studied all the names and could bring them back in an instant, the drawings clawing at his mind, the pen and ink sketches of them coming alive for him: Stede Bonnet, Charles Vane, John Rackam, Bartholomew Portugues, and Edward Teach, known as Blackbeard. Perhaps Teach, more than Kidd, was the one who trekked up Vinegar Hill, dropped his wild bounty into the small aperture of a cave like the one he had found, and then departed by the river to the sea. Perhaps there were more caves than he knew about. All is possible, he told himself, seeing the gleam once more, his mind again full of the shine, the lustrous walls inside Vinegar Hill. A chain of caves, a mountain of wealth, all waiting. It was, like the lottery, a chance, but every now and then there were winners!

The sun beat thoroughly down on him as Burt had initially crossed laterally the face of Vinegar Hill, his eyes searching for old signs, remnants of earlier messages he had left for himself. Brush beat at him, low hanging limbs of maples and scraggy pines, oak teetering with age. The ancient signposts, what there were of them, had long departed. Where the stone pile might have been, in a slight declination boarded by young maples and a few laurel trees catching the sun's heat, there was a straight incline without a bump for almost thirty yards. Back over his shoulder he looked, the huge chimney of the Salter Mills marking its way yet, the red brick mickeys climbing in a tall run, like a spear, up into the blue heat of the sky, soon its red light advice to aircraft would shine in the darkness. With a line between the chimney and an old house down in the valley of the Saugus River (it had to be Smitt Paterson's house with the green roof), he aligned the route of his adolescence. It had to be here somewhere, but no lay of the land looked familiar. Boulders might have moved, sloughed off, some by a shaking of the earth itself, which dislodged them from a long home on the hillside and might now be in the river, like there had been a wild ride on a darker night.

In truth, the house above him, hanging on the rim of the hilltop it seemed, grasping the edges, was enough to throw all signs out of kilter. It loomed as a huge igloo of white plastic siding accepting every ray of sunshine, re-broadcasting those rays. And a slough of loam and gravel had stretched away from the rear retaining wall of the house. He could picture three or four cars in a paved driveway, also hanging on the edges, for he could see a steel-wire perimeter fence. Was it meant for him? For trespassers? For historians?

Even then, all things out of kilter, something kept telling him he was close to the cave mouth. The feeling was as old as the hill itself and it came out of a sense of direction, a sense of body language. It came out of the earth itself: his present height on the hill, the way Saugus looked spread out below him, the town hall spire gleaming in the sun, the Park Press catching sun like bullets, the statue in the green of the traffic circle of Saugus Center helloing the sky, the vibrations in his fingertips, Earth on the move. Hello, Earth! they said. Hello, gold!

Then he was challenged from above. It rocked him.

The man's muscled leg came off the guardrail fence. Cliff Martignetti, with a full and broad smile, suddenly taller standing straight, waved him up the hill, with a giggle beginning in his voice as if nothing was ever very serious. Easily he was seventy or eighty pounds overweight.

"I like history. Always did. Coulda been my calling maybe." He laughed a hearty laugh, the white Yankee logo on his blue T-shirt bouncing on his chest and stomach in a carefree way. In the midst of Red Sox Nation, Revere and Chelsea and Winthrop out there on the horizon, Medford and Melrose in the scramble, at night the lights at Fenway Park probably visible, Burt saw the immediate irony all too well.

His sense of judgment though, the innate feeling he had for some things, swelled his chest as he saw, when climbing past the rail, a new Mercedes sleeping in the brilliant sunshine, with the house behind it rising like some technocrat castle against the blue sky. Everything possible shone. The house. The car. The gilt of chrome and glass. The surface of the hot top pavement itself the way a mirage gathers a gleam out on Route 95 heading to Maine, or on any desert scene.

The voice of the man in the post office came back, saying, "Our ramparts have been breached. They don't build little houses anymore." Over to one side, as a signal that landscaping was not yet accomplished, gardens waiting for set-up and alignment, a huge pile of deep, rich loam sat like a pyramid in a break of the fence rail. Beside it sat, more yellow by far in the sun, a mid-sized John Deere front-end payloader mounted on large rubber wheels. It sat quietly inactive, like a toy waiting for its playmate.

Oh, how right was that unknown man at the post office: the house was huge, fifty or so windows aglow strong as tracer fire, one wall almost leaping in pure and total reflection. All the angles of the house, he noted, every last one of them, were perfect in a kind of craft only money or pride of work could bring.

Sweeping away from the house was a two-floor, four-car garage and he could not bring himself to think what might be hidden behind the doors. Immediately he thought of Jay Leno saying on a recent car collectors' show, "Ain't that a Duesy," and the trim picture of a Cord Duesenberg filtered through his mind.

This guy, he thought, this Martignetti, sure as hell wouldn't miss a little bit of gold coming off his piece of the hill. He damn well could afford it. And the shine of the cave walls gleamed anew for the young Saugonian. From below, down along Hamilton Street coming out of Saugus Center, he wondered what the house might have looked like. Had he seen it from down there, or from Round Hill, or from in front of the new police and fire station? Would he, from such a distance, have seen this expanse, this measure of wealth, while trying to mark a breach in the Vinegar Hill skyline? Agreement came quickly to him that, despite all his long views of the hill, there had been little true assessment of what the hill had become. Now the breach would be measured by his own assumptions of this man, this new stranger, this stranger to Saugus.

Would he be a Duesy?

Out of nowhere he saw the arm of the lifeguard at Nahant Beach sweeping under him. All this was meant to be, from the moment the Ice Age in its rhythm had bunched this hill in this spot, and the cave, his cave, had been cooked, stormed, pressured into cold reality.

But now, fates still at work, he'd been caught and gathered again by another stranger, this one a newcomer on a hill in Saugus, six or so miles away from Nahant Beach. Cliff Martignetti, bouncing on his stocky legs, host of hosts, ushered him into the house, pointed out his prizes, then his voice garrulous but gleeful and obviously stating the opposite of what he meant. "Here's the boss."

In a silken gown fit for any occasion, Constance Martignetti could have been a Monique or a Felicia off a model's runway, or even a Babs off the chorus line. Blond, lean, chesty, long-legged, neat exposure here and there, petulant in a way, she oozed her sensual being all over the huge main room of the house, the whole room tempered by glass from the glare of the sun, though the wide Boston skyline was visible. Her voice was immediately recognizable as Revere or Chelsea, Everett or Malden. "Glad to meet cha, Mr. History. I read your letter. Nice touch ya got." She was, of course, Burt thought, mimicking her husband, and, of course, she was also talking about her hand in his. Warmth leaped from it, a personally branded fire of its own, a loan in the making for damn sure, and her eyes, green as the waters of Nahant, swept over him in an unmistakable welcome, the hand holding on too long, sending swift messages not needing any decoding.

"You want a beer?" The hand was still there, in place, the eyes willing to be read. Her breasts danced their dance immediately below... partition, demarcation, statehood.

"I don't drink when I'm writing," Burt replied.

Constance threw her arms high in the air, her breasts bouncing, almost bubbling in a mild corruption of youth. Her eyes penetrated his brain. Deep in his loins the messages traveled, seeking out garish and Garcia. A squeal leaped from her throat and a near-full breast popped out of her sheer, silky gown. The gown was blue, an aqua touch, a sky touch, fleeting as a cloud, and her breast came abruptly tanned to a sassy line.

She cracked up all over the room, her laughter running into far corners, bringing a new and wider grin to Cliff Martignetti's face. "I coulda told ya about her." He slapped his leg vaudevillian and laughed again and the pair of laughing sounds hustled off to a far corner of room large enough for a dance to be held in.

It was warm in the Martignetti house. It was comfortably warm. She was so lovely, so exposed in a semi-sexy way at first, not being what it appeared to be, yet as warm as the room itself. She was a fresh apple pie on a windowsill that taste buds immediately knew. She would pour. She would unnerve any tongue. And Cliff, his hands on his hips, a bright smile on his ever-tough face, the nose marked forever, the chin too and the row of scar tissue above the brows, was being a most gracious host in front of his delectable wife. Burt felt the sweet glaze run through his body, touching all the places, all the secret places. She was magnificent. Cliff was property-proud. It showed on him as bright as the face of a new coin.

In the air, as if selected from breeding, was pure debauchery. It ran over Burt like a Walter Snow-King, pummeled him with longing and desire.

Burt's eyes ran again across another wall where a huge collection of paintings or copies or illustrations, all neatly framed and set in impeccably even rows, covered the whole wall from floor to ceiling. Artist names tried to find their way into his mind. He recognized a few pieces. Assessments came with recognition. Gold, or the touch of gold, loomed everywhere.

Then it hit him. In the midst of that personal glee the two Martignettis had loosed, came the thought: Do they know about the cave? Have they found it? Found me out? Is this all a charade to skin me? To knock me off guard? To keep it all for themselves? They must know about the cave. I must have been right on top of it. He remembered his last look over his shoulder at the Salter Mills chimney and the line off to Smitty's house, how it was so perfectly straight, as if from it he could drop into the mouth of the cave.

He must have been right on top of the cave and they had been watching him. Had been watching him all along.

Constance, slowly, without alarm or nerve, cupped that near-bare breast back home where it belonged, somewhat belonged. Her beauty was broadcasting itself in a hundred ways. He could feel it. See it.

Smell it. She was, he agreed, the most sensual woman he had ever seen. Cliff Martignetti was smiling at him, reading his mind no doubt. A discomfort worked its way. How did he see this man who walked, plopped, strutted, sauntered, hunkered in his paces? What was he really like? Was he a chameleon? An upstart? A pure mustang who had powered or maneuvered his way through some boss's ranks? How far could questions be extended? How could the cave mix in?

I have to get out of here. Burt thought his words could be heard all over the room.

Cliff made the decision and was on his feet. "Listen, kid, I have to go do an errand and get some more suds while I'm at it. Do me a big favor and keep your eye on Bunny here until I get back." He pointed his finger at Burt. "And ya keep your paws off Miss Beautiful, ya hear me?" He clapped Burt on the back and was gone from the room in a shake, his movements suddenly clear and athletic, a man in control.

Burt turned to look at Constance. The name didn't ring for her, the breast working its way again, her legs longer and higher in the thin gown, her eyes burning into his. She rolled slowly to one side on the couch, and gathered no clothing close to her. Thighs leaped their promised livelihood, a huge expanse of white loveliness, a thin dark grove of mystery in the mix. This, he thought, was the banker coming through with the promised loan. She was liquid and nearly on fire, her lips wet, red, pouting.

"You know how much man you are? Especially compared to Mr. Obnoxious himself." Her head angled in its message, its direction. "You're so smooth, Burtie, so young. God, you look so good to me."

She paused again, exhibited, smiled, her eyes lighting in a new shade, and said, "You know where he's going? To play his numbers. He swears the lottery is crooked, but can't stop playing. We came back from Maine once, all the way down from Bar Harbor just to play the numbers when we had been away for a week, then drove right back up there. Wouldn't trust a soul to do it by phone. Jezus, what a bore that was, him talking his crap all the way, me thinking of the good things. Some days I can go all day without hearing what he says. Thinks he's got me pegged. I know how he passes things through his mind. Can't fool me for a second. He'll be gone an hour or two and is holding you to the promise that you have to watch over me. Goddamn sweet, huh, ain't he?"

She inched ahead on the couch, flows and folds of the gown staying put, doing their newly appointed job, exposure at the near ultimate, the solid black couch like a matte on one of the paintings on the wall. He had spied the copy of the painting when he first walked into the room. It was one he had fallen in love with as an adolescent and searching boy, and Constance, here in front of him, spinning his head and making him dizzy, could have posed for Amedo Modigliani's *Nude Sdraiato*. "He'll be on your back forever," she added, "if you don't do what he says." Her eyes shut down, her lips parted anew their brighter redness, and her hand patted one of her invitational knees. "Come over here, young, beautiful Burtie, and watch over me like the man said." The firepot with the name Constance smiled at the signal of erection, and said, "Don't say you don't know, sweet boy! Don't ever say you don't know."

Slowly she drew him down in front of her. "Just the way you like it, Burtie. Just the way you like it. All you beautiful kids are the same. Just the way you like it, all the fire on Earth is yours. You own it all. For a few minutes of life you own it all, Burtie, all the fire on Earth."

And a long while later said, "Oh, honey, do I know my men! Do I know my men! I read their brains, I do. The living sweetness, I swear! I swear!"

Constance gave up no more secrets, told no more tales, and did not ask questions about his purpose on the hill. She simply said, "You can go now, Burtie. I'll tell him you just left because you've got to meet a girlfriend or something. Remember me, but only to yourself. And good luck with your story about this hill. Remember me living up here on top of it all, just the way I like it." She shrugged her shoulders, folded the blue gown with an assured propriety, smiled and kissed him on the lips. She still smelled like loveliness itself, bloom with a long grasp. As Burt turned to go, he looked at the Modigliani copy and knew he'd remember it as long as he lived, and also remember the purported model. Perhaps he and Modigliani, somehow in creation's bent, in the twist of centuries, had shared the purpose of beauty.

He slipped over the fence, noting that the Mercedes was still in the yard, though the sun was lost on its chrome, house shade throwing new angles of new shadows. For a moment, gauging the shadow's interruptions upon the Mercedes' framework, blue coming off black in places, measurements being altered, the body sitting closer to the pavement, the year and the model of the car seemed changed. Why, he wondered, would Martignetti alter a classic and expensive and obviously new automobile? That question could easily be answered, he assumed. The man himself had already supplied the answer: King of the Hill, a minor territory here on Vinegar Hill, but King of the Hill nonetheless.

Then, alertness asserting itself at some brighter realization, knowing his mind was back at work, he wondered if Cliff Martignetti had taken one of the other super cars out of the garage, or if he had not left the property on the lottery errand. A doubt lingered, a shadow fully thrown at him. Then the Cord Duesenberg came back into focus, and with it Jay Leno's words, but he altered them as he said, "Ain't she the Duesy." And Modigliani, a master once more, brought back wholly by his subject, had shown off his best work. As Burt slipped over the rail to start his downhill trek, he marveled that he and the old master painter had most likely shared at least a facsimile of one true beauty, that beauty now trailing him out of the house like the tendrils of a most beautiful plant, the flower of her still on the couch, still at bloom, her signals radiating. He inhaled her on a thin sheet of air.

Other minor shadows reached for him, even on the rise of the hill. They came from single entities on the hillside, and then from a cluster of tree and brush, from a clutch of greenery. A maple touched him with its evening hand, its abrupt coolness. One aged oak stretched. A growth of brush looked solid and impenetrable. He felt as if he had come out of the tropics into one of the temperate zones. The Congo come Chicago or Cleveland. The Duesy had shifted gears. His breath rode easily up through his chest; convictions departed and sailed away; the energy of want dissipated. For a brief moment, sleep beckoned at parts of his body, and then let go.

Down the trail less than a thirty or fourty feet, he saw, behind another small, thick bush, a fissured opening, a slit. In his chest the aorta pumped, the heart leaped, the gold walls returned to a singular view at the back of his head, and he could feel both the arm of the Nahant lifeguard grasp him, and in encirclement the sudden, aromatic loveliness of Constance Martignetti. Life had been so fair to him after a tough start, the foul ball seen once more bouncing off a tree limb at Stackpole Field. Still, he had not heard the engine of the motorcycle that sent him to the hospital.

Of course, at first attempt, the opening to the cave was too small. He was entering feet first and his belt buckle caught on a small projection, caught again. Expanding his chest, he narrowed his gut, and slipped closer. He managed, with one arm, to dislodge a large stone that rushed downhill. A blast of breath hung itself in his chest as it careened, bounced, and abruptly came to rest against a rugged oak tree managing to keep its place on the side of the hill. It's a good thing I'm in decent shape, he thought, as he managed to slip his entire body in through the slight opening, which had turned to the left almost immediately.

Oh, God, he was ten years old again! The slight glare hit him as of old, a wall of substance run through with lines of color, sassy, impudent color that even minimal sunlight evoked. Bars, rays, strands, poles of light leaped out like the Northern Lights. Once there had been, in a swift recall, a kaleidoscope at hand, a varied treasure of colors and prismatic reflections, the odd values of a mad geometry playing with both retinas. His uncle Jim had brought the telescope-shaped instrument back from China at the end of one cruise. He couldn't remember the last time he had seen it, or his uncle Jim, gone at sea for a dozen years.

The want was piling up in him.

A single thought of property lines came at him, trying to fathom their ways across the hillside. Nobody, he figured, had been in the cave in the more than fifteen years since his other entry. He struck a match. The color struck back! Cliff Martignetti could not have gotten in here in a hundred years of dieting. No way. He was home in the middle of the glare, and all his dreams, the wants of his youth, rushed over him again as if they had never left.

There had to be a way to get at all of this, all this that was evidently on Cliff Martignetti's property. He could buy the house if he had enough money, if he had a venture capitalist to take interest, a partner. It could not be Martignetti, who would, most likely, find a way to keep it all for himself. He could romance Constance until the end was inevitable. But, no, that would not work. He shook his head in disgust at his ravenous thoughts, even as she hung on another thin sheet of air.

Then, from a distance, perhaps from the core of Earth itself, he felt the vibrations, the way he had once envisioned Pacific platelets touching upon one another in endless search of cataclysm. A sound came to him too, a deep-throated, diesel moaning of a huge engine. The Earth itself was pummeled; he could feel it, the shaking and baking of worldly things right then might be coming down on him. The ledge at his hand shook, vibrated, came like a Morse code of its own making. He had to get out of here. He had to get out. There'd be no lifeguard down here in the bowels of the earth.

With the same terror he had known at Nahant Beach, he screwed himself into the exit, the slim exit, as the vibrations continued, as his ears slowly opened to new sounds. At his left shoulder one solid, shivering quake and tremor signaled its long extension. One ear popped as if he had been riding down off a hill on Vermont's Route 100. From nowhere he saw the rolling quahogs and sea clams and a bottle bouncing with the tide change. As he slipped, finally, with great exertion, from the cave's slim opening, he heard the clear coughs and grunts of a diesel engine above him.

He stood against the small copse of trees, air rushing around him with the same warmth he had known in the sand of Nahant Beach. He had a clear auditory trail of the diesel engine, and then saw the front end of a payloader bucket lifted in the air above the guard rail.

Cliff Martignetti was playing with another one of his toys.

Burt knew he'd have to go back, offer up a proposition, shake hands with the devil in short pants. The whole deal was cemented in his mind when Constance Martignetti came to him again, more vivid, lovelier, richer, on another sheet of fresh air.

THE DUKE'S BLACK BAG

J ust pronounced *ex-Navy* and having breakfast in
a small diner in Idaho, road dust claiming him as
much as it did his old Ford convertible gracing the
parking lot like an abused antique, he met Maybelle
Hustings slinging homemade hash, the air full of
morning's riches. She was tall, neat in her apron for
a hash-house waitress, wore her hair pinned back
severely yet evoking promise in its loosing. Corded
movements in her neck, supple and graceful but fully
pronounced as a woman's, brought him early
hungers, caught him leaning in the booth. Their eyes
locked, gave out announcements, were decoded, and
then, so as not to embarrass the other, were allowed
to wander. Initial signals had been made, and
illustrated, acceptance, of some order, duly noted.

Between the two the attractions were limitless,
yet were essentially bound up in her needing to get
out of the one-horse town and his, being as horny as
three full months at sea, each of them airing their
own broadcast.

"Breakfast can do that to some of us," he remembered a wise old shipmate saying, about shore leave in general and women in particular, "but only if you're lucky."

Drake Ulban Kincaid (*Duke* to all), forty-two, looked like a bag of razor blades, tough as a bag of nails and for almost ten years running had been the Navy middleweight boxing champ. His face was a series of acute edges and angles, and he could be the model for a bronze bust on a foyer table, any table in any foyer. The boxing leavings were permanent but worn badge-like, and lifted his eyes. All first impressions made him, at once, serious and of keen interest. He came to Idaho's foothills from twenty-seven years in Uncle's Navy hardly trusting anybody who didn't pack it up as he did himself (like comrades in deck-hidden gun mounts, knowing each other's sweat, arm strengths, their attention to detail, their own page of saltiness). Men pass the test or they don't; women might ride the fence.

All he wanted was a big wad of money in his hands, to lay it out on a motel bed, count it, sleep on it. Shore leaves about the world had created certain hungers. The motel money dream had been the one most insistently repeated. More often than not, tide reaches and changes setting up his thoughts, rapacious reading of favored Patrick O'Brian novels done for the day, he dreamed of finding a gold mine in the mountains of Idaho or Utah or Montana, not being too particular where, or perhaps, all things of the dream world at extension, of taking a lot of money from a bank.

He had declared those wishes to a few of his last shipmates before parting from Uncle's Navy. Leaving a ship was about the saddest thing he had ever known, and though he had done it almost a dozen times, the feeling still rang true. It was the saddest thing, he agreed, because the marks left were indelible on a man; most men would carry them a long time; the lucky man would carry them forever; any time the tide changed, salt stung an open eye, the wind shifted out of the northeast, a boat bobbled its fenders against a dock, the marks would be known again, old marks in a new setting.

And all along he knew what the chances were of finding gold in Idaho or Montana or Utah.

Dropping the menu at his table in a window booth, Maybelle said outright, as part of her introduction (along with already assuring two buttons were open on her blouse), "I'm Maybelle and I bet you got a story or two. Guys in here know you, at least what you're like. I can tell. They noticed you when you walked into the place, sized things up. I see three or four of them by the window pegging you right off the bat just after you parked your car. Like how they thought they might have been, way back. You know, when they had it all together, not like now." She punched the last comment with a gesture of futility. "They know the swagger, the instincts in your tote bag. I saw the signs myself, you coming across the parking lot after you tossed a travel bag from the back seat into the trunk of your car. The strut's personal, like your name's on it. Says you've been around, know things, places." She looked about, dropped an empty hand in a peremptory salute, and said, "More'n this."

Her whole life had been swept up in quick changes since she had left home: behind the barn with Ricky

Sims, him shooting his mouth off later about his fourteen-year-old blow job, her father packed off to jail for two months for beating the crap out of Ricky and then his father, her mother on a continual crying jag about her own failures as a mother; the trucker who drove her the first one hundred and fifty-five miles out of town and dropped her at a motel, paid for her room for two nights, went home to his own daughters too long ignored.

A hundred jobs she'd had coming here to this diner, long hauls and short hauls and no cemented romances. When she saw him get out of his old car, the tingle began, the old tingle, the good stuff rearing its head. Where it started out she never knew, but it would seep a while, crawl around on its belly, touch here and there, and then leap for the core of feeling. More than once since he had come into the diner she swore she had touched herself in secret, with a phantom hand, like some amputees have a phantom pain. All of it brought a flicker of a smile to her face.

Her *more'n this* gesture he loved, the idea of loneliness that went with it, so innocent, so open. A sense of grace filtered through her movements. Not in a long time had he been so impressed.

"You always go at it this early in the day? Is it trade talk, making me sociable and easy, digging for a tip? Take it from me, you don't have to do much of anything for a tip. You dress this place up from the git-go. Ought to pay you for that. Put your name up in lights. Drag every boy in here from miles around. Empty the hills. Cowboys and glow boys and weed whackers, they'd all come."

"You're as smooth as I thought you were," she answered, "and a peck of trouble with it, I bet."

But with that one line from him, she was suddenly more upright, two inches taller beside the booth, it seemed. Her morning, she was thinking, hadn't started that brightly. Now, a pellet of sweat walked easily on her forehead. A small vein ran its bluish scar-like run across one temple telling him part of a story. The brows and lashes were dark, lightly massed, yet ran their routes with a quick slimness, a neatness. If she stood other than nude in front of a morning mirror, he didn't want to know, preferring his own picture show, and found, above eggs and bacon, above morning grease, a thin sheet of new air carrying her signatures, all of them.

The tie-back of her hair promised again a softness once let go, him thinking it was a perfect matting for a pillow. It matched an elegant ankle bracelet looking much out of place in the a.m. diner. The bracelet was pure gold, he knew; probably from some long-hidden lode of riches a far mountain might have yielded. It was one of the first things he noticed in the whole room, that most intimate promise a woman deals with daily, that thin, delicate letter opener of sorts, that bearer of ultimate secrets. He wondered how long it would be before he could look sideways at the bracelet, measuring, looking for an inscription. Perhaps it would say, "Welcome aboard, Captain."

With that thought, the jumble of arms and legs, the early motions of a morning erection came and went, as if an electrical plug had been pulled from a socket. Yet she was not a stray, not at all, having a carriage, using it, lessons accrued in its employment. He could tell that she was alert to everything going on around her, the early morning talk, the cigarette coughs, the rough faces talking of their rough evenings, the long eyes coming out of long nights, nights breaking loose in the morning in occasional repetition. An early stain worked on her pink shirt by her left underarm. In the midst of the morning hash crowd, eggs and bacon floating their grease in layers of air, like pages in a book or a menu, one breast rode its early titillation behind a damp spot on the shirt. Duke knew the code, waited to reciprocate.

He liked her eyes first, even before her hips sent messages walking away from the opening coffee pour. The pink dress rode her the way silk rides its prisoners, the hips engaged. He thought about two ships on the tide change, might have been in Honolulu or Singapore or somewhere in the Leyte Gulf, with a hawser swinging between them, tempo, music, a beat; man becomes electra, and then his woman whenever she comes from landside. When she came back with his plate of home-made hash and two-over light, he gave her the twenty-seven-year eye from his shore leaves.

"Women know you too," she said in rejoinder, exploring his eyes, his assessment, owning up to her own portions. "At least I do, and there's a blond in the corner booth thinks you're a smooth hunk." Looking back over her shoulder, she added, "Told her I'd let you know, just in case, but I think you call your own shots, don't you?"

"What's your take on it?" Duke said, putting a hand on the corner of the table so she could lean against his hand if she wanted to.

She did, the message running right up his arm.

"What time you get off?" he said, seeing the smoke float across the green of her eyes, more stories being told.

"I'm done now if you want. Nothing holding me, not even two day's work coming to me. Where you headed?" She didn't know why she had asked, it sounding as distinct as an invitation.

He thought about his last ship, leaving Mahoney and DePalma and Moxley in the gun mount. The slow taste of all the years was in his mouth. He gave her the whole salvo, all barrels at once. "I'm going to find a gold mine in Idaho or Montana, or maybe rob a bank. I haven't made up my mind yet."

"They both sound exciting, but I like 14-carat stuff, if I have a choice." She leaned over, tapped a finger on her ankle bracelet. Her breasts gave promise the way she bent over.

When she walked past the blond's booth, the blond said, "What'd he say? Is he jake or joke? I won't quit easy." Her hands were pressed on the table, as if deliverance was hers.

"He's taking me with him," the waitress said, a sudden hitch in her strut, and an approximately measured caesura pointing out the balance of her message. "Says he's going to find gold in the hills, or rob a bank. You want my job, you got it. Tell Marvin behind the counter." She pulled her apron off and dropped it on the counter, looking at a small mustached man standing there in his starchy white apron, his eyes still sleepy, his cheeks puffy, saying, "I quit, Marvin. I told you it'd be fast," and looking over her shoulder added, "and his breakfast is on me. Take it out of my pay. Blondie over here might take my job if you talk to her like a sheriff. She likes her men hard, too. Same as me."

They were more than a hundred miles into the road dust and the hills promising never to flatten.

His attractive looks became a smoothing agent to her excitement at being alone with a man, little but the land their company. In that quick travel they learned what the other liked, in food, entertainment, sex and books, the intrusions that television carried with it into silence, appreciation, deep thought, loneliness when loneliness was wanted. It was, they agreed, a miracle that each one of them liked to read, would spend hours at it when able. At sea it had been a snap, with a ship's library always open. "Two guys with one mule found a gold mine in Montana once. One shot the other, and then he froze to death with his pack full of Twinkies and gold dust. I don't know who wrote it or what the title was, but it had a picture on the cover of the two of them looking down two trails in the mountains."

"Make you think about the gold mine all the time? Where'd the bank come into all of it?"

They were in Pocatello, across the street from a bank with high, wide windows, a few banners stating a special day for new investors. "The high come on," she mouthed, then giggled lightly seeing a quick antipodal scene rush across the back of her mind... Duke with a bag filled with money, walking out the front door, getting in beside her, driving off into the sunset, silence sitting behind them like Buddha, all Pocatello lethargic, still, unperturbed.

The face of the building rose seven or eight floors high, yet still seemed an impenetrable fortress. A vision of one of his battleships came to her, one he had described in such intricate detail that she knew he was missing it, had trouble letting it go. The understanding of such longing in the face of reality was abruptly hers; she'd been home only twice in sixteen years. When she looked up, at the topmost floor, the sun's last reflection gleamed into her eyes off the glass of a large window, and came down like a silent shot. Duke made noise putting coins in the parking meter, the new investor at the first move of money moving.

He came back to her side of the car, and said, "You on for the long ride?" His eyes sank right down to where she was having her tingles again; she could absolutely feel them dropping down through her body, abrading all the way but with a smooth touch, an old hand at an old game.

Gawd, he owns me, she thought, closing her knees tightly, holding on to the tingle for a brief minute as it began to fade, losing itself in a quick contraction in her throat, on an unsaid word.

She looked around, both ways on the street, seeing the traffic flow, both car and pedestrian, life at its full level in a slow gear, evening beginning to settle its claims, the sun falling fully behind one hill.

He could tell she was in measurement, looking for her play in his thing, trying to find an answer in herself. At length she said, "I'm still here."

Then he was standing at the back of the car, those deep character lines still vibrant but near-bronzed in his face, marking him the way no man had ever been marked. In the rear view mirror she saw his lips pucker up as if he were going to whistle a salty tune, with a new adventure at hand. He keyed the trunk, pulled out the black bag, closed the trunk, tossed the keys in beside her in the front seat and walked into the bank.

A swell of admiration came upon her; I'll bet he's going to fill the damn bag up with money!

Thirty minutes later he was still in the bank. She tried not to fidget, but fidget she did, all the while saying what was apparent really wasn't apparent, or so she thought. It was an underworld argument, possibly deep in her soul, or on the fringe of a kind of immediate madness. Eventually, minutes more dragging by, she assented voluntarily to what had come across her mind: she would be painted an accessory to robbery, armed robbery most likely, thinking about the bag and what might have been in it. Only once had she touched it in the ride from Marvin's diner, reaching over to get a sweater out of her own bag, shoving his black bag aside, feeling it full of something, never guessing that it mattered what it was. After that, at a gas stop, he put the bag in the trunk.

Here in the middle of somewhere nowhere, evening dropped around her as if it had arms. Yet in the midst of that curried favor she waited for signals, signs, noise, the hallelujah trumpet itself, the call to accounting. Not a single siren's wail was heard. No alarms went off on the bank's outside wall as if a knockout punch had been thrown. No klaxons doing their haughty deed, raising the skin bumps galore, bopping the ears with the wild static of the universe in full throttle. The new investor banners, against the face of the bank and spanning the width of the street, rattled their plastic sounds in a slight breeze. A rope caught on the breeze and tried to whistle a small tune.

A gum wrapper and a used napkin rolled in the gutter aimless as hobos looking for one more haven for the night. She knew where she was, who she was. Barn smells came back to her as thick as yesterday. She saw Ricky Sims's ultimate smile and dismissed it as quickly as it had appeared. A man passing by, looking at her face over the car door, noting the convertible's sexy intrusion in the middle of the city, smiled a message she had seen before. He nearly fell down when she gave him eyes, rolled her tongue across full red lips. It made her wonder how long it would be before Duke took off her underpants, brought everything home. She thought, on a second accounting, she'd save him the trouble.

The tingle came again. Spinning about in the seat, looking back over her shoulder, she saw no police car coming down the street, heard no siren. She tingled again, trying to gauge the impact, the true message. Suddenly she pulled the keys from the ignition block, thought a moment, put them back. She slipped out of the convertible, stood at the open door in contemplation. When she closed the door, she walked across the street and stood against the window of a small delicatessen. Inside and below her belt, where the tingle had been, a slight hunger tantrum evoked its yearning. Rich odors rode on the breeze, while the breeze still worked the ropes of the banners. A few cars passed by, then a bus and a truck spitting a taste of monoxide. Another man passing close by dared look into her eyes for a second, as if he had been there before. He hurried off at her return gaze.

She thought she could have walked off down the street with him. She could walk off in the other direction. In a split second, she could! What the hell, the bank was like any other building, any other barn. It was easy to leave. It was not like a ship, not like leaving a ship. She understood him, understood the differences.

And there he was, coming across the street with the black bag bouncing at his knee. And he was all dressed up in his sailor suit! My God! Her eyes fastened on the cut of man he was, on the stripes that raced up and down his sleeves, at the conglomeration of colored ribbons pinned across his chest, the way the salty, white sailor hat sat across his forehead, cocked in a cocky way. Nothing ever like it. He was elegance and confidence and man galore and she knew what had kept her in place.

Into the back seat he tossed the black bag. She listened for sounds. None came. No klaxon. No sirens. When he turned the key and the engine came to life, she slipped in beside him. The car slid away from the curb, joined traffic, aimed for the distant hills. Again she listened for life to scream out behind them its impossible possibilities. Nothing came. They cruised. The wind came over the windshield as stiff as a sea breeze. He tossed his hat into the back seat and put his arm around her. She snuggled comfortably close, inhaling her own dream. Eventually his hand slipped down into her lap, moved easily on its way, found the triangle, found her tingle. Twice he turned her loose into her own feelings. A trucker, passing by them on a wide stretch of road, blared his diesel horn at such roadway gaiety. Before the third episode on the ride to wherever, she slipped off her underpants without an exchange of words. She touched him lightly. He touched back.

At the Moosehead Motel, cranked tightly against a high cliff rise, they registered. In the room he asked her to go to the office to get some ice for a few drinks while he changed. She went off to the office, smiled easily at the woman behind the counter smiling at her. When she came back, he was out of his uniform but in Navy skivvies and was lying on the double bed on which was spread a million dollars in hundreds, fifties and twenties. The floor was covered with assorted money bands: hundreds, fifties, twenties, tens, the whole floor littered, accountant's mosaics.

"We're going to sleep," he said, and rolled over on his side. She took off her clothes and lay down beside him. At three in the morning they were properly introduced. And then he told her everything.

"I had a hard time with my father. He had no give, none at all. It was always my mother who would cement things, put things back in place after an argument, crazy words bouncing all around us."

He sipped on a drink. "Suddenly, she wasn't really there. She just evaporated. Withered away. She went down to about eighty pounds you could pick up with one hand and move her to a clean bed. We had two beds for her, changed beds for her a couple of times a day. But she just withered. Her arms got so thin I was afraid they'd break on me. Arms wretched as toothpicks. The frailest things I've ever seen in my life. Worse than any newborn on a farm or what you see in films about hunger and famine, like in Africa."

He paused and she knew he was scaling differences in things he had known, had seen. "The only thing she had left was the look in her eyes. It always said, 'I love you; it's been worth it. Keep things neat. I'll be watching.' My father lost it all when she stopped breathing one morning just as the sun came in the window. He couldn't count on her any more. She was the real iron in the family and he knew it. My grandfather tried to plan on college for me. He had a few bucks put aside he said, could take care of me. I didn't want any part of college. So, at fifteen, things breaking apart for me, for us, just about every day, I left, faked some papers, joined the Navy. It was the best place in the world for me. I found out on one return visit that my grandfather had set up a trust for me that I could tap into when I was twenty-five. Into that bank back there. I just made believe it was not there. Pulled my twenty-seven-plus years, but the dream kept coming at me.

"So, here we are. I never have to work if I don't want to. You'll never have to sling hash again. You can write your own ticket, with me or without me. I bring no pressures."

She told him about Ricky Sims, the big mouth on him, the rotten looks she'd get from classmates and their parents, from Ricky himself.

Duke kept rubbing her back where the spinal column made the sexiest groove he could remember. Once he promised, "I'm going to look at that in the daylight, see what it does for you." She laughed and hugged him. He passed his fingers down over the groove again, knew her spine moved in response, felt the bills sticking to her skin and loved the idea.

For her, Ricky was gone forever. Duke's dream was real. One time during the night, after knowing him all over again, head to toe, front to back, she woke with a start when she heard a distant siren. Soon, silence flowing its weight in the room, his breath beside her as steady as a ship's wake, she went back to sleep.

Even with the smell of money filling the room, seeping up under her, making slight noises when she moved on the sheet of it, she marked him forever.

On the small bureau of the Moosehead Motel, the black bag sat empty for the rest of the night.

In the morning they filled it up, left a hundred dollar bill for the maid, along with all the printed money bands.

RURAL FREE DELIVERY

T he meltdown, in earnest, had begun. From his porch during the past few days he had seen the mailbox, inch by secret inch, protrude from the harsh mound of snow downhill from him in the dumping area. The red flag on the box, as if raised in signal by the mailman, quickly came into view as did the decorative bars and blue field of a hand-painted Stars and Stripes posing a minute mural on one side.

With both flags fully exposed, Danforth "Jazz" Colbere finally came to attention.

The March lamb had pranced away with much of the huge pile of snow where the town workers had dumped it through the rough winter, most of the snow coming from the center of Saugus during a half dozen storms. The melt, leaving map-like dark patches over much of the top soil, was now nearly complete, and Jazz Colbere sat on his porch watching the ultimate transition. When he closed his eyes the sun left slight tracks across his forehead in a path easily followed. A scented breeze with a mysterious musical note aboard carried him for an abrupt second to a distant post in his army days, *Reveille* about in the air. Somewhere south of the 38th Parallel he thought it to be, perhaps Mung-Dung-ni or Sae-pori, or off on one of the islands in the Philippines, but he could not lock it down.

For another full minute of staring at the mailbox, he was aware of maple leaf buds scrambling for a touch of the same sunlight. Continuity and life force worked on him their long fingers. A sudden hunger tantrum, beginning deep in his gut, scratching about, touching elsewhere, tried for resolution. His last female company had been three full years ago. Maggie D'Urbenville, after a six month stay and after bitter testimony over the chance meeting of an old acquaintance, had gone off in a huff and never returned. She had been a soft presence against him all night long and fully known. Under covers her hand would often slide across his turned hip; that would be hours after her voice haunted him with her reading a story out loud, the rest of the kitchen dark, her chair by the woodstove creaking out snappy punctuation.

For a few months, on the sly, he asked questions around town about Maggie, but did not get answers. So one more time he let go of the past. Long earlier he decided that he did not have time to argue, to hold a grudge, or even to give advice. Holding pretty well to those resolves, Maggie, as warm as she made the night, fell away from his mind; peace, intruding silences, comfortable memories, seemed sufficient. It was enough for him that he had not cast his net about for more company. He remembered his father saying some man once said he also serves who stands and waits. For these three years he held fast to that tenet. And the strange circumstance of the mailbox had surfaced as a minor surprise, him awaiting it, expecting it, or something like it, for a long time. It was, perhaps, a dream enacted.

Nearing sixty years of age, he was yet slim and somewhat wiry from decently good habits and long walks in black boots, jeans and seasonal tops and outer wear. At a distance townsfolk could recognize him. Thick, dark hair hid the tops of his ears, and made his eyebrows out as chevrons. Jazz Colbere, for thirty or more years, lived on the bluff above the old swamp, a semi-hermit to a good portion of Saugus. He appeared not to have had a steady job for many years. People who talked about him said he lived on "old money," but never said what that money was. They knew he read a lot, had no television they knew of, and recycled all his paper waste so that his wide reading habit was well-known. What shopping he did, he did locally, but took a long time between trips.

The small log house with the wide porch had been his father's home for forty years. Then, by a quickly enacted law, the town had appropriated the land below the house, the whole range of the swamp, for a refuse dump. The swamp, or The Pit as town youngsters had called it, once had been the source of rock iron ore for the first iron works in America, a short distance away. Suddenly the catfish were gone, the owls, the coons and the occasional fox, all as if obliterated. They had gone almost overnight, the way boyhood leaves, sometimes vague, unknown and unannounced, yet often offered up as a challenge to what comes after. And here, at least thirty years later, that site, capped off by new environmental demands, had become the sole place for town snow disposal.

And on this new April day, after a ravaging winter people would do their best to forget, the final thaw had come in the silence of the night, like katydids from their long, deep sleep.

Jazz's gait was unhurried as he finally ambled down the hill towards the mailbox. He could not see any vehicle on the incoming road for over half a mile. Alders and a few gnarly oaks in scattered copses threatened the skyline with their lumpy arms and their arthritic, bony fingers. Huge piles of snow had withered, stretched their liquid reach, and disappeared. Blue sky leaped past the horizon with bright signals and maple aromas caught new edges at the far end of the loam-capped area. Spring, with all its signals, had a sure grip in place.

To his surprise, neither name nor address showed on the mailbox, a rugged iron dog of a mailbox, which might have been smithied in days of old. Heft freely granted its root of adjective. The mailbox had been, he presumed, uprooted by a plow, picked up by a front loader, dropped into a dump truck, and brought out here for the meltdown. Old Glory painted on one side came off clear and shiny in abbreviated contour. Traces of rust ran a slight patina on the other side, a patina with a moccasin texture. But there was no pole attached to the box and no mounting holes penetrating the bottom, so he wondered how it had served its owner. That curiosity worked him through and through. What appears to be one thing is often another, he might have said. A small amazement told him adventure might be at hand. Surprise and containment often mix well, he could have vouchered.

With an easy heave, he tossed the mailbox onto his shoulders and started back uphill to the house.

Odors of residue snow and ice hung around him, particulates of the rough winter now done holding sway. And he felt that something was in the metal container. Probably snow, he decided, but other and choicer options came quickly to his mind, even as the maple odor climbed on the air, as winter let go its deep handclasp.

Atop scattered newspapers on the kitchen floor he propped the mailbox, but after thirty minutes little water flowed from it and he was sure it had not been full of snow or ice. Yet, with the sense of adventure, of apprehension, of surprise, all playing at the edges of his mind, he deliberated at opening the box. Time, he felt, had no measurements for him, no rush. Impatience had no place out here on the far edge of town, where a lone man ambled his days away in observation, contemplation, now and then a piece of wood being whittled into another shape, a good book taking him deeply past sundown.

Acknowledging his comfort, yet feeling a sense of intrigue, he sat back and tried to resurrect the happening of the mailbox. No pictures or details came in a rush; only the smell of his own heavy coffee assailed him. He felt rooted. A third cup was still a celebration. The aroma cut off the maple advances, the winter departure.

He sipped his coffee, bit at the final taste, marked morning once again. When he tipped the mailbox on one end, popped the small door open, a flood of envelopes fell out. An unknown richness elbowed him aside, good as a late strike in an abandoned mine. Each envelope was protected by a plastic bag with fasteners, a grip of edges that fashioned a tight seam. Each envelope had writing on it, but no address, no stamp; there was a number and a small title on the face of each one. Branded. Titled. Distinguished. The writing was neat, small, feminine, and left-handed at first glance. He inhaled a scent from the first envelope he picked up, which said, "No. 17, How Gardens Grow." The scent was alive, was almost green and growing, and gave a hint of something he must have known before. He thought, gladiola. It was only guessing.

Something else was trying to dictate to him. He struggled to find that dictation. It would not come clearly from its place. "No. 22" simply bore one word, "Moonplace." All the vastness of possibilities crowded him, rushed at him in a torrent. Imagination's sake. A neat, left-handed woman aware of aroma's dodge, full of intrigue, energetic, romantic, perhaps a vegetarian or an environmentalist of sorts, came into being. One part of the message told him the mailbox was deposited in the snow during the winter, said that it was not accidentally knocked down and dumped out here at the end of town.

When the legend on "No. 50" popped up, "The Finding Man," the barb of the hook went deep under his skin.

To You Who Finds My Messages:

I do not use a bottle cast out upon an irreverent sea. I use a factor of the USPS, believing in America, hope and attendant salvation forming around a lonely life. I painted the flag you have seen on this container. This box has not been torn up by a plow. It has been delivered. I am at the end of things and look for someone who can find me, some person who is keen and observant, and has firm beliefs. And someone

314

who craves company the way I do, but sincere company. Know that my passion leaps for attention, and my curiosity.

Loneliness Itself.

No. 37 was scribed, "Partial Delivery," and said, *Some of me comes here from the end of things. If you listen there will be soft notes on the wind, musical notes that I send, that have transported me elsewhere.*

Jazz was mesmerized by a few of the messages, some much more lyrical than others, a few waxing almost prophetic, now and then one or more clawing for a scant sense of awareness, of recognition, not of the writer, but of the person.

For four days he studied many of the notes, found acceptance, joy, a sense of sharing. Finally, the natural hungers came upon him when he read No. 13, "My Poem in the Mix":

I am a gift to him who finds me.
I lie in wait.
The touching is terrible and lonely.
Please absolve me.
Please.

Jazz Colbere felt the terror of that loneliness. The hunger tantrum, the awful needs, leaped through him, their passages wide and compelling. The whole concoction was an SOS sent out by a desperate woman. Surely, without a doubt, he was being sought, for he alone had a constant view of the old swamp area. Of all people, he would see the mailbox first. No known or forgotten friend filled the unknown.

That evening the street map of the town fell open on his table. Coffee aroma layered the air in the room so that the maple tendencies had trouble coming through to him. Stars moved across the windows in their endless cycles. He kept reading the words of each message, finding simple repetition coming to the front. That repetition was, at a sudden realization, *I am at the end of things.* He did not think it meant the last straw in life, but rather something physical, a clue of sorts. The repetition was marked, deliberate, and came in every seventh message. There were seven such messages.

For three days Jazz studied the map of the town. He wrote names of certain streets, grouped them in classes, by other distinctions, and found nothing. He looked for the merest opening. In the grip of an excitement he found himself. It pursued him at all hours. One day, just at the start of May, in bright sunlight, he walked streets of the town, under the popping maples, as if he were on a simple constitutional. Nothing came out of the walk. He trudged back uphill and returned to the map. He wrote more names, thought of some he had seen, trying to make connections. At the fourth list of names, one name leaped out in the repetition. *Old Terminal Road.* It too might have said, *I am at the end of things.*

As he passed down Old Terminal Road the next morning, his breath a bit heavy and expectant, sunshine falling all around him, coming down through tree limbs and new buds in a near-wanton laziness, his gaze fell on the last house on the road. He caught a kind of sparkle from its lines: a neat, weather-beaten, old Cape Cod cottage with clean, blue trim. A small porch was braced by four white columns. Four window flower boxes stood empty in perfect alignment across the front porch. A few fruit trees clustered in a side yard. The mail box out front, plain and austere, bore the legend:

Maybelle Frond
49 Old Terminal Road

From a distance, kicked unevenly by tantrum's languor and heady needs as identifiable as written words, the maple buds leaped their beginnings upon him all over again. At a significant pause in his step, at a critical turn of his head, he saw a curtain in a front window move slowly apart, as if any moment, in full declaration, someone would step through the opening. Jazz Colbere could only hazard a guess that that someone might elicit a nightlong presence, a hand full of signals, a voice in the kitchen.

THE RESCUES OF BRITTAN COURVALAIS

I t did not come with electricity or a smash of static on the air, but it was there. Brittan Courvalais, five minutes into the darkness of a new day, a streetlight's glow falling through his window like a subtle visitor, was caught on the edge of his chair. Knowledge flowed to him, information of a most sublime order, privacy, intimacy, all in one slow sweep of the air: his grandson was just now, just this minute, into this world, his only grandson. He could feel him, that child coming, making way his debut into the universe, and his name would be Shag. And for this life he and Shag would be in a mysterious and incomprehensible state of connection. This, in the streetlight's glow, in the start of a new day though dawn not yet afoot, he was told.

People of the neighborhood shortly said that the oldest man among them, white-bearded, dark-eyed, seventy-five-year-old Brittan Courvalais, loved his only grandchild Shag in a deep and special way. They said there was a virtual connection, a most generous connection between them, more than the usual. At times they dwelled on the love ingredient, and then on the old and the young, the near gone and the coming. On days when young Shag came by, just an infant in his mother's arms, the old man's step changed, his gait changed, his shoulders stiffened, his voice went lyrical. Some heard him singing under the silver maple tree in the side yard, the tone reaching, ascendant, carrying more than day in it or cool evening or a new stab at dawn. Shag would come, put his arms out, and nestle against the old man's beard. The pair would look into each other's eyes and the world about them seemed lost, distant, at odds with the very young and the very old. Brittan's daughter Marta could only beam when the topic was broached, or say, "I don't know what it is. It mystifies me, but it's as if they share an infinite else." She'd smile broadly when she said it, shrug her shoulders, be fully happy in her puzzle.

From just about every aspect, Brittan Courvalais was a very ordinary man, until such time as an extraordinary demand was placed upon him. Neighbors of the old war dog only knew what they saw and heard, but little of the hidden parts of his life, where valor had surfaced when needed. Stories had been told, sometimes whispered. In Korea, it was said, he'd taken on a mountain and the enemy and beat them both. Just after Korea, out on the highway, he'd pulled an unconscious truck driver from the cab of his truck minutes before the whole rig exploded in a huge ball of fire that shut down an overpass for nearly five months. Later, on a cold spring day, skies heavy, off the wash of Egg Rock out in Lynn Harbor, he'd gone under a capsized boat and extracted two unconscious sailors. And every year since then, without exception, and for the everlasting grace of the neighborhood, the two sailors, on the morning of the Fourth of July, would set up a flag on Brittan's front lawn, plank down three or four cases of beer and drink them off in a day long salute. Three or four times the truck driver came to celebrate. People said that other unknown visitors would drop by, have a beer, casually say a word or two to Brittan, shake hands and quietly leave, like shadows in a man's life. Such shadows made more stories, and naturally, with such kicks for a starter, the Fourth always came up a party.

Otherwise, in his quiet and retiring life, Brittan Courvalais raised an exceptionally small patch of tomatoes with an exceptionally good yield, so good that from that little patch some neighbors could preserve a great deal of tomato sauce. That a seventy-five-year-old man had such a green thumb was quite acceptable: *he's been around, hasn't he?* That's why his lawn was generally trimmed and healthy looking, a few beds of flowers hosted a smash of colors every year. His small cottage stood as a marker of time, of the seasons, a sort of contentment in itself. Retirement in a very tolerable neutral gear, life ebbing out in a comfortable wake, long days astern.

And then one day, at a nearby park, when the seat of a swing hit another child and Marta rushed to help, Shag disappeared. Nobody, in all the hue and cry, had seen him go. Nobody had seen anyone carry him off. Hundreds hunted all the fields and pathways. No Shag. On the second day the two sailors came by to help. And the old man sat on his porch sad, morose, and ready to scream. The authorities declared it a kidnapping. Brittan, for four days, sitting on his porch, waited for some word. Marta started to speak one day coming up the stairs and the old man held his hand up, as if listening. He kept his hand in the air for a full five minutes. Marta did not speak. Later that afternoon, when the mailman came by, Brittan Courvalais once more held his hand up for silence. At his next gossip stop, at Jed Hendry's Barbershop, and again back at the post office, the mailman repeated the story; "The old soldier is listening for something, as if it's going to come from out of space, a space probe, mind you. Should have seen his eyes, would scare the pants off you. Like he was *hearing* something!"

Marta and her husband came by each day after their visit to the police station. She'd make coffee, put nibbling food on the porch table, and look at her father's face. She wanted to reach out and touch him, to be a child again for him, but the look in her father's eyes frightened her. "I don't know what he's going to do, Earl," she said, "he's so locked up into something, something so very different." Then she'd go into the house and cry for an hour or more.

The weight of the world, thus, crushed down on the old man who sat waiting for good news only.

On the sixth day, all hope fading, to some all of it gone, one neighbor saw Brittan Courvalais standing on his porch, his head tipped, as if listening for a bird's call or someone calling from out of sight, perhaps in the house or down the street. Brittan held his hand in the air as though he was asking for quiet or noting peaceful intentions to an unseen guest. The neighbor looked about and saw no other person except a delivery driver stepping down from his truck eight or nine houses away. Slanting rays of

May sunlight were flashing down through young leaves and limbs and falling on Courvalais like pieces of newly minted coin. On the porch floor pieces of shadow or shade were cast like dominoes. A slight breeze talked in the same leaves and began to whisper on the edges of gutters and downspouts. Two or three times the old man cocked his head, his mouth slightly ajar, stony in intent, inert. The wind whispered, the sun's rays played tag, the gutters and downspouts answered. Then, as if coming from a slight paralysis, unfrozen for a moment, he picked his jacket off a chair, got into his old Plymouth Duster and drove down the road. At the end of the road he turned left, toward the highway.

Three days later he was still gone.

Marta was beside herself, now with a double worry. And the police came to the house, eventually asking odd questions. First, a uniformed sergeant came, questioning, slowly inserting the knife under thin skin. Then, after the topic was broached, a lieutenant of detectives came, a cigar in his mouth as he stepped from the car and came up the front walk. He didn't stumble or trip over his words, bringing them up quickly and darkly from the cavern of his chest, half cough and half words. "Why was your father so attached to the child? *Harrumph. Hack. Hack. Harrumph.*"

"He's his grandchild. He loves him."

"Was it not an unusual love? Is it possible that the old man has taken the baby? *Harrumph. Hack. Hack. Harrumph.* That right now he's with him someplace?"

People of the neighborhood began to talk. The mailman heard the talk and carried it. *Some of those old stories were, in fact, made up. The old man wasn't what he appeared to be after all. What have we made him? What kind of a man would drive his daughter into this near madness? You really don't know, do you, what lurks in the heart of a man.*

HE'D BEEN MYSTIFIED by many things in life: the small man down in Homestead, Florida who secretly moved stones weighing many tons, supposedly by himself; a rocking chair sculpted from stone and weighing thousands of pounds; a tall vertical solid stone gate of equal tonnage that swung on small points of balance, seemingly immovable yet moved and placed. How the all-state halfback he played behind when he was a young man told him, just before the big game of the year, that his turn was coming, and there he was, rushing on the field breathless in the first quarter. What had pulled him up that mountain in Korea to what he thought was certain death? How had he been able to go into the cold water to save those men after almost drowning under a raft in Lake Hwachon when his unit crossed by rafts mounted on boats with outboard motors and a mortar round had landed right beside them, all of them trussed in full gear? He couldn't remember how he'd gotten out of the clutches of all that web equipment, or Sanders's hands pulling at him, hauling him down.

And he never professed to understand the knowledge that came to him about Shag from the moment of the boy's birth. That they were connected was enough for him. The corners of the boy's mouth when he smiled up at him were locked behind his eyes.

And here he was, seven days later, vaguely answering some unlimited connection, some communication, coming at him. He didn't know where it was coming from, and he had driven endlessly it seemed from the day he had left home, sometimes three or four hundred miles a day, sometimes fifty to sit in the middle of a park or a village green, listening.

Now, on the seventh day, hearing his name and description aired over the radio, also a subject of search, he was on the outskirts of Schenectady. He did not know how he had gotten here, but the urge was unarguable, unimpeachable. Shag was calling him. It had been that way in the beginning. It would always be that way. He knew he was near. The parts of the city spread out, and the possible routes cluttered his mind, but there was notice of a kind pulling him. It was unmistakable. It was Shag. He drove around for three hours, like a moth around a huge glowing light, the last light of the year, October light crowding down on the life of the moth.

And then it was stronger than it ever was. He was beside a mall. The voice on the radio was giving out the description of his car, the registration number, and his description. He was at least three hundred miles from home. Nobody would know him. He parked the car. Six hours later, tired, exhaustion finally coming down upon his body, he sat in a small diner and ate his first meal of the day. Shag had come and gone, but he knew this was the place. It had been so from the beginning. Sanders, all the way from Chicago, had been from the beginning, and the mountain in Korea had been from the beginning. The trucker had always been coming at him, a journey started a long time in the past, like the two sailors caught under their craft, unconscious, waiting for him.

He finished his meal and walked back outside. As he neared the Duster, he saw the policeman sitting in a patrol car a few spaces away. Brittan turned to move in the other direction.

"Sir!" the voice said. "Sir!" It was a strong young voice, somewhat friendly in tone.

He turned back to the voice. The young policeman stepped from his car. "May I ask you some questions, sir? Is this your car? Do you have some ID? Are you Brittan Courvalais? Someone spotted you earlier and called it in, said you were hanging around too much. There's a warrant out for you."

"I'm looking for my grandson. That is no crime."

"Why are you here in Schenectady? You must be hundreds of miles from home." Blue-eyed, pink-cheeked, probably shaved only three times a week, the young officer was dubious, but not uncomfortable. "I checked out your car, and you in the diner. I know you don't have your grandson with you. Not unless he's with someone else local. Why's his name Shag?" He was pleasant in an unpleasant situation.

"I'll tell you, son. I don't know why his name is Shag, but it was always going to be that. And I don't know why I'm here, but something is telling me that he's near here. I cannot leave this place. I've driven over two thousand miles, some of it in circles, around mountains, across bridges and rivers, down beside the huge Finger Lakes, Canandegua on the crown of a hill perhaps just because of its name, something pulling at me, drawing me, and it's brought me here. I can't leave here. I've done nothing but look for that boy. It's like he keeps calling for me, but I never hear his voice. It's a kind of impulse, the only way I can describe it. It beats or hums, but no words to it."

"I know about names," the officer said. "My father named me Sawyer. I am Sawyer Billings and had a hell of a time with the name as a kid. My father says he has no idea why it came to him. I handle my dukes pretty good. Had a lot of scrapes over that name."

"Ever think that's why your father did it? I know of someone named Lawyer and he makes tackles and interceptions, and he's pretty tough at that."

"Not until now, sir. Is there any way I can help you? I can make a report or hold it up. The only one who'd get upset about any delay would be the captain, and he takes enough time off, so it won't matter."

"Just let me be around here. Whatever it is, it's very strong. I have to check it out."

"Where? In a particular store? Nearby?"

"I don't know. If I knew I'd be there now. I'd have you by the collar pulling you with me. I just don't know."

"Well, sir, I'll sit on it for a while. My sister was crying about Shag the other day, saying how sad it was. She has two of her own. Father named her Cameron. Never hurt her. She's a fighter, too. But gets sad." He walked to his patrol car. "I'll be around. Good hunting, sir." The car slipped out of the mall like a small animal passing through the brush.

A FEW HOURS AFTER the patrol car had departed the parking lot, his neck stiff, an old injury talking through his knee, he woke with a start. Now it was stronger, that call of Shag, that disruption on the air. He shook his head, looked for the patrol car, walked toward the mall. It came again, stronger, not a voice, not words, not his name, but a humming, a vibration, near electrical. Twice he went past one store, only to come back and feel the announcement again. This was it. Again he looked for Sawyer Billings or his car and saw neither.

He entered the store, an open building that seemed to spread as wide as three football fields. He could smell popcorn, flowers, and the burnt skin of chicken frying. Should he stay by the door? Was it the only way out of the store? Would he be here for hours? No, he would be active. He would pursue the feeling, the sensation, that vibrating hum still coming at him.

Scanning the store for the silhouette of someone carrying a child, he picked an aisle and started down it. Back over his shoulder he looked, afraid he might miss something, and looked down side aisles. A hum of voices came to him, a caustic static that intruded on the vibrating hum. A wife arguing with her husband. A father calling for his son to hurry. A brother teasing a younger sister. Then, from another aisle, the next one over, beyond the display of electric cords and lamps and shades and rows of batteries and bulbs in blue and white boxes, he felt his grandson. He felt Shag.

Back he went to the main aisle, crossed over, looked down the aisle. The silhouette was exclusive: a woman holding a child. A man near her was looking at a display of security alarms, a big man, wide across the shoulders, in worn dungarees and work boots.

The woman was in her late thirties, dark hair, red lips. She hummed to the infant in her arms.

The eyes of Brittan Courvalais met the eyes of his grandson Shag. The boy's head came up off the woman's shoulder. Brittan stepped closer, saw the curve of a smile on the child's lip as if it were juxtaposed on the back of his brain. He was ready to grab the boy when Shag said, "Gampa."

The woman spun on her heels, looked into Brittan Courvalais's eyes, saw some kind of trouble or ownership there, said, "Harry," in a very demanding voice. "We have to go. Now! Now, Harry!"

The big man also spun around. Courvalais screamed, "Get the police. This baby's been kidnapped. This is my grandson Shag." He reached for the child. The woman spun away. The man pushed him. His knee pained its whole length. The mountain was in front of him again. The frigid waters of Lake Hwachon were there again for him. He reached, grabbed the man's arm, pulled him at himself, and tossed him against a display. Boxes tumbled.

The woman screamed. "Help! Help! He's trying to steal my baby!"

A man rushed down the aisle and went to grab Brittan's arm. Brittan yelled, "Quick, get the police. Sawyer Billings is outside in the police car. Get him! Hurry." His fist closed around the woman's wrist. The baby let out a yell. Their eyes locked again. Then Brittan's eyes locked with the woman's eyes. It was then she knew her first terror. It was so very real, so unexpected. They had only been looking for a simple night-light. A simple night-light.

Officer Sawyer Billings was Johnny-on-the-spot, having spent some off-duty hours at the mall, watching the old man from a distance. Cuffs were soon on the big man. The baby was taken from the woman's arms and put into the arms of his grandfather, who was feeling the ultimate joy, who could already hear the phone ringing at his daughter's home three hundred miles away.

AUTHOR
Tom Sheehan

TOM SHEEHAN has been nominated for six Pushcart Prizes, the PEN/Martha Albrand Award for Memoirs, the Million Writer's Award for Fiction, the *Zine Yearbook,* and the *E-2 Ink Project.* His story, *"The Man Who Hid Music,"* won a Silver Rose Award for Excellence in the Art of the Short Story and was anthologized in *Silver Rose Anthology: Award-Winning Short Stories 2001.* He is a two-time winner of the Saugus.net Ghost Story Contest, was winner of Eastoftheweb's non-fiction competition (London) and has been Featured Writer in several publications, including *Nuvein, Eclectica, New Works Review,* and *Tryst.*

Tom avidly follows Saugus hockey and football. He is a member of the Saugus High School Sports Hall of Fame, along with cover artist Jeff Fiovaranti.

He has been retired from Raytheon Company since 1990, and life changed then with the gift of a computer on retirement day from his family. Eight novels, eighty or ninety short stories and almost five hundred poems later, he is still at it. His wife Beth, a hospice and Alzheimer's nurse, is the most compassionate person he has ever met. All his life he has told his children they have come here with two things in their kit bag, love and energy, and it's up to them to use both to their full extent, to get them going in synch. He knows there are new poets and writers in that mix.

He is a graduate of Saugus High School (1947), Marianapolis Prep School in Thompson, Connecticut (1948), Boston College (1956). As an infantry veteran of the Korean War, he served during 1950-1952 with the 278th Regimental Combat Team and in Korea with the 31st Infantry Regiment of the 7th Infantry Division, earning the Combat Infantryman's Badge.

He forever celebrates his family, his comrades, and his hometown of Saugus, Massachusetts.

COVER ARTIST
Jeff Fioravanti

THERE HAS NOT BEEN a time in Jeff Fioravanti's life when art has not played a major role. From the first time he put color to paper, this talented artist has sought to capture the world and all its wonders. A life-long resident of Massachusetts, Jeff is a nationally recognized award-winning artist who creates spellbinding works of art, offering each viewer a very powerful and moving experience on the legacy of America.

"Pastels are my medium of choice for all my finished work," Jeff says. "They are pure, immediate, and luminous—all important components in my interaction with and interpretation of the American landscape. They are durable and offer great flexibility, which I find allows me the freedom to express and apply a wide range of techniques necessary to capture the power and strength of the treasured lands, shores, and properties of our country.

Since August of 2001, Jeff has been on a mission, utilizing his talents to showcase the historic lands of America by bringing attention to the history of our nation and the need to protect and preserve these natural and man-made treasures. It is a mission he calls: "Painting today, to preserve the past, for tomorrow."

Jeff is a Signature Member of the Pastel Painters Society of Cape Cod, the Connecticut Pastel Society, and one of the most recognized and respected art organizations in North America, the Pastel Society of America. He has been published in *American Artist Magazine* and *Pastel Artist International,* and his work can be found in many private collections throughout the US and Europe, as well as in the permanent collection of the Cape Ann Historical Museum.

Jeff has won awards at both the local and national level, including "Best in Show" at the *2000 Renaissance in Pastel,* a national juried exhibition sponsored by the Connecticut Pastel Society. Jeff's work can be viewed online at www.fioravanti-fineart.com, or at the following galleries: Art Research Associates, in South Hamilton, Massachusetts; Art 3 Gallery, in Manchester, New Hampshire; and Gallery 30, in Gettysburg, Pennsylvania.

A Note on the Type

~

The text of this book is set in Bookman Old Style, designed by Alexander Phemister, a punchcutter at Miller & Richard foundry in Edinburgh, Scotland, in the 1850s. Phemister ended his career at the Dickson foundry in Boston, Massachusetts, where he became a partner and continued designing type until he retired in 1891. Alexander Phemister was born in Edinburgh, Scotland, in 1829 and died in Boston, Massachusetts, in 1894.

Printed in the United States
42029LVS00003BA/121-144